APPLAUD CLARKE'S WITH RAMA"

RENDEZVOUS WITH RAMA

BEST NOVEL OF THE YEAR
1973

Hugo Award
Nebula Award
John W. Campbell Memorial Award
and
The Jupiter Award

Inside Rama...

Commander Bill Norton and his crew landed on the mysterious space vessel and made their way into its hollow interior. There they found a completely self-contained world that must have been cruising through space for at least 200,000 years . . . but was now seemingly dead.

Then, as Norton and his fellow astronauts began to explore the spaceship, Rama suddenly—and incredibly—came to life . . .

A DAZZLING ADVENTURE

CRITICS
ARTHUR C.
"RENDEZVOUS

"Clarke is in good form here, providing something for everybody — politics, religion and all kinds of science wrapped up in a taut mystery-suspense."
> —*Publishers Weekly*

"Arthur has done it again — proved that the chief ingredient of superior science fiction is *story*. His sense of presence and of real people involved in real experiences is unfailing.
> —*Frank Herbert*

"What an absolute pleasure . . . imagine, an astronomical story by someone who knows astronomy. It was delightful to be presented with a scene to stagger the imagination and yet have it described so exactly and meticulously as to know you have been there."
> —*Isaac Asimov*

Rendezvous with Rama

Arthur C. Clarke

A Del Rey Book

BALLANTINE BOOKS • NEW YORK

A Del Rey Book
Published by Ballantine Books

Library of Congress Catalog Card Number: 73-3497

ISBN 0-345-27344-3

This edition published by arrangement with
Harcourt Brace Jovanovich, Inc.

Manufactured in the United States of America

First Ballantine Books Edition: September 1974
Eighth Printing: October 1977

First Special Printing: January 1975

Cover art by Stanislaw Fernandes

To Sri Lanka,
where I climbed the
stairway of the Gods

Rendezvous
with Rama

1

Spaceguard

SOONER OR LATER, it was bound to happen. On June 30, 1908, Moscow escaped destruction by three hours and four thousand kilometers—a margin invisibly small by the standards of the universe. On February 12, 1947, another Russian city had a still narrower escape, when the second great meteorite of the twentieth century detonated less than four hundred kilometers from Vladivostok, with an explosion rivaling that of the newly invented uranium bomb.

In those days there was nothing that men could do to protect themselves against the last random shots in the cosmic bombardment that had once scarred the face of the Moon. The meteorites of 1908 and 1947 had struck uninhabited wilderness; but by the end of the twenty-first century there was no region left on Earth that could be safely used for celestial target practice. The human race had spread from pole to pole. And so, inevitably . . .

At 0946 GMT on the morning of September 11 in the exceptionally beautiful summer of the year 2077, most of the inhabitants of Europe saw a dazzling fireball appear in the eastern sky. Within seconds it was brighter than the Sun, and as it moved across the heavens—at first in utter silence—it left behind it a churning column of dust and smoke.

Somewhere above Austria it began to disintegrate, producing a series of concussions so violent that more than a million people had their hearing permanently damaged. They were the lucky ones.

Moving at fifty kilometers a second, a thousand tons of rock and metal impacted on the plains of northern Italy, destroying in a few flaming moments the labor of centuries. The cities of Padua and Verona were wiped from the face of the Earth; and the last glories of Venice sank forever beneath the sea as the waters of the Adriatic came thundering landward after the hammer blow from space.

Six hundred thousand people died, and the total damage was more than a trillion dollars. But the loss to art, to history, to science—to the whole human race, for the rest of time—was beyond all computation. It was as if a great war had been fought and lost in a single morning; and few could draw much pleasure from the fact that, as the dust of destruction slowly settled, for months the whole world witnessed the most splendid dawns and sunsets since Krakatoa

After the initial shock, mankind reacted with a determination and a unity that no earlier age could have shown. Such a disaster, it was realized, might not occur again for a thousand years—but it might occur tomorrow. And the next time, the consequences could be even worse.

Very well; *there would be no next time.*

A hundred years earlier, a much poorer world, with far feebler resources, had squandered its wealth attempting to destroy weapons launched, suicidally, by mankind against itself The effort had never been successful, but the skills acquired then had not been forgotten. Now they could be used for a far nobler purpose, and on an infinitely vaster stage. No meteorite large enough to cause catastrophe would ever again be allowed to breach the defenses of Earth.

So began Project SPACEGUARD. Fifty years later—and in a way that none of its designers could ever have anticipated—it justified its existence.

2

Intruder

By the year 2130, the Mars-based radars were discovering new asteroids at the rate of a dozen a day. The SPACEGUARD computers automatically calculated their orbits and stored the information in their own enormous memories, so that every few months any interested astronomer could have a look at the accumulated statistics. These were now quite impressive.

It had taken more than 120 years to collect the first thousand asteroids, since the discovery of Ceres, largest of these tiny worlds, on the very first day of the nineteenth century. Hundreds had been found and lost and found again; they existed in such swarms that one exasperated astronomer had christened them "vermin of the skies." He would have been appalled to know that SPACEGUARD was now keeping track of half a million.

Only the five giants—Ceres, Pallas, Juno, Eunomia, and Vesta—were more than two hundred kilometers in diameter; the vast majority were merely oversized boulders that would fit into a small park. Almost all moved in orbits that lay beyond Mars. Only the few that came far enough sunward to be a possible danger to Earth were the concern of SPACEGUARD. And not one in a thousand of these, during the entire future history of the solar system, would pass within a million kilometers of Earth.

The object first catalogued as 31/439, according to the year and the order of its discovery, was detected while it was still outside the orbit of Jupiter. There was nothing unusual about its location; many asteroids went beyond Saturn before turning once more toward their distant master, the Sun. And Thule II, most far-ranging of all, traveled so close to Uranus that it might well be a lost moon of that planet.

But a first radar contact at such a distance was unprecedented; clearly, 31/439 must be of exceptional size. From the strength of the echo, the computers deduced a diameter of at least forty kilometers. Such a giant had not been discovered for a hundred years. That it had been overlooked for so long seemed incredible.

Then the orbit was calculated, and the mystery was resolved—to be replaced by a greater one. 31/439 was not traveling on a normal asteroidal path, along an ellipse which it retraced with clockwork precision every few years. It was a lonely wanderer among the stars, making its first and last visit to the solar system —for it was moving so swiftly that the gravitational field of the Sun could never capture it. It would flash inward past the orbits of Jupiter, Mars, Earth, Venus, and Mercury, gaining speed as it did so, until it rounded the Sun and headed out once again into the unknown.

It was at this point that the computers started flashing their "We have something interesting" sign, and, for the first time, 31/439 came to the attention of human beings. There was a brief flurry of excitement at SPACEGUARD headquarters, and the interstellar vagabond was quickly dignified by a name instead of a mere number. Long ago, the astronomers had exhausted Greek and Roman mythology; now they were working through the Hindu pantheon. And so 31/439 was christened Rama.

For a few days, the news media made a fuss over the visitor, but they were badly handicapped by the sparsity of information. Only two facts were known about Rama: its unusual orbit and its approximate size. Even this last was merely an educated guess, based upon the strength of the radar echo. Through the telescope, Rama still appeared as a faint, fifteenth-magnitude star—much too small to show a visible disc. But as it plunged in toward the heart of the solar system, it would grow brighter and larger month by month; before it vanished forever, the orbiting observatories would be able to gather more precise information about its shape and size. There was plenty of time, and perhaps during the next few years some spaceship on its ordinary business might be routed close enough to get good photographs. An actual rendezvous was most unlikely; the energy cost would be far too great to permit physical contact with an object cutting across the orbits of the planets at more than a hundred thousand kilometers an hour.

So the world soon forgot about Rama. But the astronomers did not. Their excitement grew with the passing months as the new asteroid presented them with more and more puzzles.

First of all, there was the problem of Rama's light curve. It didn't have one.

All known asteroids, without exception, showed a

slow variation in their brilliance, waxing and waning in a period of a few hours. It had been recognized for more than two centuries that this was an inevitable result of their spin and their irregular shape. As they toppled end over end along their orbits, the reflecting surfaces they presented to the sun were continually changing, and their brightness varied accordingly.

Rama showed no such changes. Either it was not spinning at all or it was perfectly symmetrical. Both explanations seemed unlikely.

There the matter rested for several months, because none of the big orbiting telescopes could be spared from their regular job of peering into the remote depths of the universe. Space astronomy was an expensive hobby, and time on a large instrument could easily cost a thousand dollars a minute. Dr. William Stenton would never have been able to grab the Farside two-hundred-meter reflector for a full quarter of an hour if a more important program had not been temporarily derailed by the failure of a fifty-cent capacitor. One astronomer's bad luck was his good fortune.

Stenton did not know what he had caught until the next day, when he was able to get computer time to process his results. Even when they were finally flashed on his display screen, it took him several minutes to understand what they meant.

The sunlight reflected from Rama was not, after all, absolutely constant in its intensity. There was a very small variation—hard to detect, but quite unmistakable, and extremely regular. Like all the other asteroids, Rama was indeed spinning. But whereas the normal "day" for an asteroid was several hours, Rama's was only four *minutes*.

Stenton did some quick calculations, and found it hard to believe the results. At its equator, this tiny world must be spinning at more than a thousand kilometers an hour. It would be rather unhealthy to attempt a landing anywhere except at the poles, because the centrifugal force at the equator would be powerful enough to flick any loose objects away from it at an acceleration of almost one gravity. Rama was a rolling stone that could never have gathered any cosmic moss. It was surprising that such a body had managed to hold itself together, and had not long ago shattered into a million fragments.

An object forty kilometers across, with a rotation period of only four minutes—where did that fit into the astronomical scheme of things? Dr. Stenton was a somewhat imaginative man, a little too prone to jump to conclusions. He now jumped to one that gave him an uncomfortable few minutes indeed:

The only specimen of the celestial zoo that fitted this description was a collapsed star. Perhaps Rama was a dead sun, a madly spinning sphere of neutronium, every cubic centimeter weighing billions of tons.

At this point, there flashed briefly through Stenton's horrified mind the memory of that timeless classic, H. G. Wells's "The Star." He had first read it as a small boy, and it had helped to spark his interest in astronomy. Across more than two centuries of time it had lost none of its magic and its terror. He would never forget the images of hurricanes and tidal waves, of cities sliding into the sea, as that other visitor from the stars smashed into Jupiter and then fell sunward past the Earth. True, the star that old Wells described was not cold, but incandescent, and wrought much of its destruction by heat. That scarcely mattered; even if Rama was a cold body, reflecting only the light of the Sun, it could kill by gravity as easily as by fire.

Any stellar mass intruding into the solar system would completely distort the orbits of the planets. The Earth had only to move a few million kilometers sunward—or starward—for the delicate balance of climate to be destroyed. The antarctic icecap could melt and flood all low-lying land; or the oceans could freeze and the whole world be locked in eternal winter. Just a nudge in either direction would be enough. . . .

Then Stenton relaxed and breathed a sigh of relief. This was all nonsense; he should be ashamed of himself.

Rama could not possibly be made of condensed matter. No star-sized mass could penetrate so deeply into the solar system without producing disturbances that would have betrayed it long ago. The orbits of all the planets would have been affected; that, after all, was how Neptune, Pluto, and Persephone had been discovered. No, it was utterly impossible for an object as massive as a dead sun to sneak up unobserved.

In a way, it was a pity. An encounter with a dark star would have been quite exciting.

While it lasted . . .

3

Rama and Sita

THE EXTRAORDINARY MEETING of the Space Advisory Council was brief and stormy. Even by the twenty-second century, no way had yet been discovered of keeping elderly and conservative scientists from occupying crucial administrative positions. Indeed, it was doubted if the problem ever would be solved.

To make matters worse, the current chairman of SAC was Professor Emeritus Olaf Davidson, the distinguished astrophysicist. Professor Davidson was not much interested in objects smaller than galaxies, and never bothered to conceal his prejudices. And though he had to admit that ninety per cent of his science was now based upon observations from space-borne instruments, he was not at all happy about it. No fewer than three times during his distinguished career, satellites specially launched to prove one of his pet theories had done precisely the opposite.

The question before the Council was straightforward enough. There was no doubt that Rama was an unusual object—but was it an important one? In a few months it would be gone forever, so there was little time in which to act. Opportunities missed now would never recur.

At a rather horrifying cost, a space-probe soon to be launched from Mars to go beyond Neptune could be modified and sent on a high-speed trajectory to meet Rama. There was no hope of a rendezvous; it would be the fastest fly-by on record, for the two bodies would pass each other at two hundred thousand kilometers an hour. Rama would be observed intensively for only a few minutes, and in real close-up for less than a second. But with the right instrumentation, that would be long enough to settle many questions.

Although Davidson took a jaundiced view of the Neptune probe, it had already been approved and he saw no point in sending more good money after bad. He spoke eloquently on the follies of asteroid-chasing, and on the urgent need for a new high-resolution interferometer on the Moon to prove the newly revived "big bang" theory of creation, once and for all.

That was a grave tactical error, because the three most ardent supporters of the "modified steady state" theory were also members of the Council. They secretly agreed with Davidson that asteroid-chasing was a waste of money; nevertheless . . .

He lost by one vote.

Three months later, the space-probe, rechristened Sita, was launched from Phobos, the inner moon of Mars. The flight time was seven weeks, and the instrument was switched to full power only five minutes before interception. Simultaneously, a cluster of camera pods was released, to sail past Rama, so that it could be photographed from all sides.

The first images, from ten thousand kilometers

away, brought to a halt the activities of all mankind. On a billion television screens, there appeared a tiny, featureless cylinder, growing rapidly second by second. By the time it had doubled its size, no one could pretend any longer that Rama was a natural object.

Its body was a cylinder so geometrically perfect that it might have been turned on a lathe—one with centers fifty kilometers apart. The two ends were quite flat, apart from some small structures at the center of one face, and were twenty kilometers across; from a distance, when there was no sense of scale, Rama looked almost comically like an ordinary domestic boiler.

Rama grew until it filled the screen. Its surface was a dull, drab gray, as colorless as the Moon, and completely devoid of markings except at one point. Halfway along the cylinder there was a kilometer-wide stain or smear, as if something had once hit and splattered, ages ago.

There was no sign that the impact had done the slightest damage to Rama's spinning walls; but this mark had produced the slight fluctuation in brightness that had led to Stenton's discovery.

The images from the other cameras added nothing new. However, the trajectories their pods traced through Rama's minute gravitational field gave one other vital piece of information: the mass of the cylinder.

It was far too light to be a solid body. To nobody's great surprise, it was clear that Rama must be hollow.

The long-hoped-for, long-feared encounter had come at last. Mankind was about to receive the first visitor from the stars.

4

Rendezvous

COMMANDER NORTON REMEMBERED those first TV transmissions, which he had replayed so many times, during the final minutes of the rendezvous. But there was one thing no electronic image could possibly convey—and that was Rama's overwhelming size.

He had never received such an impression when landing on a natural body like the Moon or Mars. Those were worlds, and one expected them to be big. Yet he had also landed on Jupiter VIII, which was slightly larger than Rama—and that had seemed quite a small object.

It was easy to resolve the paradox. His judgment was wholly altered by the fact that this was an artifact, millions of times heavier than anything that man had ever put into space. The mass of Rama was at least ten trillion tons; to any spaceman, that was not only an awe-inspiring but also a terrifying thought. No wonder that he sometimes felt a sense of insignificance, and even depression, as that cylinder of sculptured, ageless metal filled more and more of the sky.

There was also a sense of danger here that was wholly novel to his experience. In every earlier landing, he had known what to expect, there was always the possibility of accident, but never of surprise. With Rama, surprise was the only certainty

Now, *Endeavour* was hovering less than a thousand meters above the North Pole of the cylinder, at the very center of the slowly turning disc This end had been chosen because it was the one in sunlight, as Rama rotated, the shadows of the short, enigmatic structures near the axis swept steadily across the metal plain. The northern face of Rama was a gigantic sundial, measuring the swift passage of its four-minute day.

Landing a five-thousand-ton spaceship at the center of a spinning disc was the least of Norton's worries. It was no different from docking at the axis of a large space station; *Endeavour's* lateral jets had already given her a matching spin, and he could trust Lieutenant Joe Calvert to put her down as gently as a snowflake, with or without the aid of the navigation computer.

"In three minutes," said Calvert, without taking his eyes from the display screen, "we'll know if it's made of antimatter."

Norton grinned, recalling some of the more hair-raising theories about Rama's origin. If that unlikely speculation was true, in a few seconds there would be the biggest bang since the solar system had been formed. The total annihilation of ten thousand tons would, briefly, provide the planets with a second sun.

Yet the mission profile had allowed for even this remote contingency. *Endeavour* had squirted Rama with one of her jets from a safe thousand kilometers away. Nothing whatsoever had happened when the expanding cloud of vapor arrived on target, and a matter-anti-timatter reaction involving even a few milligrams would have produced an awesome fireworks display.

Norton, like all space commanders, was a cautious man. He had looked long and hard at the northern face of Rama in choosing the point of touch-down. After much thought, he had decided to avoid the obvious spot—the exact center, on the axis itself. A clearly marked circular disc, a hundred meters in diameter, was centered on the pole, and he had a strong suspicion that this must be the outer seal of an enormous air lock. The creatures who had built this hollow world must have had some way of taking their ships inside. This was the logical place for the main entrance, and he thought it might be unwise to block the front door with his own vessel.

But this decision generated other problems. If *Endeavour* touched down even a few meters from the axis, Rama's rapid spin would start her sliding away from the pole. At first, the centrifugal force would be very weak, but it would be continuous and inexorable. Norton did not relish the thought of his ship slithering across the polar plain, gaining speed minute by minute until she was slung off into space at a thousand kilometers an hour when she reached the edge of the disc.

It was possible that Rama's minute gravitational field—about one-thousandth of Earth's—might prevent this from happening. It might hold *Endeavour* against the plain with a force of several tons, and if the surface was sufficiently rough, the ship might stay near the pole. But Norton had no intention of balancing an unknown frictional force against a quite certain centrifugal one.

Fortunately, Rama's designers had provided an answer Equally spaced around the polar axis were three low pillbox-shaped structures, about ten meters in diameter. If *Endeavour* touched down between any two of these, the centrifugal drift would fetch her up against them, and she would be held firmly in place, like a ship glued against a quayside by the incoming waves.

"Contact in fifteen seconds," said Calvert.

As he tensed himself above the duplicate controls, which he hoped he would not have to touch, Norton became acutely aware of all that had come to focus on this instant of time. This, surely, would be the most momentous landing since the first touch-down on the Moon, over a century and a half ago

The gray pillboxes drifted slowly upward outside the control port. There was the last hiss of a reaction jet, and a barely perceptible jar

In the weeks that had just passed, Commander Norton had often wondered what he would say at this moment. But now that it was upon him, history chose his words, and he spoke almost automatically, barely aware of the echo from the past:

"Rama Base. *Endeavour* has landed."

As recently as a month ago, he would never have believed it possible. The ship had been on a routine mission, checking and emplacing asteroid warning beacons, when the order came. *Endeavour* was the only spacecraft in the solar system that could possibly make a rendezvous with the intruder before it whipped around the Sun and hurled itself back toward the stars. Even so, it had been necessary to rob three other ships of the Solar Survey, which were now drifting helplessly until tankers could refuel them. Norton was afraid that it would be a long time before the skippers of *Calypso*, *Beagle*, and *Challenger* would speak to him again.

Even with all the extra propellant it had been a long, hard chase. Rama was already inside the orbit of Venus when *Endeavour* caught up with it. No other ship could have done so; this privilege was unique, and not a moment of the weeks ahead was to be wasted. A thousand scientists on Earth would have cheerfully mortgaged their souls for this opportunity; now they could only watch over the TV circuits, biting their lips and thinking how much better *they* could do the job. They were probably right, but there was no alternative. The inexorable laws of celestial mechanics had decreed that *Endeavour* would be the first, and the last, of all man's ships to make contact with Rama.

The advice he was continually receiving from Earth did little to alleviate Norton's responsibility. If split-second decisions had to be made, no one could help him; the radio time lag to Mission Control was already ten minutes, and increasing. He often envied the great navigators of the past, before the days of electronic communications, who could interpret their sealed orders without continual monitoring from headquarters. When *they* made mistakes, no one ever knew.

Yet at the same time, he was glad that some decisions could be delegated to Earth. Now that *Endeavour's* orbit had coalesced with Rama's, they were heading sunward like a single body. In forty days they would reach perihelion, and pass within twenty-million kilometers of the Sun. That was far too close for comfort. Long before then *Endeavour* would have to use her remaining fuel to nudge herself into a safer orbit. The crew would have perhaps three weeks of exploring time before they parted from Rama forever.

After that, the problem would be Earth's. *Endeavour* would be virtually helpless, speeding on an orbit that could make her the first ship to reach the stars—in approximately fifty thousand years. There was no need to worry, Mission Control had promised. Somehow, regardless of cost, *Endeavour* would be refueled, even if it proved necessary to send tankers and abandon them in space once they had transferred every gram of propellant. Rama was a prize worth any risk short of a suicide mission.

And, of course, it might even come to that. Commander Norton had no illusions on this score. For the first time in a hundred years, an element of total uncertainty had entered human affairs, and uncertainty was one thing that neither scientists nor politicians could tolerate. If that was the price of resolving it, *Endeavour* and her crew would be expendable.

5

First EVA

RAMA WAS SILENT as a tomb—which, perhaps, it was. There were no radio signals, on any frequency; no vibrations that the seismographs could pick up, apart from microtremors undoubtedly caused by the Sun's increasing heat; no electrical currents; no radioactivity. It was almost ominously quiet. One might have expected that even an asteroid would be noisier.

What did we expect? Norton asked himself. A committee of welcome? He was not sure whether to be disappointed or relieved The initiative, at any rate, appeared to be his.

His orders were to wait for twenty-four hours, then to go out and explore. Nobody slept much that first day. Even the crew members not on duty spent their time monitoring the ineffectually probing instruments or simply looking out the observation ports at the starkly geometrical landscape. Is this world alive? they asked themselves, over and over again. Is it dead? Or is it merely sleeping?

On the first EVA, Norton took only one companion: Lieutenant Commander Karl Mercer, his tough and resourceful life-support officer. He had no intention of getting out of sight of the ship, and if there was any trouble it was unlikely that a larger party would be safer. As a precaution, however, he had two more crew members, already suited up, standing by in the air lock.

The few grams of weight that Rama's combined gravitational and centrifugal fields gave them were neither help nor hindrance; they had to rely entirely on their jets. As soon as possible, Norton decided, he would string a cat's cradle of guide ropes between the ship and the pillboxes, so that they could move around without wasting propellant.

The nearest pillbox was only ten meters from the air lock, and Norton's first concern was to check that the contact had caused no damage to the ship. *Endeavour*'s hull was resting against the curving wall with a thrust of several tons, but the pressure was evenly distributed. Reassured, he began to drift around the circular structure, trying to determine its purpose.

He had traveled only a few meters when he came across an interruption in the smooth, apparently metallic wall. At first, he thought it was some peculiar decoration, for it seemed to serve no useful function. Six radial grooves, or slots, were deeply recessed in the metal, and lying in them were six crossed bars, like the spokes of a rimless wheel, with a small hub at the center. But there was no way in which the wheel could be turned, because it was embedded in the wall.

Then he noticed, with growing excitement, that there were deeper recesses at the ends of the spokes nicely shaped to accept a clutching hand. (Claw? Tentacle?) If one stood *so*, bracing against the wall, and pulled on the spokes so . . .

Smooth as silk, the wheel slid out of the wall. To his utter astonishment—for he had been virtually certain that any moving parts would have become vacuum-welded ages ago—Norton found himself holding a spoked wheel. He might have been the captain of some old windjammer standing at the helm of his ship.

He was glad that his helmet's sunshade did not allow Mercer to read his expression. He was startled, but also angry with himself. Perhaps he had already made his first mistake. Were alarms now sounding inside Rama, and had his thoughtless action already triggered some implacable mechanism?

But *Endeavour* reported no change; her sensors still detected nothing except faint thermal crepitations and his own movements.

"Well, Skipper, are you going to turn it?"

Norton thought once more of his instructions: "Use your own discretion, but proceed with caution." If he checked every single move with Mission Control, he would never get anywhere.

"What's your diagnosis, Karl?" he asked.

"It's obviously a manual control for an air lock—probably an emergency back-up system in case of power failure. I can't imagine *any* technology, however advanced, that wouldn't take such precautions."

And it would be fail-safe, Norton told himself. It could be operated only if there was no possible danger to the system.

He grasped two opposing spokes of the windlass, braced his feet against the ground, and tested the wheel. It did not budge.

"Give me a hand," he said to Mercer.

Each took a spoke. Exerting their utmost strength, they were unable to produce the slightest movement.

Of course, there was no reason to suppose that clocks and corkscrews on Rama turned in the same direction as they did on Earth.

"Let's try the other way," suggested Mercer.

This time, there was no resistance. The wheel rotated almost effortlessly through a full circle. Then, very smoothly, it took up the load.

Half a meter away, the curving wall of the pillbox started to move, like a slowly opening clamshell. A few particles of dust, driven by wisps of escaping air, streamed outward like dazzling diamonds as the brilliant sunlight caught them.

The road to Rama lay open.

6

Committee

IT HAD BEEN a serious mistake, Dr. Bose often thought, to put the United Planets Headquarters on the Moon. Inevitably, Earth tended to dominate the proceedings—as it dominated the landscape beyond the dome. If they *had* to build here, perhaps they should have gone to Farside, where that hypnotic disc never shed its rays.

But, of course, it was much too late to change, and, in any case, there was no real alternative. Whether the colonies liked it or not, Earth would be the cultural and economic overlord of the solar system for centuries to come.

Dr. Bose had been born on Earth, and had not emigrated to Mars until he was thirty, so he felt that he could view the political situation fairly dispassionately. He knew now that he would never return to his home planet, even though it was only five hours away by shuttle. At age 115, he was in perfect health, but he could not face the reconditioning needed to accustom him to three times the gravity he had enjoyed for most of his life. He was exiled forever from the world of his birth. Not being a sentimental man, he had never let this depress him unduly.

What did depress him sometimes was the need for dealing, year after year, with the same familiar faces. The marvels of medicine were all very well—and certainly he had no desire to put back the clock—but there were men around this conference table with whom he had worked for more than half a century. He knew exactly what they would say and how they would vote on any given subject. He wished that, someday, one of them would do something totally unexpected—even something quite crazy.

And probably they felt exactly the same way about him.

The Rama Committee was still manageably small, though doubtless that would soon be changed. His six colleagues—each representing one of the members of the United Planets—were all present in the flesh. They had to be; electronic diplomacy was not possible over solar-system distances. Some elder statesmen, accustomed to the instantaneous communications that Earth had long taken for granted, had never reconciled themselves to the fact that radio waves took minutes, or even hours, to journey across the gulfs between the planets. "Can't you scientists do something about it?" they had been heard to complain bitterly when told that immediate face-to-face conversation was impossible between Earth and any of its remoter children. Only the Moon had the barely acceptable one-and-a-half-second delay—with all the political and psychological consequences that implied. Because of this fact of astronomical life, the Moon—and *only* the Moon —would always be a suburb of Earth.

Also present in person were specialists who had been co-opted to the committee. Professor Davidson, the astronomer, was an old acquaintance. Today he did not seem his usual irascible self. Bose knew nothing of the infighting that had preceded the launch of the first probe to Rama, but the Professor's colleagues had not let him forget it.

Dr. Thelma Price was familiar through her numerous television appearances, though she had first made her reputation fifty years ago during the archeological explosion that had followed the draining of that vast marine museum the Mediterranean.

Bose could still recall the excitement of that time, when the lost treasures of the Greeks, the Romans, and a dozen other civilizations were restored to the light of day. That was one of the few occasions when he was sorry to be living on Mars.

The exobiologist Carlisle Perera was another obvious choice; so was Dennis Solomons, the science historian. Bose was slightly less happy about the presence of Conrad Taylor, the celebrated anthropologist, who had made his reputation by uniquely combining scholarship and eroticism in his study of puberty rites in late-twentieth-century Beverly Hills.

No one, however, could possibly have disputed the right of Sir Lewis Sands to be on the committee. A man whose knowledge was matched only by his urbanity, Sir Lewis was reputed to lose his composure only when called the Arnold Toynbee of his age. The great historian was not present in person, however. He stubbornly refused to leave Earth, even for so momentous a meeting as this. His stereo image, indistinguishable from the real one, apparently occupied the chair to Bose's right, and, as if to complete the illusion, someone had placed a glass of water in front of him. Bose considered this sort of technological tour de force an unnecessary gimmick, but it was surprising how many undeniably great men were childishly delighted to be in two places at once. Sometimes this electronic miracle produced comic disasters. Bose had been at one diplomatic reception when somebody had tried to walk through a stereogram, and discovered, too late, that it was the real person. And it was even funnier to watch projections trying to shake hands.

Now, His Excellency the Ambassador from Mars to the United Planets called his wandering thoughts to order, cleared his throat, and said: "Gentlemen, the committee is now in session. I think I am correct in saying that this is a gathering of unique talents, assembled to deal with a unique situation. The directive that the Secretary-General has given us is to evaluate that situation, and to advise Commander Norton when necessary."

This was a miracle of oversimplification, and everyone knew it. Unless there was a real emergency, the committee might never be in direct contact with Commander Norton—if, indeed, he ever heard of its existence. The committee was a temporary creation of the United Planets Science Organization, reporting through its director to the Secretary-General. It was true that the Solar Survey was part of the U.P.—but on the operations, not the science, side. In theory, this should not make much difference; there was no reason why the Rama Committee—or anyone else, for that matter—should not call up Commander Norton and offer helpful advice.

But deep-space communications were expensive. *Endeavour* could be contacted only through PLANETCOM, which was an autonomous corporation famous for the strictness and efficiency of its accounting. It took a long time to establish a line of credit with PLANETCOM. Somewhere, someone was working on this, but, at the moment, PLANETCOM's hardhearted computers did not recognize the existence of the Rama Committee.

"This Commander Norton," said Sir Robert Mackay, the Ambassador from Earth, "has a tremendous responsibility. What sort of person is he?"

"I can answer that," said Professor Davidson, his fingers flying over the keyboard of his memory pad. He frowned at the screenful of information, and started to make an instant synopsis.

"William Tsien Norton, born 2077, Brisbane, Oceana. Educated Sydney, Bombay, Houston. Then five years at Astrograd, specializing in propulsion. Commissioned 2102. Rose through usual ranks . . . lieutenant on the third Persephone expedition . . . distinguished himself during fifteenth attempt to establish base on Venus . . . um . . um . . . exemplary record . . . dual citizenship, Earth and Mars . . . wife and one child in Brisbane, wife and *two* in Port Lowell, with option on third . . ."

"Wife?" asked Taylor innocently.

"No. Child, of course," snapped the Professor, before he caught the grin on the other's face. Mild laughter rippled around the table, though the overcrowded terrestrials looked more envious than amused. After a century of determined effort, Earth had still failed to get its population below the target of one billion. . . .

"Appointed commanding officer Solar Survey research vessel *Endeavour*. First voyage to retrograde satellites of Jupiter . . um, that was a tricky one . . . one asteroid mission when ordered to prepare for this operation . . . managed to beat deadline . . ."

The Professor cleared the display and looked at his colleagues. "I think we were extremely lucky, considering that he was the only man available at such short notice. We might have had the usual run-of-the-mill captain." He sounded as if he was referring to the typical peg-legged scourge of the spaceways, pistol in one hand and cutlass in the other.

"The record proves only that he's competent," objected the Ambassador from Mercury (population: 112,500, but growing). "How will he react in a wholly novel situation like this?"

On Earth, Sir Lewis Sands cleared his throat. A second and a half later, he did so on the Moon. "Not exactly a novel situation," he reminded the Hermian, "even though it's three centuries since it last occurred. If Rama is dead, or unoccupied—and so far all the evidence suggests that it is—Norton is in the position of an archeologist discovering the ruins of an extinct culture." He bowed politely to Dr Price, who nodded in agreement. "Obvious examples are Schliemann at Troy and Mouhot at Angkor Vat. The danger is minimal, though of course accident can never be completely ruled out."

"But what about the booby traps and trigger mechanisms these Pandora people have been talking about?" asked Dr Price.

"Pandora?" asked the Hermian Ambassador quickly. "What's that?"

"It's a crackpot movement," explained Sir Robert, with as much embarrassment as a diplomat was ever likely to show, "that is convinced that Rama is a grave potential danger. A box that shouldn't be opened, you know." He doubted if the Hermian *did* know, classical studies were not encouraged on Mercury

"Pandora—paranoia," snorted Taylor. "Oh, of course such things are *conceivable*, but why should any intelligent race want to play childish tricks?"

"Well, even ruling out such unpleasantness," Sir Robert continued, "we still have the much more ominous possibility of an active, inhabited Rama. Then the situation is one of an encounter between two cultures—at very different technological levels. Pizzaro and the Incas. Peary and the Japanese. Europe and Africa. Almost invariably, the consequences have been disastrous—for one or both parties. I'm not making any recommendations; I'm merely pointing out precedents."

"Thank you, Sir Robert," replied Bose. It was a mild nuisance, he thought, having two "Sirs" on one small committee; in these latter days, knighthood was an honor few Englishmen escaped. "I'm sure we've all thought of these alarming possibilities. But if the creatures inside Rama are . . . er . . . malevolent, will it really make the slightest difference what we do?"

"They might ignore us if we go away."

"What—after they've traveled billions of miles and thousands of years?"

The argument had reached the take-off point, and was now self-sustaining. Bose sat back in his chair, said little, and waited for a consensus to emerge.

It was just as he had predicted. Everyone agreed that, once he had opened the first door, it was inconceivable that Commander Norton should not open the second.

7

Two Wives

IF HIS WIVES ever compared his videograms, Commander Norton thought, with more amusement than concern, it would involve him in a lot of extra work. Now, he could make one long gram and dupe it, adding only brief personal messages and endearments before shooting the almost identical copies off to Mars and to Earth.

Of course, it was highly unlikely that his wives ever would do such a thing; even at the concessionary rates allowed to spacemen's families, it would be expensive. And there would be no point in it. His families were on excellent terms with each other, and exchanged the usual greetings on birthdays and anniversaries. Yet, on the whole, perhaps it was just as well that the girls had never met, and probably never would. Myrna had been born on Mars, and so could not tolerate the high gravity of Earth. And Caroline hated even the twenty-five minutes of the longest possible terrestrial journey.

"Sorry I'm a day late with this transmission," said Norton after he had finished the general-purpose preliminaries, "but I've been away from the ship for the last thirty hours, believe it or not.

"Don't be alarmed—everything is under control, going perfectly. It's taken us two days, but we're almost through the air-lock complex. We could have done it in a couple of hours if we'd known what we do now. But we took no chances, sent remote cameras ahead, and cycled all the locks a dozen times to make sure they wouldn't seize up behind us—*after* we'd gone through.

"Each lock is a simple revolving cylinder with a slot on one side. You go in through this opening, crank the cylinder around a hundred and eighty degrees, and the slot then matches up with another door so you can step out of it. Or float, in this case.

"The Ramans really made sure of things. There are three of these cylinder locks, one after the other, just inside the outer hull and below the entry pillbox. I can't imagine how even one would fail, unless someone blew it up with explosives, but if it did, there would be a second back-up, and then a third.

"And *that's* only the beginning. The final lock opens into a straight corridor, almost half a kilometer long. It looks clean and tidy, like everything else we've seen. Every few meters there are small ports that probably held lights, but now everything is completely black, and, I don't mind telling you, scary. There are also two parallel slots, about a centimeter wide, cut in the walls and running the whole length of the tunnel. We suspect that some kind of shuttle runs inside these, to tow equipment—or people—back and forth. It would save us a lot of trouble if we could get it working.

"I mentioned that the tunnel was half a kilometer long. Well, from our seismic soundings we knew that

that's about the thickness of the shell, so obviously we were almost through it. And at the end of the tunnel we weren't surprised to find another of those cylindrical air locks.

"Yes, *and* another. *And* another. These people seem to have done everything in threes. We're in the fnal lock chamber now, waiting for the OK from Earth before we go through. The interior of Rama is only a few meters away. I'll be a lot happier when the suspense is over.

"You know Jerry Kirchoff, my exec, who's got such a library of *real* books that he can't afford to emigrate from Earth? Well, Jerry told me about a situation just like this, back at the beginning of the twenty-first—no, twentieth century. An archeologist found the tomb of an Egyptian king, the first one that hadn't been looted by robbers. His workmen took months to dig their way in, chamber by chamber, until they came to the final wall. Then they broke through the masonry, and he held out a lantern and pushed his head inside. He found himself looking into a whole roomful of treasure —incredible stuff, gold and jewels.

"Perhaps this place is also a tomb; it seems more and more likely. Even now, there's still not the slightest sound, or hint of any activity.

"Well, tomorrow we should know."

Norton switched the recorder to HOLD. What else, he wondered, should he say about the work before he began the separate personal messages to his families? Normally, he never went into so much detail, but these circumstances were scarcely normal. This might be the last gram he would ever send to those he loved. He owed it to them to explain what he was doing.

By the time they saw these images, and heard these words, he would be inside Rama—for better or for worse.

8

Through the Hub

NEVER BEFORE HAD Norton felt so strongly his kinship with that long-dead Egyptologist. Not since Howard Carter had first peered into the tomb of Tutankhamen could any man have known a moment such as this. Yet the comparison was almost ridiculously ludicrous.

Tutankhamen had been buried only yesterday—not even four thousand years ago; Rama might be older than mankind. That little tomb in the Valley of the Kings could have been lost in the corridors through which they had already passed, but the space that lay beyond this final seal was at least a million times greater. And as for the treasure it might hold—that was beyond imagination.

No one had spoken over the radio circuits for at least five minutes; the well-trained team had not even reported verbally when all the checks were complete. Mercer had simply given him the OK sign and waved

him toward the open tunnel. It was as if everyone realized that this was a moment for history, not to be
spoiled by unnecessary small talk. That suited Norton,
for at the moment he, too, had nothing to say. He
flicked on the beam of his flashlight, triggered his jets,
and drifted slowly down the short corridor, trailing his
safety line behind him. Only seconds later, he was inside.

Inside *what?* All before him was total darkness; not
a glimmer of light was reflected back from the beam.
He had expected this, but he had not really believed it.
All the calculations had shown that the far wall was
tens of kilometers away; now his eyes told him that
this was indeed the truth. As he drifted slowly into
that darkness, he felt a sudden need for the reassur-
ance of his safety line, stronger than any he had ever
experienced before, even on his first EVA. And that
was ridiculous. He had looked out across the light-
years and the megaparsecs without vertigo; why
should he be disturbed by a few cubic kilometers of
emptiness?

He was queasily brooding over this problem when
the momentum damper at the end of the line braked
him gently to a halt, with a barely perceptible rebound. He swept the vainly probing beam of the flashlight down from the nothingness ahead, to examine the
surface from which he had emerged.

He might have been hovering over the center of a
small crater, which was itself a dimple in the base of a
much larger one. On either side rose a complex of terraces and ramps—all geometrically precise and obviously artificial—which extended for as far as the
beam could reach. About a hundred meters away he
could see the exits of the other two air-lock systems,
identical with this one.

And that was all. There was nothing particularly exotic or alien about the scene. In fact, it bore a considerable resemblance to an abandoned mine. He felt a vague sense of disappointment; after all this effort, there should have been some dramatic, even transcendental, revelation. Then he reminded himself that he could see only a couple of hundred meters. The darkness beyond his field of view might yet contain more wonders than he cared to face.

He reported briefly to his anxiously waiting companions, then added: "I'm sending out the flare—two-minute delay. Here goes."

With all his strength, he threw the little cylinder straight upward—or outward—and started to count seconds as it dwindled along the beam. Before he had reached the quarter minute, it was out of sight; when he had got to a hundred, he shielded his eyes and aimed the camera. He had always been good at estimating time; he was only two seconds off when the world exploded with light. And this time there was no cause for disappointment.

Even the millions of candle power of the flare could not light up the whole of this enormous cavity, but he could see enough to grasp its plan and appreciate its titanic scale. He was at one end of a hollow cylinder at least ten kilometers wide, and of indefinite length. From his viewpoint at the central axis, he could see such a mass of detail on the curving walls surrounding him that his mind could not absorb more than a minute fraction of it. He was looking at the landscape of an entire world by a single flash of lightning, and he tried by a deliberate effort of will to freeze the image in his mind.

All around him, the terraced slopes of crater rose up until they merged into the solid wall that rimmed the sky No—that impression was false; he must discard the instincts both of Earth and of space, and reorientate himself to a new system of co-ordinates.

He was not at the lowest point of this strange, inside-out world, but the highest. From here, all directions were *down*, not up. If he moved away from this central axis, toward the curving wall which he must no longer think of as a wall, gravity would steadily increase. When he reached the inside surface of the cylinder, he could stand upright on it at any point, feet toward the stars and head toward the center of the spinning drum. The concept was familiar enough; since the earliest dawn of space flight, centrifugal force had been used to simulate gravity. It was only the scale of this application that was so overwhelming, so shocking. The largest of all space stations, Syncsat Five, was less than two hundred meters in diameter. It would take some little while to grow accustomed to one hundred times that size.

The tube of landscape that enclosed him was mottled with areas of light and shade that could have been forests, fields, frozen lakes, or towns; the distance, and the fading illumination of the flare, made identification impossible. Narrow lines that could be highways, canals, or well-trained rivers formed a faintly visible geometrical network; and far along the cylinder, at the very limit of vision, was a band of deeper darkness. It formed a complete circle, ringing the interior of this world, and Norton suddenly recalled the myth of Oceanus, the sea that, the ancients believed, surrounded the Earth.

Here, perhaps, was an even stranger sea—not circular, but *cylindrical*. Before it became frozen in the interstellar night, did it have waves and tides and currents—and fish?

The flare guttered and died; the moment of revelation was over. But Norton knew that as long as he lived these images would be burned in his mind. Whatever discoveries the future might bring, they could never erase this first impression. And history could never take from him the privilege of being the first of all mankind to gaze upon the works of an alien civilization.

9

Reconnaissance

"WE HAVE NOW launched five long-delay flares down the axis of the cylinder, and so have a good photo-coverage of its full length. All the main features are mapped. Though there are few that we can identify, we've given them provisional names.

"The interior cavity is fifty kilometers long and sixteen wide. The two ends are bowl-shaped, with rather complicated geometries. We've called ours the Northern Hemisphere and are establishing our first base here at the axis.

"Radiating from the central hub, 120 degrees apart, are three ladders that are almost a kilometer long. They all end at a terrace, or ring-shaped plateau, that runs right around the bowl. And leading on from that, continuing the direction of the ladders, are three enormous stairways, which go all the way down to the plain. If you imagine an umbrella with only three ribs, equally spaced, you'll have a good idea of this end of Rama.

"Each of those ribs is a stairway, very steep near the axis and then slowly flattening out as it approaches the plain below. The stairways—we've called them Alpha, Beta, Gamma—aren't continuous, but break at five more circular terraces. We estimate there must be between twenty and thirty thousand steps. Presumably they were used only for emergencies, since it's inconceivable that the Ramans—or whatever we're going to call them—had no better way of reaching the axis of their world.

"The Southern Hemisphere looks quite different. For one thing, it has no stairways and no flat central hub. Instead, there's a huge spike, kilometers long, jutting along the axis, with six smaller ones around it. The whole arrangement is very odd, and we can't imagine what it means.

"The fifty-kilometer-long cylindrical section between the two bowls we've called the Central Plain. It may seem crazy to use the word 'plain' to describe something so obviously curved, but we feel it's justified. It will appear flat to us when we get down there —just as the interior of a bottle must seem flat to an ant crawling around inside it.

"The most striking feature of the Central Plain is the ten-kilometer-wide dark band running completely around it at the halfway mark. It looks like ice, so we've christened it the Cylindrical Sea. Right out in the middle there's a large oval island, about ten kilometers long and three wide, and covered with tall structures. Because it reminds us of Old Manhattan, we've called it New York. Yet I don't think it's a city; it seems more like an enormous factory or chemical processing plant.

"But there are some cities—or, at any rate, towns —at least six of them. If they were built for human beings, they could each hold about fifty thousand people. We've called them Rome, Peking, Paris, Moscow, London, Tokyo. They are linked with highways and something that seems to be a rail system.

"There must be enough material for centuries of research in this frozen carcass of a world. We've four thousand square kilometers to explore, and only a few weeks to do it in. I wonder if we'll ever learn the answer to the two mysteries that have been haunting me ever since we got inside: who were they, *and what went wrong?*"

The recording ended. On Earth and Moon, the members of the Rama Committee relaxed, then started to examine the maps and photographs spread in front of them. Though they had already studied these for many hours, Commander Norton's voice added a dimension no pictures could convey He had actually been there, had looked with his own eyes across this extraordinary inside-out world, during the brief moments while its age-long night had been illuminated by the flares. And he was the man who would lead any expedition to explore it.

"Dr. Perera, I believe you have some comments to make?"

Ambassador Bose wondered briefly if he should have given the floor first to Professor Davidson, as senior scientist and the only astronomer. But the old cosmologist still seemed to be in a mild state of shock, and was clearly out of his element All his professional career he had looked upon the universe as an arena for the titanic impersonal forces of gravitation, magnetism, radiation; he had never believed that life played an important role in the scheme of things, and he regarded its appearance on Earth, Mars, and Jupiter as an accidental aberration.

But now there was proof that life not only existed outside the solar system, but also had scaled heights far beyond anything that man had achieved, or could hope to reach for centuries to come. Moreover, the discovery of Rama challenged another dogma that Davidson had preached for years. When pressed, he would reluctantly admit that life probably did exist in other star systems; but it was absurd, he had always maintained, to imagine that it could ever cross the interstellar gulfs.

Perhaps the Ramans had indeed failed, if Commander Norton was correct in believing that their world was now a tomb. But at least they had attempted the feat, on a scale that indicated a high confidence in the outcome. If such a thing had happened once, it must surely have happened many times in this galaxy of a hundred billion suns. And someone, somewhere, would eventually succeed.

This was the thesis that, without proof but with considerable arm-waving, Dr. Carlisle Perera had been preaching for years. He was now a very happy man, though also a most frustrated one. Rama had spectacularly confirmed his views, but he could never set foot inside it, or even see it with his own eyes. If the devil had suddenly appeared and offered him the gift of instantaneous teleportation, he would have signed the contract without bothering to look at the small print.

"Yes, Mr. Ambassador, I think I have some information of interest. What we have here is undoubtedly a 'space ark.' It's an old idea in the astronautical literature. I've been able to trace it back to the British physicist J. D. Bernal, who proposed this method of interstellar colonization in a book published in 1929 —yes, two hundred years ago! And the great Russian pioneer Tsiolkovsky put forward somewhat similar proposals even earlier.

"If you want to go from one star system to another, you have a number of choices. Assuming that the speed of light is an absolute limit—and that's *still* not completely settled, despite anything you may have heard to the contrary" (there was an indignant sniff, but no formal protest, from Davidson)—"you can make a fast trip in a small vessel, or a slow journey in a giant one.

"There seems no technical reason why spacecraft cannot reach ninety per cent, or more, of the speed of light. That would mean a travel time of five to ten years between neighboring stars—tedious, perhaps, but not impracticable, especially for creatures whose life spans might be measured in centuries. One can imagine voyages of this duration carried out in ships not much larger than ours.

"But perhaps such speeds are impossible, with reasonable pay loads. Remember, you have to carry the fuel to slow down at the end of the voyage, even if you're on a one-way trip. So it may make more sense to take your time—ten thousand, a hundred thousand years.

"Bernal and others thought this could be done with mobile worldlets a few kilometers across, carrying thousands of passengers on journeys that would last for generations. Naturally, the system would have to be rigidly closed, recycling all food, air, and other expendables. But, of course, that's just how the Earth operates—on a slightly larger scale.

"Some writers suggested that these space arks should be built in the form of concentric spheres; others proposed hollow, spinning cylinders so that centrifugal force could provide artificial gravity—exactly what we've found in Rama—"

Davidson could not tolerate this sloppy talk. "No such thing as centrifugal *force*. It's an engineer's phantom. There's only inertia."

"You're quite right, of course," admitted Perera, "though it might be hard to convince a man who'd just been slung off a carrousel. But mathematical rigor seems unnecessary—"

"Hear, hear," interjected Bose, with some exasperation. "We all know what you mean, or think we do. Please don't destroy our illusions."

"Well, I was merely pointing out that there's nothing conceptually novel about Rama, though its size is startling. Men have imagined such things for two hundred years.

"Now I'd like to address myself to another question. Exactly how long has Rama been traveling through space?

"We now have a very precise determination of its orbit and its velocity. Assuming that it's made no navigational changes, we can trace its position back for millions of years. We expected that it would be coming from the direction of a nearby star. But that isn't the case at all.

"It's more than *two hundred thousand years* since Rama passed near any star, and that particular one turns out to be an irregular variable—about the most unsuitable sun you could imagine for an inhabited solar system. It has a brightness range of over fifty to one; any planets would be alternately baked and frozen every few years."

"A suggestion," put in Dr. Price. "Perhaps that explains everything. Maybe this was once a normal sun and became unstable. That's why the Ramans had to find a new one."

Perera admired the old archeologist, so he let her down lightly. But what would *she* say, he wondered, if he started pointing out the instantly obvious in her own specialty?

"We did consider that," he said gently. "But if our present theories of stellar evolution are correct, this star could *never* have been stable, could never have had lifebearing planets. So Rama has been cruising through space for at least two hundred thousand years, and perhaps for more than a million.

"Now it's cold and dark and apparently dead, and I think I know why. The Ramans may have had no choice—perhaps they were indeed fleeing from some disaster—but they miscalculated.

"No closed ecology can be one-hundred-per-cent efficient; there is always waste, loss—some degradation of the environment and build-up of pollutants. It may take billions of years to poison and wear out a planet, but it will happen in the end. The oceans will dry up; the atmosphere will leak away.

"By our standards, Rama is enormous—yet it is still a very tiny planet. My calculations, based on the leakage through its hull, and some reasonable guesses about the rate of biological turnover, indicate that its ecology could survive for only about a thousand years. At the most, I'll grant ten thousand.

"That would be long enough, at the speed Rama is traveling, for a transit between the closely packed suns in the heart of the galaxy. But not out here, in the scattered population of the spiral arms. Rama is a ship that exhausted its provisions before it reached its goal. It's a derelict, drifting among the stars.

"There's just one serious objection to this theory, and I'll raise it before anybody else does. Rama's orbit is aimed so accurately at the solar system that coincidence seems ruled out. In fact, I'd say it's now heading much too close to the Sun for comfort. *Endeavour* will have to break away long before perihelion, to avoid overheating.

"I don't pretend to understand this. Perhaps there is some form of automatic terminal guidance still operating, steering Rama to the nearest suitable star ages after its builders died.

"And they *are* dead; I'll stake my reputation on

that. All the samples we've taken from the interior are absolutely sterile. We've not found a single microorganism. As for the talk you may have heard about suspended animation, you can ignore it. There are fundamental reasons why hibernation techniques will work for only a few centuries—and we're dealing with time spans a thousandfold longer.

"So the Pandorans and their sympathizers have nothing to worry about. For my part, I'm sorry. It would have been wonderful to have met another intelligent species.

"But at least we have answered one ancient question. We are not alone. The stars will never again be the same to us."

10

Descent into Darkness

COMMANDER NORTON WAS sorely tempted, but, as captain, his first duty was to his ship. If anything went badly wrong on this initial probe, he might have to run for it.

So that left his second officer, Lieutenant Commander Mercer, as the obvious choice. Norton willingly admitted that Karl was better suited for the mission.

The authority on life-support systems, Mercer had written some of the standard textbooks on the subject. He had personally checked out innumerable types of equipment, often under hazardous conditions, and his biofeedback control was famous. At a moment's notice he could cut his pulse rate by fifty per cent, and reduce respiration to almost zero for up to ten minutes. This useful little trick had saved his life on more than one occasion.

Yet despite his great ability and intelligence, he was

almost wholly lacking in imagination. To him, the most dangerous experiments or missions were simply jobs that had to be done. He never took unnecessary risks, and he had no use at all for what was commonly regarded as courage.

The two mottoes on his desk summed up his philosophy of life. One asked, WHAT HAVE YOU FORGOTTEN? The other said, HELP STAMP OUT BRAVERY. The fact that he was widely regarded as the bravest man in the fleet was the only thing that ever made him angry.

Given Mercer, that automatically selected the next man: his inseparable companion, Lieutenant Joe Calvert. It was hard to see what the two had in common. The lightly built, rather highly strung navigation officer was ten years younger than his stolid and imperturbable friend, who certainly did not share his passionate interest in the art of the primitive cinema.

But no one can predict where the lightning will strike, and years ago Mercer and Calvert had established an apparently stable liaison. That was common enough. Much more unusual was the fact that they also shared a wife back on Earth, who had borne each of them a child. Norton hoped that he could meet her one day; she must be a most remarkable woman. The triangle had lasted for at least five years, and still seemed to be an equilateral one.

Two men were not enough for an exploring team. Long ago it had been found that three was the optimum—for if one man was lost, two might still escape where a single survivor would be doomed. After a good deal of thought, Norton had chosen Technical Sergeant Willard Myron. A mechanical genius who could make anything work, or design something better if it wouldn't, Myron was the ideal man to identify alien pieces of equipment. On a long sabbatical from his regular job as associate professor at Astrotech, the Sergeant had refused to accept a commission on the grounds that he did not wish to block the promotion of more deserving career officers. No one took this explanation seriously, and it was generally agreed that Will rated zero for ambition. He might make it to space sergeant, but he would never be a full professor. Myron, like countless NCO's before him, had discovered the ideal compromise between power and responsibility.

As they drifted through the last air lock and floated out along the weightless axis of Rama, Calvert found himself, as he so often did, in the middle of a movie flashback. He sometimes wondered if he should attempt to cure himself of this habit, but he could not see that it had any disadvantages. It could make even the dullest situations interesting and—who could tell? —one day it might save his life. He would remember what Fairbanks or Connery or Hiroshi had done in similar circumstances.

This time, he was about to go over the top, in one of the early twentieth-century wars; Mercer was the sergeant, leading a three-man patrol on a night raid into no man's land. It was not too difficult to imagine that they were at the bottom of an immense shell crater, though one that had somehow become neatly tailored into a series of ascending terraces. The crater was flooded with light from three widely spaced plasma arcs, which gave an almost shadowless illumination over the whole interior. But beyond that, over the rim of the most distant terrace, were darkness and mystery.

In his mind's eye, Calvert knew perfectly well what lay there. First there was the flat circular plain over a kilometer across. Trisecting it into three equal parts, and looking much like broad railroad tracks, were three wide ladders, their rungs recessed into the surface so that they would provide no obstruction to anything sliding over them. Since the arrangement was completely symmetrical, there was no reason to choose one ladder rather than another; that nearest to air lock Alpha had been selected purely as a matter of convenience.

Though the rungs of the ladders were uncomfortably far apart, that presented no problem. Even at the rim of the hub, half a kilometer from the axis, gravity was still barely one-thirtieth of Earth's. Although they were carrying almost a hundred kilos of equipment and life-support gear, they would be able to move easily hand over hand.

Commander Norton and the back-up team accompanied them along the guide ropes that had been stretched from air lock Alpha to the rim of the crater. Then, beyond the range of the floodlights, the darkness of Rama lay before them. All that could be seen in the dancing beams of the helmet lights was the first few hundred meters of the ladder, dwindling away across a flat and otherwise featureless plain.

And now, Mercer told himself, I have to make my first decision. Am I going *up* that ladder, or *down* it?

The question was not a trivial one. They were still essentially in zero gravity, and the brain could select any reference system it pleased. By a simple effort of will, Mercer could convince himself that he was looking out across a horizontal plain or up the face of a vertical wall or over the edge of a sheer cliff. Not a few astronauts had experienced grave psychological problems by choosing the wrong co-ordinates when they started on a complicated job.

Mercer was determined to go head-first, for any other mode of locomotion would be awkward. Moreover, that way he could more easily see what was in front of him. For the first few hundred meters, therefore, he would imagine he was climbing upward; only when the increasing pull of gravity made it impossible to maintain the illusion would he switch his mental directions one hundred and eighty degrees.

He grasped the first rung and gently propelled himself along the ladder. Movement was as easy as swimming along the sea bed—easier, in fact, for there was no backward drag of water. It was so easy that there was a temptation to go too fast, but Mercer was much too experienced to hurry in a situation as novel as this.

In his earphones he could hear the regular breathing of his two companions. He needed no other proof that they were in good shape, and wasted no time in conversation. Though he was tempted to look back, he decided not to risk it until they had reached the platform at the end of the ladder.

The rungs were spaced a uniform half-meter apart, and for the first portion of the climb Mercer missed the alternate ones. But he counted them carefully, and at around two hundred noticed the first distinct sensations of weight. The spin of Rama was starting to make itself felt.

At rung four hundred, he estimated that his apparent weight was about five kilos, or about eleven pounds. This was no problem, but it was getting hard to pretend that he was climbing when he was being firmly dragged *upward*.

The five hundredth rung seemed a good place to pause. He could feel the muscles in his arms responding to the unaccustomed exercise, even though Rama was now doing all the work and he had merely to guide himself.

"Everything OK, Skipper," he reported. "We're just passing the halfway mark. Joe, Will, any problems?"

"I'm fine. What are you stopping for?" Calvert answered.

"Same here," added Myron. "But watch out for the Coriolis force. It's starting to build up."

So Mercer had already noticed. When he let go of

the rungs, he had a distinct tendency to drift off to the right. He knew perfectly well that this was merely the effect of Rama's spin, but it seemed as if some mysterious force was gently pushing him away from the ladder.

Perhaps it was time to start going feet-first, now that "down" was beginning to have a physical meaning. He would run the risk of a momentary disorientation.

"Watch out—I'm going to swing around."

Holding firmly to the rung, he used his arms to twist himself around a hundred and eighty degrees, and found himself momentarily blinded by the lights of his companions. Far above them—and now it really *was* above—he could see a fainter glow along the rim of the sheer cliff. Silhouetted against it were the figures of Norton and the back-up team, watching him intently. They seemed very small and far away, and he gave them a reassuring wave.

He released his grip and let Rama's still-feeble pseudo-gravity take over. The drop from one rung to the next required more than two seconds; on Earth, in the same time, a man would have fallen thirty meters.

The rate of fall was so painfully slow that he hurried things up a trifle by pushing with his hands, gliding over spans of a dozen rungs at a time, and checking himself with his feet whenever he felt he was traveling too fast.

At rung seven hundred, he came to another halt and swung the beam of his helmet lamp downward. As he had calculated, the beginning of the stairway was only fifty meters below.

A few minutes later, they were on the first step. It was a strange experience, after months in space, to stand upright on a solid surface, and to feel it pressing against one's feet. Their weight was still less than ten kilograms, but that was enough to give a feeling of stability. When he closed his eyes, Mercer could believe that he once more had a real world beneath him.

The ledge or platform from which the stairway descended was about ten meters wide, and curved upward on each side until it disappeared into the darkness. Mercer knew that it formed a complete circle and that if he walked along it for five kilometers, he would come right back to his starting point, having circumambulated Rama.

At the fractional gravity that existed here, however, real walking was impossible; one could only bound along in giant strides. And therein lay danger. The stairway that swooped down into the darkness, far below the range of their lights, would be deceptively easy to descend. But it would be essential to hold on to the tall handrail that flanked it. Too bold a step might send an incautious traveler arching far out into space. He would hit the surface again perhaps a hundred meters lower down. The impact would be harmless, but its consequences might not be, for the spin of Rama would have moved the stairway off to the left. And so a falling body would hit against the smooth curve that swept in an unbroken arc to the plain almost seven kilometers below.

That, Mercer told himself, would be a hell of a toboggan ride. The terminal speed, even in this gravity, could be several hundred kilometers an hour. Perhaps it would be possible to apply enough friction to check such a headlong descent; if so, this might even be the most convenient way to reach the inner surface of Rama. But some very cautious experimenting would be necessary first.

"Skipper," reported Mercer, "there were no problems getting down the ladder. If you agree, I'd like to continue toward the next platform. I want to time our rate of descent on the stairway."

Norton replied without hesitation. "Go ahead." He did not need to add, "Proceed with caution."

It did not take Mercer long to make a fundamental discovery. It was impossible, at least at this one-twentieth-of-a-gravity level, to walk down the stairway in the normal manner. Any attempt to do so resulted in a slow-motion dreamlike movement that was intolerably tedious. The only practical way was to ignore the steps and to use the handrail to pull oneself downward.

Calvert had come to the same conclusion. "This stairway was built to walk *up*, not down!" he exclaimed. "You can use the steps when you're moving against gravity, but they're just a nuisance in this direction. It may not be dignified, but I think the best way down is to slide along the handrail."

"That's ridiculous," protested Myron. "I can't believe the Ramans did it that way."

"I doubt if they ever used this stairway. It's obviously only for emergencies. They must have had some mechanical transport system to get up here. A funicular, perhaps. That would explain those long slots running down from the hub."

"I always assumed they were drains—but I suppose they could be both. I wonder if it ever rained here?"

"Probably," said Mercer. "But I think Joe is right, and to hell with dignity. Here we go."

The handrail—presumably it *was* designed for something like hands—was a smooth flat metal bar supported by widely spaced pillars a meter high. Mercer straddled it, carefully gauged the braking power he could exert with his hands, and let himself slide.

Sedately, slowly picking up speed, he descended into the darkness, moving in the pool of light from his helmet lamp. He had gone about fifty meters when he called the others to join him.

None of them would admit it, but they all felt like

boys again, sliding down the banisters. In less than two minutes, they had made a kilometer descent in safety and comfort. Whenever they felt they were going too fast, a tightened grip on the handrail provided all the braking that was necessary.

"I hope you enjoyed yourselves," Norton called when they stepped off at the second platform. "Climbing back won't be quite so easy."

"That's what I want to check," replied Mercer, who was walking experimentally back and forth, getting the feel of the increased gravity. "It's already a tenth of a gee here. You really notice the difference."

He walked—or, more accurately, glided—to the edge of the platform and shone his helmet light down the next section of the stairway. As far as his beam could reach, it appeared identical with the one above —though careful examination of photos had shown that the height of the steps steadily decreased with the rising gravity. The stair had apparently been designed so that the effort required to climb it was more or less constant at every point in its long curving sweep.

Mercer glanced up toward the hub of Rama, now almost two kilometers above him. The little glow of light, and the tiny figures silhouetted against it, seemed horribly far away. For the first time he was glad that he could not see the whole length of this enormous stairway. Despite his steady nerves and lack of imagination, he was not sure how he would react if he could see himself like an insect crawling up the face of a vertical saucer more than sixteen kilometers high—and with the upper half hanging above him. Until this moment, he had regarded the darkness as a nuisance; now he almost welcomed it.

"There's no change of temperature," he reported to Norton. "Still just below freezing. But the air pressure is up, as we expected—around three hundred millibars. Even with this low oxygen content, it's almost breathable; farther down, there will be no problems at all. That will simplify exploration enormously. What a find—the first world on which we can walk without breathing gear! In fact, I'm going to take a sniff."

Up on the hub, Norton stirred a little uneasily. But Mercer, of all men, knew exactly what he was doing. He would already have made enough tests to satisfy himself.

Mercer equalized pressure, unlatched the securing clip of his helmet, and opened it a crack. He took a cautious breath; then a deeper one.

The air of Rama was dead and musty, as if from a tomb so ancient that the last trace of physical corruption had disappeared ages ago. Even Mercer's ultra-sensitive nose, trained through years of testing life-support systems to and beyond the point of disaster, could detect no recognizable odors. There was a faint metallic tang, and he suddenly recalled that the first men on the Moon had reported a hint of burned gun-powder when they repressurized the lunar module. Mercer imagined that the moon-dust-contaminated cabin of *Eagle* must have smelled rather like Rama.

He sealed the helmet again and emptied his lungs of the alien air. He had extracted no sustenance from it; even a mountaineer acclimatized to the summit of Everest would die quickly here. But a few kilometers farther down, it would be a different matter.

What else was there to do here? He could think of nothing, except the enjoyment of the gentle, unaccustomed gravity. But there was no point in growing used to that, since they would be returning immediately to the weightlessness of the hub.

"We're coming back, Skipper," he reported. "There's no reason to go farther—until we're ready to go *all* the way."

"I agree. We'll be timing you, but take it easy."

As he bounded up the steps, three or four at a stride, Mercer agreed that Calvert had been perfectly correct; these stairs were built to be walked *up*, not down. As long as one did not look back, and ignored the vertiginous steepness of the ascending curve, the climb was a delightful experience. After about two hundred steps, however, he began to feel some twinges in his calf muscles, and decided to slow down. The others had done the same; when he ventured a quick glance over his shoulder, they were considerably farther down the slope.

The climb was wholly uneventful, merely an apparently endless succession of steps. When they stood once more on the highest platform, immediately beneath the ladder, they were barely winded, and it had taken them only ten minutes. They paused for another ten, then started on the last vertical kilometer.

Jump—catch hold of a rung—jump—catch—jump —catch . . . It was easy, but so boringly repetitious that there was danger of becoming careless. Halfway up the ladder they rested for five minutes. By this time their arms as well as their legs had begun to ache. Once again Mercer was glad that they could see so little of the vertical face on which they were clinging. It was not too difficult to pretend that the ladder extended only a few meters beyond their circle of light, and would soon come to an end.

Jump—catch a rung—jump—then, quite suddenly, the ladder *really* ended. They were back in the weightless world of the axis, among their anxious friends. The whole trip had taken under an hour, and they felt a sense of modest achievement.

But it was much too soon to feel pleased with themselves. For all their efforts, they had traversed less than an eighth of that Cyclopean stairway.

11

Men, Women, and Monkeys

SOME WOMEN, COMMANDER Norton had decided long ago, should not be allowed aboard ship; weightlessness did things to their breasts that were too damn distracting. It was bad enough when they were motionless; but when they started to move, and sympathetic vibrations set in, it was more than any warm-blooded male should be asked to take. He was quite sure that at least one serious space accident had been caused by acute crew distraction, after the transit of an unholstered lady officer through the control cabin.

He had once mentioned this theory to Surgeon Commander Laura Ernst, without revealing who had inspired his particular train of thought. There was no need; they knew each other much too well. On Earth, years ago, in a moment of mutual loneliness and depression, they had once made love. Probably they would never repeat the experience (but could one ever be *quite* sure of that?), because so much had changed for both of them. Yet whenever the well-built surgeon oscillated into the Commander's cabin he felt a fleeting echo of the old passion, she knew that he felt it, and both were happy.

"Bill," she began, "I've checked our mountaineers, and here's my verdict. Karl and Joe are in good shape —all indications normal for the work they've done. But Will shows signs of exhaustion and body loss. I won't bother you with the details. I don't believe he's been getting all the exercise he should, and he's not the only one. There's been some cheating in the centrifuge; if there's any more, heads will roll. Please pass the word."

"Yes, ma'am. But there's some excuse. The men have been working very hard."

"With their brains and fingers, certainly. But not with their bodies—not *real* work in kilogram-meters. And that's what we'll be dealing with, if we're going to explore Rama."

"Well, can we?"

"Yes, if we proceed with caution. Karl and I have worked out a very conservative profile—based on the assumption that we can dispense with breathing gear below the second level. Of course, that's an incredible stroke of luck, and changes the whole logistics picture. I still can't get used to the idea of a world with oxygen. . . . So we need to supply only food and water and thermosuits, and we're in business. Going down will be easy; it looks as if we can slide most of the way, on that very convenient banister."

"I've got Chips working on a sled with parachute-braking. Even if we can't risk it for the crew, we can use it for stores and equipment."

"Fine; *that* should do the trip in ten minutes. Otherwise it will take about an hour. Climbing up is harder to estimate. I'd like to allow six hours, including two one-hour periods. Later, as we get experience—*and develop some muscles*—we may be able to cut this back considerably."

"What about psychological factors?"

"Hard to assess, in such a novel environment. Darkness may be the biggest problem."

"I'll establish searchlights on the hub. Besides its own lamps, any party down there will always have a beam playing on it."

"Good—that should be a great help."

"One other point: should we play safe and send a party only halfway down the stair and back or should we go the whole way, on the first attempt?"

"If we had plenty of time, I'd be cautious. But time is short, and I can see no danger in going all the way —and looking around when we get there."

"Thanks, Laura—that's all I want to know. I'll get the Exec working on the details. And I'll order all hands to the centrifuge—twenty minutes a day at half a gee. Will that satisfy you?"

"No. It's point six gee down there in Rama, and I want a safety margin. Make it three-quarters—"

"Ouch!"

"For ten minutes—"

"I'll settle for that."

"*Twice* a day."

"Laura, you're a cruel, hard woman. But so be it. I'll break the news just before dinner. That should spoil a few appetites."

It was the first time Commander Norton had ever seen Karl Mercer slightly ill at ease. He had spent fifteen minutes discussing the logistics problems in his usual competent manner, but something was obviously worrying him. His captain, who had a shrewd idea of what it was, waited patiently until he brought it out.

"Skipper," Mercer said, finally, "are you *sure* you

should lead this party? If anything goes wrong, I'm considerably more expendable. And I've been farther inside Rama than anyone else—even if only by fifty meters."

"Granted. But it's time the commander led his troops, and we've decided that there's no greater risk on this trip than on the last. At the first sign of trouble, I'll be back up that stairway fast enough to qualify for the Lunar Olympics."

He waited for any further objections, but none came, though Mercer still looked unhappy. So he took pity on him and added gently: "And I bet Joe will beat me to the top."

The big man relaxed, and a slow grin spread across his face. "All the same, Bill, I wish you'd taken someone else."

"I wanted *one* man who'd been down before, and we can't both go. As for Herr Doctor Professor Sergeant Myron, Laura says he's still two kilos overweight. Even shaving off that mustache didn't help."

"Who's your number three?"

"I still haven't decided. That depends on Laura."

"She wants to go herself."

"Who doesn't? But if she turns up at the top of her own fitness list, I'll be very suspicious."

As Mercer gathered his papers and launched himself out of the cabin, Norton felt a brief stab of envy. Almost all the crew—about eighty-five per cent, by his minimum estimate—had worked out some sort of emotional accommodation to their lives in space. He had known ships where the captain had done the same, but theirs was not his way. Though discipline aboard *Endeavour* was based largely on the mutual respect between highly trained and intelligent men and women, the commander needed something more to underline his position. His responsibility was unique, and demanded a certain degree of isolation, even from his closest friends. Any liaison could be damaging to morale, for it was almost impossible to avoid charges of favoritism. For this reason, affairs spanning more than two degrees of rank were firmly discouraged; but apart from this, the only rule regulating shipboard sex was "So long as you don't do it in the corridors and frighten the simps."

There were four superchimps aboard *Endeavour*, though strictly speaking the name was inaccurate, because the ship's nonhuman crew did not come from chimpanzee stock. In zero gravity, a prehensile tail is an enormous advantage, and all attempts to supply these to humans had turned into embarrassing failures. After equally unsatisfactory results with the great apes, the Superchimpanzee Corporation had turned to the monkey kingdom.

Blackie, Blondie, Goldie, and Brownie had family trees whose branches included the most intelligent of the Old and New World monkeys, plus synthetic genes that had never existed in nature. Their rearing and education had probably cost as much as that of the average spaceman, and they were worth it. Each weighed less than thirty kilos and consumed only half the food and oxygen of a human being, but each could replace 2.75 men for housekeeping, elementary cooking, tool-carrying, and dozens of other routine jobs.

That 2.75 was the Corporation's claim, based on innumerable time-and-motion studies. The figure, though surprising and frequently challenged, appeared to be accurate, for simps were quite happy to work fifteen hours a day and did not get bored by the most menial and repetitious tasks. So they freed human beings for human work; and on a spaceship, that was a matter of vital importance.

Unlike the monkeys who were their nearest relatives, *Endeavour*'s simps were docile, obedient, and uninquisitive. Being cloned, they were also sexless, which eliminated awkward behavioral problems. Carefully house-trained vegetarians, they were clean and didn't smell. They would have made perfect pets, except that nobody could possibly have afforded them.

Despite these advantages, having simps on board involved certain problems. They had to have their own quarters—inevitably labeled "The Monkey House." Their little mess room was always spotless, and was well equipped, with TV, games equipment, and programmed teaching machines. To avoid accidents, they were absolutely forbidden to enter the ship's technical areas; the entrances to all these were color-coded in red, and the simps were conditioned so that it was psychologically impossible for them to pass these visual barriers.

There was also a communications problem. Though they had an equivalent IQ of sixty, and could understand several hundred words of English, they were unable to talk. It had proved impossible to give useful vocal cords to either apes or monkeys, and they therefore had to express themselves in sign language.

The basic signs were obvious and easily learned, so that everyone on board ship could understand routine messages. But the only man who could speak fluent Simplish was their handler: Chief Steward McAndrews.

It was a standing joke that Sergeant Ravi McAndrews *looked* rather like a simp—which was hardly an insult, for with their short, tinted pelts and graceful movements they were very handsome animals. They were also affectionate, and everyone on board had his favorite. Norton's was the aptly named Goldie.

But the warm relationship one could so easily establish with simps created another problem, often used as a powerful argument against their employment in space. Since they could be trained only for routine, low-grade tasks, they were worse than useless in an emergency; they could then be a danger to themselves and to their human companions. In particular, teaching them to use spacesuits had proved impossible, the concepts involved being quite beyond their understanding.

No one liked to talk about it, but everybody knew what had to be done if a hull was breached or the order came to abandon ship. It had happened only once; then, the simp handler had carried out his instructions more than adequately. He was found with his charges, killed by the same poison. Thereafter, the job of euthing was transferred to the chief medical officer, who, it was felt, would have less emotional involvement.

Norton was thankful that this responsibility, at least, did not fall upon the captain's shoulders. He had known men he would have killed with far fewer qualms than Goldie.

12

The Stairway
of the Gods

IN THE CLEAR, cold atmosphere of Rama, the beam of the searchlight was completely invisible. Three kilometers down from the central hub, the hundred-meter-wide oval of light lay across a section of that colossal stairway. A brilliant oasis in the surrounding darkness, it was sweeping slowly toward the curved plain still five kilometers below; and in its center moved a trio of antlike figures, casting long shadows before them.

It had been, just as they had hoped and expected, a completely uneventful descent. They had paused briefly at the first platform, and Norton had walked a few hundred meters along the narrow, curving ledge before starting the slide down to the second level. Here they had discarded their oxygen gear and reveled in the strange luxury of being able to breathe without mechanical aids. Now they could explore in comfort, freed from the greatest danger that confronts a man in space, and forgetting all worries about suit integrity and oxygen reserve.

By the time they had reached the fifth level, and there was only one more section to go, gravity had reached almost half its terrestrial value. Rama's centrifugal spin was at last exerting its real strength; they were surrendering themselves to the implacable force that rules every planet, and that can exert a merciless price for the smallest slip. It was still easy to go downward; but the thought of the return, up those thousands upon thousands of steps, was already beginning to prey upon their minds.

The stairway had long ago ceased its vertiginous downward plunge and was now flattening out toward the horizontal. The gradient was now only about one in five; at the beginning, it had been five in one. Normal walking was now both physically and psychologically acceptable; only the lowered gravity reminded them that they were not descending some great stairway on Earth. Norton had once visited the ruins of an Aztec temple, and the feelings he had then experienced now came echoing back to him—amplified a hundred times. Here was the same sense of awe and mystery, and the sadness of the irrevocably vanished past. Yet the scale here was so much greater, both in time and in space, that the mind was unable to do it justice; after a while, it ceased to respond. Norton wondered if, sooner or later, he would take even Rama for granted.

And there was another respect in which the parallel with terrestrial ruins failed completely. Rama was hundreds of times older than any structure that had survived on Earth, even the Great Pyramid. But *everything looked absolutely new; there was no sign of wear and tear.*

Norton had puzzled over this a good deal, and had

arrived at a tentative explanation. Everything that they had so far examined was part of an emergency back-up system, seldom put to actual use. He could not imagine that the Ramans—unless they were physical-fitness fanatics of the kind not uncommon on Earth—ever walked up and down this incredible stairway, or its two identical companions completing the invisible Y far above his head. Perhaps they had been required only during the actual construction of Rama, and had served no purpose since that distant day. That theory would do for the moment; yet it did not feel right. There was something wrong, somewhere.

They did not slide for the last kilometer, but went down the steps two at a time in long, gentle strides; this way, Norton decided, they would give more exercise to muscles that would soon have to be used. And so the end of the stairway came upon them almost un-awares; suddenly, there were no more steps—only a flat plain, dull gray in the now weakening beam of the hub search-light, fading away into the darkness a few hundred meters ahead.

Norton looked back along the beam, toward its source up on the axis more than eight kilometers away. He knew that Mercer would be watching through the telescope, so he waved to him cheerfully.

"Captain here," he reported over the radio. "Every-one in fine shape—no problems. Proceeding as planned."

"Good," replied Mercer. "We'll be watching."

There was a brief silence; then a new voice cut in. "This is the Exec, on board ship. Really, Skipper, this isn't good enough. You know the news services have been screaming at us for the last week. I don't expect deathless prose, but can't you do better than that?"

"I'll try," Norton said, chuckling. "But remember—there's nothing to see yet. It's like . . . well . . . being on a huge, darkened stage, with a single spotlight. The first few hundred steps of the stairway rise out of it until they disappear into the darkness overhead. What we can see of the plain looks perfectly flat. The curvature's too small to be visible over this limited area. And that's about it."

"Like to give any impressions?"

"Well, it's still very cold—below freezing—and we're glad of our thermostats. And *quiet*, of course; quieter than anything I've ever known on Earth, or in space, where there's always some background noise. Here, every sound is swallowed up. The space around us is so enormous that there aren't any echoes. It's weird, but I hope we'll get used to it."

"Thanks, Skipper. Anyone else? Joe, Boris?"

Joe Calvert, never at a loss for words, was happy to oblige.

"I can't help thinking that this is the first time—*ever*—that we've been able to walk on another world, breathing its natural atmosphere—though I suppose 'natural' is hardly the word you can apply to a place like this. Still, Rama must resemble the world of its builders; our own spaceships are all miniature earths. Two examples are damned poor statistics, but does this mean that all intelligent life forms are oxygen eaters? What we've seen of their work suggests that the Ramans were humanoid, though perhaps about fifty percent taller than we are. Wouldn't you agree, Boris?"

Is Joe teasing Boris? Norton asked himself. I wonder how he's going to react.

To all his shipmates, Lieutenant Boris Rodrigo was something of an enigma. The quiet, dignified communications officer was popular with the rest of the crew, but he never entered fully into their activities and always seemed a little apart—marching to the music of a different drummer.

As indeed he was, being a devout member of the

Fifth Church of Christ, Cosmonaut. Norton had never been able to discover what had happened to the earlier four, and he was equally in the dark about the church's rituals and ceremonies. But the main tenet of its faith was well known. Its members believed that Jesus Christ was a visitor from space, and an entire theology had been constructed on that assumption.

It was perhaps not surprising that an unusually high proportion of the church's devotees worked in space in some capacity or other. Invariably, they were efficient, conscientious, and absolutely reliable. They were universally respected, and even liked, especially since they made no attempt to convert others. Yet there was also something slightly spooky about them. Norton could never understand how men with advanced scientific and technical training could possibly believe some of the things he had heard Cosmo Christers state as incontrovertible fact.

As he waited for Boris to answer Joe's possibly loaded question, the Commander had a sudden insight into his own hidden motives. He had chosen Rodrigo because he was physically fit, technically qualified, and completely dependable. At the same time, he wondered if some part of his mind had not selected the Lieutenant out of an almost mischievous curiosity. How would a man with such religious beliefs react to the awesome reality of Rama? Suppose he encountered something that confounded his theology—or, for that matter, confirmed it?

But Rodrigo, with his usual caution, refused to be drawn.

"They were certainly oxygen breathers, and they *could* be humanoid. But let's wait and see. With any luck, we should discover what they were like. There may be pictures, statues—perhaps even bodies, over in those towns. If they are towns."

"And the nearest is only eight kilometers away," said Calvert hopefully.

Yes, thought Norton. But it's also eight kilometers back—and then there's that overwhelming stairway to climb again. Can we take the risk?

A quick sortie to the "town" they had named Paris had been among the first of his contingency plans, and now he had to make his decision. They had ample food and water for a stay of twenty-four hours; they would always be in full view of the back-up team on the hub, and any kind of accident seemed virtually impossible on this smooth, gently curving metal plain. The only foreseeable danger was exhaustion; when they got to Paris, which they could do easily enough, could they do more than take a few photographs and perhaps collect some small artifacts before they had to return?

But even such a brief foray would be worth it. There was so little time, as Rama hurtled sunward toward a perihelion too dangerous for *Endeavour* to match.

In any case, part of the decision was not his to make. Up in the ship, Dr. Ernst would be watching the outputs of the biotelemetering sensors attached to his body. If she turned thumbs down, that would be that.

"Laura, what do you think?"

"Take thirty minutes' rest, and a five-hundred-calorie energy module. Then you can start."

"Thanks, Doc," interjected Calvert. "Now I can die happy. I always wanted to see Paris. Montmartre, here we come."

13

The Plain of Rama

AFTER THOSE INTERMINABLE stairs, it was a strange luxury to walk once more on a horizontal surface. Directly ahead, the ground was indeed completely flat; to right and left, at the limits of the floodlit area, the rising curve could just be detected. They might have been walking along a very wide, shallow valley; it was quite impossible to believe that they were really crawling along the inside of a huge cylinder, and that beyond this little oasis of light the land rose up to meet —no, to *become*—the sky.

Though they all felt a sense of confidence and subdued excitement, after a while the almost palpable silence of Rama began to weigh heavily upon them. Every footstep, every word, vanished instantly into the unreverberant void. After they had gone little more than half a kilometer, Joe Calvert could stand it no longer.

Among his minor accomplishments was a talent now rare, though many thought not rare enough: the art of whistling. With or without encouragement, he could reproduce the themes from most of the movies of the last two hundred years. He started appropriately with "Heigh-ho, heigh-ho, it's off to work we go," found that he couldn't stay down comfortably in the bass with Disney's marching dwarfs, and switched quickly to the *River Kwai* song. Then he progressed, more or less chronologically, through half a dozen epics, culminating with the theme from Sid Krassman's famous late-twentieth-century "Napoleon."

It was a good try, but it didn't work, even as a morale builder. Rama needed the grandeur of Bach or Beethoven or Sibelius or Tuan Sun, not the trivia of popular entertainment. Norton was on the point of suggesting that Joe save his breath for later exertions when the young officer realized the inappropriateness of his efforts. Thereafter, apart from an occasional consultation with the ship, they marched on in silence. Rama had won this round.

On this initial traverse, Norton had allowed for one detour. Paris lay straight ahead, halfway between the foot of the stairway and the shore of the Cylindrical Sea, but only a kilometer to the right of their track was a very prominent, and rather mysterious, feature, which had been christened the Straight Valley. It was a long groove or trench, forty meters deep and a hundred wide, with gently sloping sides; it had been provisionally identified as an irrigation ditch or canal. Like the stairway, it had two similar counterparts, equally spaced on the curve of Rama.

The three valleys were almost ten kilometers long, and they stopped abruptly just before they reached the sea—which was strange if they were intended to carry water. And on the other side of the sea the pattern was repeated: three more ten-kilometer trenches continued on to the region of the South Pole.

They reached the near end of the Straight Valley after only fifteen minutes' comfortable walking, and stood for a while staring thoughtfully into its depths. The perfectly smooth walls sloped down at an angle of sixty degrees; there were no steps or footholds. Filling the bottom was a sheet of flat white material that looked much like ice. A specimen could settle a good many arguments. Norton decided to get one.

With Calvert and Rodrigo acting as anchors and playing out a safety rope, he rappelled slowly down the steep incline. When he reached the bottom, he fully expected to find the familiar slippery feel of ice underfoot, but he was mistaken. The friction was too great; his footing was secure. This material was some kind of glass or transparent crystal. When he touched it with his finger tips, it was cold, hard, and unyielding.

Turning his back to the searchlight and shielding his eyes from its glare, Norton tried to peer into the crystalline depths, as one may attempt to gaze through the ice of a frozen lake. But he could see nothing. Even when he tried the concentrated beam of his own helmet lamp, he was no more successful. This stuff was translucent, but not transparent. If it was a frozen liquid, it had a melting point much higher than water.

He tapped it gently with the hammer from his geology kit. The tool rebounded with a dull, unmusical "clunk." He tapped harder, with no more result, and he was about to exert his full strength when some impulse made him desist.

It seemed most unlikely that he could crack this material; but what if he did? He would be like a vandal smashing some enormous plate-glass window. There would be a better opportunity later, and at least he had discovered valuable information. It now seemed most unlikely that this was a canal. It was simply a peculiar trench that stopped and started abruptly, but led nowhere. And if at any time it had carried liquid, where were the stains, the encrustations of dried-up sediment, that one would expect? Everything was bright and clean, as if the builders had left only yesterday.

Once again he was face to face with the fundamental mystery of Rama, and this time it was impossible to evade it. Norton was a reasonably imaginative man, but he would never have reached his present position if he had been liable to the wilder flights of fancy. Yet now, for the first time, he had a sense, not exactly of foreboding, but of anticipation. Things were not what they seemed; there was something very odd indeed about a place that was simultaneously brand new and a million years old.

Deep in thought, he began to walk slowly along the length of the little valley, while his companions, still holding the rope that was attached to his waist, followed him along the rim. He did not expect to make any further discoveries, but he wanted to let his curious emotional state run its course. For something else was worrying him; and it had nothing to do with the inexplicable newness of Rama.

He had walked no more than a dozen meters when it hit him like a thunderbolt.

He knew this place. *He had been here before.*

Even on Earth, or on some familiar planet, that experience is disquieting, though it is not particularly rare. Most men have known it at some time or other, and usually they dismiss it as the memory of a forgotten photograph, a pure coincidence—or, if they are mystically inclined, some form of telepathy from another mind, or even a flashback from their own future.

But to recognize a spot that *no* other human being can possibly have seen—that is quite shocking. For several seconds, Norton stood rooted to the smooth crystalline surface on which he had been walking, trying to straighten out his feelings. His well-ordered universe had been turned upside down, and he had a dizzying glimpse of those mysteries at the edge of existence that he had successfully ignored for most of his life.

Then, to his immense relief, common sense came to the rescue. The disturbing sensation of *déjà vu* faded out, to be replaced by a real and identifiable memory from his youth.

It was true, he had once stood between such steeply sloping walls, watching them drive into the distance until they seemed to converge at a point indefinitely far ahead. But they had been covered with neatly trimmed grass; and underfoot had been broken stone, not smooth crystal.

It had happened thirty years ago, during a summer vacation in England. Largely because of another student (he could remember her face, but he had forgotten her name), he had taken a course in industrial archeology, then very popular among science and engineering graduates. They had explored abandoned coal mines and cotton mills, climbed over ruined blast furnaces and steam engines, goggled unbelievingly at primitive (and still dangerous) nuclear reactors, and driven priceless turbine-powered antiques along restored motor roads.

Not everything that they saw was genuine. Much had been lost during the centuries, for men seldom bother to preserve the commonplace articles of everyday life. But where it was necessary to make copies, they had been reconstructed with loving care.

And so, young Bill Norton had found himself bowling along at an exhilarating hundred kilometers an hour while he furiously shoveled precious coal into the firebox of a locomotive that looked two hundred years old but was actually younger than he was. The thirty-kilometer stretch of the Great Western Railway, however, was quite genuine, though it had required a good deal of excavating to get it back into commission.

With whistle screaming, they had plunged into a hillside and raced through a smoky, flame-lit darkness. An astonishingly long time later, they had burst out of the tunnel into a deep, perfectly straight cutting between steep grassy banks. The long-forgotten vista was almost identical with the one before him now.

"What is it, Skipper?" called Rodrigo. "Have you found something?"

As Norton dragged himself back to present reality, some of the oppression lifted from his mind. There was mystery here—yes; but it might not be beyond human understanding. He had learned a lesson, though it was not one that he could readily impart to others. At all costs, he must not let Rama overwhelm him. That way lay failure, perhaps even madness.

"No," he answered. "There's nothing down here. Haul me up. We'll head straight to Paris."

14

Storm Warning

"I'VE CALLED THIS meeting of the committee," said His Excellency the Ambassador from Mars to the United Planets, "because Dr. Perera has something important to tell us. He insists that we get in touch with Commander Norton right away, using the priority channel we've been able to establish—after, I might say, a good deal of difficulty Dr. Perera s statement is rather technical, and, before we come to it, I think a summary of the present position might be in order. Dr. Price has prepared one Oh yes—some apologies for absence. Sir Lewis Sands has had to leave for Earth for a conference he's chairing, and Dr. Taylor asked to be excused."

He was rather pleased about that last absence. The anthropologist had rapidly lost interest in Rama when it became obvious that it would present little scope for him. Like many others, he had been bitterly disap-

pointed to learn that the mobile worldlet was dead;
now there would be no opportunity for sensational
books and "viddies" about Raman rituals and behavioral patterns. Others might dig up skeletons and clas-
sify artifacts, but *that* sort of thing did not appeal to
Conrad Taylor. Perhaps the only discovery that would
bring him back in a hurry would be some highly ex-
plicit works of art, like the notorious frescoes of Thera
and Pompeii.

Thelma Price took exactly the opposite point of
view. She preferred excavations and ruins uncluttered
by inhabitants who might interfere with dispassionate
scientific studies. The bed of the Mediterranean had
been ideal—at least until the city planners and landscape artists had started getting in the way. And Rama
would have been perfect except for the maddening detail that it was a hundred million kilometers away and
she would never be able to visit it in person.

"As you all know," she began, "Commander Norton has completed one traverse of almost thirty kilometers without encountering any problems. He explored the curious trench shown on your maps as the
Straight Valley. Its purpose is still quite unknown, but
it is clearly important, because it runs the full length
of Rama—except for the break at the Cylindrical Sea
—and there are two identical structures 120 degrees
apart on the circumference of the world.

"Next, the party turned left—or east, if we adopt
the North Pole convention—until they reached Paris.
As you'll see from this photograph, taken by a telescopic camera at the hub, it is a group of several
hundred buildings, with wide streets between them.

"Now *these* photographs were taken by Commander Norton's group when they reached the site. If Paris
is a city, it is a most peculiar one. Note that none of
the buildings have windows, or even doors! They are
all plain, rectangular structures, an identical thirty-five

meters high. And they appear to have been extruded from the ground. There are no seams or joints. Look at this close-up of the base of a wall—there's a smooth transition into the ground.

"My own feeling is that this place is not a residential area, but a storage or supply depot. In support of that theory, look at this photo.

"These narrow slots or grooves, about five centimeters wide, run along all the streets, and there is one leading to every building—going straight into the wall. There is a striking resemblance to the streetcar tracks of the early twentieth century. They are obviously part of some transport system.

"We've never considered it necessary to have public transport direct to every house. It would be economically absurd; people can always walk a few hundred meters. But if these buildings are being used for the storage of heavy materials, it would make sense."

"May I ask a question?" said the Ambassador from Earth.

"Of course, Sir Robert."

"Commander Norton couldn't get into a single building?"

"No. When you listen to his report, you can tell he was quite frustrated. At one time he decided that the buildings could be entered only from underground; then he discovered the grooves of the transport system, and changed his mind."

"Did he try to break in?"

"There was no way he could, without explosives or heavy tools. And he doesn't want to do that until all other approaches have failed."

"I have it!" Dennis Solomons suddenly interjected. "Cocooning!"

"I beg your pardon?"

"It's a technique developed a couple of hundred years ago," continued the science historian. "Another name for it is mothballing. When you have something you want to preserve, you seal it inside a plastic envelope, and then pump in an inert gas. The original use was to protect military equipment between wars; it was once applied to whole ships. It's still widely used in museums that are short of storage space. No one knows what's inside some of the hundred-year-old cocoons in the Smithsonian basement."

Patience was not one of Perera's virtues. He was aching to drop his bombshell, and could restrain himself no longer. "*Please*, Mr. Ambassador! This is all very interesting, but I feel my information is rather more urgent."

"If there are no other points—very well, Dr. Perera."

The exobiologist, unlike Taylor, had not found Rama a disappointment. It was true that he no longer expected to find life; but sooner or later, he felt quite sure, some remains would be discovered of the creatures who had built this fantastic world. Exploration had barely begun, although the time available was horribly brief before *Endeavour* would be forced to escape from her present sun-grazing orbit.

But now, if his calculations were correct, man's contact with Rama would be even shorter than he had feared. One detail had been overlooked—because it was so large that no one had noticed it before.

"According to our latest information," Perera began, "one party is now on its way to the Cylindrical Sea, while Commander Norton has another group setting up a supply base at the foot of Stairway Alpha. When that's established, he intends to have at least two exploratory missions operating at all times. In this way he hopes to use his limited manpower at maximum efficiency.

"It's a good plan, but there may be no time to carry it out. In fact, I would advise an immediate alert, and a preparation for total withdrawal at twelve hours' notice. Let me explain.

"It is surprising how few people have commented on a rather obvious anomaly about Rama. It is now well inside the orbit of Venus, yet the interior is still frozen. And the temperature of an object in direct sunlight at this point is about five hundred degrees!

"The reason, of course, is that Rama has not had time to warm up. It must have cooled down to near absolute zero—270 degrees below—while it was in interstellar space. Now, as it approaches the Sun, the outer hull is already almost as hot as molten lead. But the inside will stay cold until the heat works its way through that kilometer of rock.

"There's some kind of fancy dessert with a hot exterior and ice cream in the middle—I don't remember what it's called—"

"Baked Alaska. It's a favorite at U.P. banquets, unfortunately."

"Thank you, Sir Robert. That's the situation in Rama at the moment, but it won't last. All these weeks, the solar heat has been working its way through, and we can expect a sharp temperature rise to begin in a few hours. *That's* not the problem, however. By the time we'll have to leave anyway, it will be no more than comfortably tropical."

"Then what's the difficulty?"

"I can answer in one word, Mr. Ambassador: *hurricanes.*"

15

The Edge of the Sea

THERE WERE NOW more than twenty men and women inside Rama—six of them down on the plain, the rest ferrying equipment and expendables through the air-lock system and down the stairway. The ship itself was almost deserted, with the minimum possible staff on duty. The joke went around that *Endeavour* was really being run by the four simps, and that Goldie had been given the rank of acting commander.

For these first explorations, Norton had established a number of ground rules; the most important dated back to the earliest days of man's space-faring. Every group, he had decided, must contain one person with prior experience. But not *more* than one. In that way, everybody would have an opportunity to learn as quickly as possible.

And so, the first party to head for the Cylindrical Sea, though it was led by Surgeon Commander Laura

Ernst, had as its one-time veteran Boris Rodrigo, just back from Paris. The third member, Sergeant Pieter Rousseau, had been with the back-up teams at the hub. He was an expert on space-reconnaissance instrumentation, but on this trip he would have to depend on his own eyes and a small portable telescope.

From the foot of Stairway Alpha to the edge of the sea was just under fifteen kilometers, or an Earth equivalent of eight under the low gravity of Rama. Laura Ernst, who had to prove that she lived up to her own standards, set a brisk pace. They stopped for thirty minutes at the midway mark, and made the whole trip in a completely uneventful three hours.

It was also quite monotonous, walking forward in the beam of the searchlight through the anechoic darkness of Rama. As the pool of light advanced with them, it slowly elongated into a long, narrow ellipse; this foreshortening of the beam was the only visible sign of progress. If the observers up on the hub had not given them continual distance checks, they could not have guessed whether they had traveled one kilometer or five or ten. They just plodded onward through the million-year-old night, over an apparently seamless metal surface.

But at last, far ahead, at the limits of the now weakening beam, there was something new. On a normal world it would have been a horizon; as they approached, they could see that the plain on which they were walking came to an abrupt stop. They were nearing the edge of the sea.

"Only a hundred meters," said Hub Control. "Better slow down."

That was hardly necessary, yet they had already done so. From the level of the plain to that of the sea —if it was a sea, and not another sheet of that mysterious crystalline material—was a sheer straight drop of fifty meters. Although Norton had impressed upon everyone the danger of taking anything for granted in Rama, few doubted that the sea was really made of ice. But for what conceivable reason was the cliff on the southern shore five hundred meters high, instead of the fifty here?

It was as if they were approaching the edge of the world. Their oval of light, cut off abruptly ahead of them, became shorter and shorter. But far out on the curved screen of the sea their monstrous foreshortened shadows had appeared, magnifying and exaggerating every movement. Those shadows had been their companions every step of the way as they marched down the beam, but now that they were broken at the edge of the cliff they no longer seemed part of them. They might have been creatures of the Cylindrical Sea, waiting to deal with any intruders into their domain.

Because they were now standing on the edge of a fifty-meter cliff, it was possible for the first time to appreciate the curvature of Rama. But no one had ever seen a frozen lake bent upward into a cylindrical surface; that was distinctly unsettling, and the eye did its best to find some other interpretation. It seemed to Dr. Ernst, who had once made a study of visual illusions, that half the time she was really looking at a *horizontally* curving bay, not a surface that soared up into the sky. It required a deliberate effort of will to accept the fantastic truth.

Only in the line directly ahead, parallel to the axis of Rama, was normality preserved. In this direction alone was there agreement between vision and logic. Here, for the next few kilometers at least, Rama looked flat, and *was* flat. And out there, beyond their distorted shadows and the outer limit of the beam, lay the island that dominated the Cylindrical Sea.

"Hub Control," Dr. Ernst radioed, "please aim your beam at New York."

The night of Rama fell suddenly upon them as the

oval of light went sliding out to sea. Conscious of the now invisible cliff at their feet, they all stepped back a few meters. Then, as if by some magical stage transformation, the towers of New York sprang into view.

The resemblance to old-time Manhattan was only superficial; this star-born echo of Earth's past possessed its own unique identity. The more Dr. Ernst stared at it, the more certain she became that it was not a city at all.

The real New York, like all of man's habitations, had never been finished; still less had it been designed. *This* place, however, had an over-all symmetry and pattern, though one so complex that it eluded the mind. It had been conceived and planned by some controlling intelligence, and then it had been completed, like a machine devised for some specific purpose. After that there was no possibility of growth or change.

The beam of the searchlight slowly tracked along those distant towers and domes and interlocked spheres and crisscrossed tubes. Sometimes there was a brilliant reflection as some flat surface shot the light back toward them. The first time this happened, they were all taken by surprise. It was exactly as if, over there on that strange island, someone was signaling to them.

But there was nothing that they could see here that was not already shown in greater detail on photographs taken from the hub. After a few minutes, they called for the light to return to them and began to walk eastward along the edge of the cliff. It had been plausibly theorized that, somewhere, there must surely be a flight of steps, or a ramp, leading down to the sea. And one crewman, who was a keen sailor, had raised an interesting conjecture.

"Where there's a sea," Sergeant Ruby Barnes had predicted, "there must be docks and harbors—and ships. You can learn everything about a culture by studying the way it builds boats." Her colleagues thought this a rather restricted point of view, but at least it was a stimulating one.

Dr. Ernst had almost given up the search, and was preparing to make a descent by rope, when Rodrigo spotted the narrow stairway. It could easily have been overlooked in the shadowed darkness below the edge of the cliff, for there was no guardrail or other indication of its presence. And it seemed to lead nowhere; it ran down the fifty-meter vertical wall at a steep angle, and disappeared below the surface of the sea.

They scanned the flight of steps with their helmet lights, could see no conceivable hazard, and Dr. Ernst got Commander Norton's permission to descend. A minute later, she was cautiously testing the surface of the sea.

Her foot slithered almost frictionlessly back and forth. The material felt exactly like ice. It *was* ice.

When she struck it with her hammer, a familiar pattern of cracks radiated from the impact point, and she had no difficulty in collecting as many pieces as she wished. Some had already melted when she held up the sample holder to the light. The liquid appeared to be slightly turbid water, and she took a cautious sniff.

"Is that safe?" Rodrigo called down, with a trace of anxiety.

"Believe me, Boris," she answered, "if there are any pathogens around here that have slipped through my detectors, our insurance policies lapsed a week ago."

But Rodrigo had a point. Despite all the tests that had been carried out, there was a slight risk that this substance might be poisonous, or might carry some unknown disease. In normal circumstances, Dr. Ernst would not have taken even this minuscule chance. Now, however, time was short, and the stakes were enormous. If it became necessary to quarantine *En-*

deavour, that would be a small price to pay for her cargo of knowledge.

"It's water, but I wouldn't care to drink it—it smells like an algae culture that's gone bad. I can hardly wait to get it to the lab."

"Is the ice safe to walk on?"

"Yes, solid as a rock."

"Then we can get to New York."

"Can we, Pieter? Have you ever tried to walk across four kilometers of ice?"

"Oh—I see what you mean. Just imagine what Stores would say if we asked for a set of skates! Not that many of us would know how to use them, even if we had any aboard."

"And there's another problem," put in Rodrigo. "Do you realize that the temperature is already above freezing? Before long, that ice is going to melt. How many spacemen can swim four kilometers? Certainly not this one."

Dr. Ernst rejoined them at the edge of the cliff, and held up the small sample bottle in triumph.

"It's a long walk for a few cc's of dirty water, but it may teach us more about Rama than anything we've found so far. Let's head for home."

They turned toward the distant lights of the hub, moving with the gentle, loping strides that had proved the most comfortable means of walking under this reduced gravity. Often they looked back, drawn by the hidden enigma of the island out there in the center of the frozen sea.

And just once, Dr. Ernst thought she felt the faint suspicion of a breeze against her cheek.

It did not come again, and she quickly forgot about it.

16

Kealakekua

"As you know perfectly well, Dr. Perera," said Ambassador Bose in a tone of patient resignation, "few of us share your knowledge of mathematical meteorology. So please take pity on our ignorance."

"With pleasure," answered the exobiologist, quite unabashed. "I can explain it best by telling you what is going to happen inside Rama—very soon.

"The temperature is now about to rise, as the solar heat pulse reaches the interior. According to the latest information I've received, it is already above freezing point. The Cylindrical Sea will soon start to thaw; and unlike bodies of water on Earth, it will melt from the bottom upward. That may produce some odd effects; but I'm much more concerned with the atmosphere.

"As it is heated, the air inside Rama will expand—and will attempt to rise toward the central axis. And this is the problem. At ground level, although it is apparently stationary, it is actually sharing the spin of Rama—over eight hundred kilometers an hour. As it rises toward the axis, it will try to retain that speed. And it won't be able to do so, of course. The result will be violent winds and turbulence. I estimate velocities of between two and three hundred kilometers an hour.

"Incidentally, very much the same thing occurs on Earth. The heated air at the Equator—which shares the Earth's sixteen-hundred-kilometer-an-hour spin—runs into the same problem when it rises and flows north and south."

"Ah, the trade winds! I remember that from my geography lessons."

"Exactly, Sir Robert. Rama will have trade winds, with a vengeance. I believe they'll last only a few hours, and then some kind of equilibrium will be restored. Meanwhile, I should advise Commander Norton to evacuate—as soon as possible. Here is the message I propose sending."

With a little imagination, Norton told himself, he could pretend that this was an improvised night camp at the foot of some mountain in a remote region of Asia or America. The clutter of sleeping pads, collapsible chairs and tables, portable power plant, lighting equipment, electrosan toilets, and miscellaneous scientific apparatus would not have looked out of place on Earth—especially because there were men and women working here without life-support systems.

Establishing Camp Alpha had been hard work, for everything had had to be manhandled through the chain of air locks, sledded down the slope from the hub, and then retrieved and unpacked. Sometimes, when the braking parachutes failed, a consignment had ended up a good kilometer away, out on the plain. Despite this, several crew members had asked permis-

sion to make the ride; Norton had firmly forbidden it.
In an emergency, however, he might be prepared to
reconsider the ban.

Almost all this equipment would stay here, for the
labor of carrying it back was unthinkable—in fact, impossible. There were times when Norton felt an irra-
tional shame to be leaving so much human litter in this
strangely immaculate place. When they finally depart-
ed, he was prepared to sacrifice some of their precious
time to leave everything in good order. Improbable
though it was, perhaps millions of years hence, when
Rama shot through some other star system, it might
have visitors again. He would like to give them a good
impression of Earth.

Meanwhile, he had a rather more immediate problem. During the last twenty-four hours he had received
almost identical messages from Mars and Earth. It
seemed an odd coincidence; perhaps they had been
commiserating with each other, as wives who lived
safely on different planets were liable to do under sufficient provocation. Rather pointedly, they had reminded him that, even though he was now a great hero, he
still had family responsibilities.

The Commander picked up a collapsible chair and
walked out of the pool of light into the darkness surrounding the camp. It was the only way he could get
any privacy, and he could also think better away from
the turmoil. Deliberately turning his back on the or-
ganized confusion behind him, he began to speak into
the recorder slung around his neck.

"Original for personal file, dupes to Mars and
Earth. Hello, darling. Yes, I know I've been a lousy
correspondent, but I haven't been aboard ship for a
week. Apart from a skeleton crew, we're all camping
inside Rama, at the foot of the stairway we've christened Alpha.

"I have three parties out now, scouting the plain,

but we've made disappointingly slow progress, because everything has to be done on foot. If only we had some means of transportation. I'd be very happy to settle for a few electric bicycles; they'd be perfect for the job.

"You've met my medical officer, Surgeon Commander Ernst—" He paused uncertainly. Laura had met *one* of his wives, but which? Better cut that out.

Erasing the sentence, he began again.

"My M/O, Surgeon Commander Ernst, led the first group to reach the Cylindrical Sea, fifteen kilometers from here. She found that it was frozen water, as we'd expected—but you wouldn't want to drink it. Dr. Ernst says it's a dilute organic soup, containing traces of almost any carbon compound you care to name, as well as phosphates and nitrates and dozens of metallic salts. There's not the slightest sign of life—not even any dead microorganisms. So we still know nothing about the biochemistry of the Ramans—though it was probably not wildly different from ours."

Something brushed lightly against his hair. He had been too busy to get it cut, and would have to do something about that before he next put on a space helmet.

"You've seen the viddies of Paris and the other towns we've explored on this side of the sea—London, Rome, Moscow. It's impossible to believe that they were ever built for anything to *live* in. Paris looks like a giant storage depot. London is a collection of cylinders linked together by pipes connected to what are obviously pumping stations. Everything is sealed up, and there's no way to find out what's inside without explosives or lasers. We won't try these until there are no alternatives.

"As for Rome and Moscow—"

"Excuse me, Skipper. Priority from Earth."

What now? Norton said to himself. Can't a man get a few minutes to talk to his families?

He took the message from the Sergeant and scanned it quickly, just to satisfy himself that it was not immediate. Then he read it again, more slowly.

What the devil was the Rama Committee? And why had he never heard of it? He knew that all sorts of associations, societies, and professional groups—some serious, some completely crackpot—had been trying to get in touch with him. Mission Control had done a good job of protection, and would not have forwarded this message unless it was considered important.

"Two-hundred-kilometer winds . . . probably sudden onset . . ." Well, that was something to think about. But it was hard to take it too seriously, on this utterly calm night; and it would be ridiculous to run away like frightened mice when they were just starting effective exploration.

Norton lifted a hand to brush aside his hair, which had somehow fallen into his eyes again. Then he froze, the gesture uncompleted.

He *had* felt a trace of wind, several times in the last hour. It was so slight that he had completely ignored it; after all, he was the commander of a *space*ship, not a sailing ship. Until now the movement of air had not been of the slightest professional concern. What would the long-dead captain of that earlier *Endeavour* have done in a situation such as this?

Norton had asked himself that question at every moment of crisis in the last few years. It was his secret, which he had never revealed to anyone. And, like most of the important things in life, it had come about quite by accident.

He had been captain of the *Endeavour* for several months before he realized that it was named after one of the most famous ships in history. True, during the last four hundred years there had been a dozen *Endeavours* of sea and two of space, but the ancestor of them all was the 370-ton Whitby collier that Captain James Cook, RN, had sailed around the world between 1768 and 1771.

With a mild interest that had quickly turned to an absorbing curiosity, almost an obsession, Norton had begun to read everything he could find about Cook. He was now probably the world's leading authority on the greatest explorer of all time, and knew whole sections of the *Journals* by heart.

It still seemed incredible that one man could have done so much with such primitive equipment. But Cook had been not only a supreme navigator, but also a scientist and—in an age of brutal discipline—a humanitarian. He treated his own men with kindness, which was unusual; what was quite unheard of was that he behaved in exactly the same way to the often hostile savages in the new lands he discovered.

It was Norton's private dream, which he knew he would never achieve, to retrace at least one of Cook's voyages around the world. He had made a limited but spectacular start, which would certainly have astonished the Captain, when he once flew a polar orbit directly above the Great Barrier Reef. It had been early morning on a clear day, and from four hundred kilometers up he had had a superb view of that deadly wall of coral, marked by its line of white foam, along the Queensland coast.

He had taken just under five minutes to travel the whole two thousand kilometers of the reef. In a single glance he could span weeks of perilous voyaging for that first *Endeavour*. And through the telescope he had caught a glimpse of Cooktown and the estuary where the ship had been dragged ashore for repairs after her near-fatal encounter with the reef.

A year later, a visit to the Hawaii Deep-Space Tracking Station had given him an even more memorable experience. He had taken the hydrofoil to Kealakekua Bay, and as he moved swiftly past the bleak volcanic cliffs he felt a depth of emotion that had surprised and even disconcerted him. The guide had led his group of scientists, engineers, and astronauts past the glittering metal pylon that had replaced the earlier monument, destroyed by the Great Tsunami of '68. They had walked on for a few more yards across black, slippery lava to the small plaque at the water's edge. Little waves were breaking over it, but Norton scarcely noticed them as he bent down to read the words.

NEAR THIS SPOT
CAPTAIN JAMES COOK
WAS KILLED
FEBRUARY 14, 1779
ORIGINAL TABLET DEDICATED AUGUST 18, 1928
BY COOK SESQUICENTENNIAL COMMISSION
REPLACED BY TRICENTENNIAL COMMISSION
FEBRUARY 14, 2079

That was years ago, and a hundred million kilometers away. But at moments like this, Cook's reassuring presence seemed very close. In the secret depths of his mind, Norton would ask: "Well, Captain, what is *your* advice?" It was a little game he played on occasions when there were not enough facts for sound judgment and one had to rely on intuition. That had been part of Cook's genius; he always made the right choice—until the end, at Kealakekua Bay.

The Sergeant waited patiently, while his commander stared silently out into the night of Rama. It was no longer unbroken, for at two spots about four kilometers away the faint patches of light of exploring parties could be clearly seen.

In an emergency, I can recall them within the hour, Norton told himself. And that, surely, should be good enough.

He turned to the Sergeant. "Take this message. Rama Committee, care of PLANETCOM. Appreciate your advice and will take precautions. Please specify meaning of phrase 'sudden onset.' Respectfully, Norton, Commander, *Endeavour* "

He waited until the Sergeant had disappeared toward the blazing lights of the camp, then switched on his recorder again. But the train of thought was broken and he could not get back into the mood. The letter would have to wait for some other time.

It was not often that Captain Cook came to his aid when he was neglecting his duty. But he suddenly remembered how rarely and briefly poor Elizabeth Cook had seen her husband in sixteen years of married life. Yet she had borne him six children—and outlived them all.

His wives, never more than ten minutes away at the speed of light, had nothing to complain about.

17

Spring

DURING THE FIRST "nights" in Rama it had not been easy to sleep. The darkness and the mysteries it concealed were oppressive, but even more unsettling was the silence. Absence of noise is not a natural condition; all human senses require some input. If they are deprived of it, the mind manufactures its own substitutes.

And so, many sleepers had later complained of strange noises, even of voices, which were obviously illusions, because those awake had heard nothing. Dr. Ernst had prescribed a simple and effective cure; during the sleeping period the camp was now lulled by gentle, unobtrusive background music.

During this night, Norton found the cure inadequate. He kept straining his ears into the darkness, and he knew what he was listening for. But though a faint breeze did caress his face from time to time, there was no sound that could possibly be taken for that of a distant, rising wind. Nor did either of the exploring parties report anything unusual.

At last, around ship's midnight, he went to sleep. There was always a man on watch at the communications console, in case of any urgent messages. No other precautions seemed necessary.

Not even a hurricane could have created the sound that did wake Norton, and the whole camp, in a single instant. It seemed that the sky was falling, or that Rama had split open and was tearing itself apart. First there was a rending crack, then a long-drawn-out series of crystalline crashes, like a million glasshouses being demolished. It lasted for minutes, though it seemed like hours. It was still continuing, apparently moving away into the distance, when Norton got to the message center.

"Hub Control! What's happened?"

"Just a moment, Skipper. It's over by the sea. We're getting the light on it."

Eight kilometers overhead, on the axis of Rama, the searchlight began to swing its beam out across the plain. It reached the edge of the sea, then started to track along it, scanning around the interior of the world. A quarter of the way around the cylindrical surface, it stopped.

Up there in the sky—or what the mind still persisted in calling the sky—something extraordinary was happening. At first it seemed to Norton that the sea was boiling. It was no longer static and frozen in the grip of an eternal winter. A huge area, kilometers across, was in turbulent movement. And it was changing color; a broad band of white was marching across the ice.

Suddenly a slab perhaps a quarter of a kilometer on a side began to tilt upward like an opening door. Slowly and majestically, it reared into the sky, glittering and sparkling in the beam of the searchlight. Then it slid back and vanished beneath the surface, while a tidal wave of foaming water raced outward in all directions from its point of submergence.

Not until then did Norton fully realize what was happening. *The ice was breaking up.* All these days and weeks the sea had been thawing, far down in the depths. It was hard to concentrate because of the crashing roar that still filled the world and echoed around the sky, but he tried to think of a reason for so dramatic a convulsion. When a frozen lake or river thawed on Earth, it was nothing like this.

But of course! It was obvious enough, now that it had happened. The sea was thawing from *beneath,* as the solar heat seeped through the hull of Rama. And when ice turns into water, it occupies less volume.

So the sea had been sinking below the upper layer of ice, leaving it unsupported. Day by day the strain had been building up; now the bank of ice that encircled the equator of Rama was collapsing, like a bridge that had lost its central pier. It was splintering into hundreds of floating islands, which would crash and jostle into each other until they, too, melted. Norton's blood ran suddenly cold when he remembered the plans that were being made to reach New York by sledge.

The tumult was swiftly subsiding; a temporary stalemate had been reached in the war between ice and water. In a few hours, as the temperature continued to rise, the water would win, and the last vestiges of ice would disappear. But in the long run ice would be the victor, as Rama rounded the Sun and set forth once more into the interstellar night.

Norton remembered to start breathing again; then he called the party nearest the sea. To his relief, Rodrigo answered at once. No, the water hadn't reached them. No tidal wave had come sloshing over the edge of the cliff. "So now we know," he added calmly, "why there *is* a cliff." Norton agreed silently. But that hardly explains, he thought, why the cliff on the southern shore is ten times higher.

The hub searchlight continued to scan around the world. The awakened sea was steadily calming, and the boiling white foam no longer raced outward from capsizing ice floes. In fifteen minutes, the main disturbance was over.

But Rama was no longer silent. It had awakened from its sleep, and ever and again there came the sound of grinding ice as one berg collided with another.

Spring had been a little late, Norton told himself, but winter had ended.

And there was that breeze again, stronger than ever. Rama had given him enough warnings; it was time to go.

As he neared the halfway mark, Norton once again felt gratitude to the darkness that concealed the view above—and below. Though he knew that more than ten thousand steps still lay ahead of him, and could picture the steeply ascending curve in his mind's eye, the fact that he could see only a small portion of it made the prospect more bearable.

This was his second ascent, and he had learned from his mistakes on the first. The great temptation was to climb too quickly in this low gravity; every step was so easy that it was hard to adopt a slow, plodding rhythm. But unless one did this, after the first few thousand steps strange aches developed in the thighs and calves. Muscles that one never knew existed started to protest, and it was necessary to take longer and longer periods of rest. Toward the end of the first climb, Norton had spent more time resting than climbing, and even then it was not enough. He had suffered painful leg cramps for the next two days, and would have been almost incapacitated had he not been back in the zero-gravity environment of the ship.

So this time he had started with almost painful slowness, moving like an old man. He had been the last to leave the plain, and the others were strung out along the half-kilometer of stairway above him. He could see their lights moving up the invisible slope ahead.

He felt sick at heart at the failure of his mission, and even now hoped that this was only a temporary retreat. When they reached the hub, they could wait until any atmospheric disturbances had ceased. Presumably there would be a dead calm there, as at the center of a cyclone, and they could wait out the expected storm in safety.

Once again he was jumping to conclusions, drawing dangerous analogies from Earth. The meteorology of a whole world, even under steady-state conditions, was a matter of enormous complexity. After several centuries of study, terrestrial weather forecasting was still not absolutely reliable. And Rama was not merely a completely novel system; it was also undergoing rapid changes, for the temperature had risen several degrees in the last few hours. Yet there was no sign of the promised hurricane, though there had been a few feeble gusts from apparently random directions.

They had now climbed five kilometers, which in this low and steadily diminishing gravity was equivalent to less than two on Earth. At the third level, three kilometers from the axis, they rested for an hour, taking light refreshments and massaging leg muscles. This was the last point at which they could breathe in comfort; like old-time Himalayan mountaineers, they had left their oxygen supplies here, and now put them on for the final ascent.

An hour later, they had reached the top of the stairway, and the beginning of the ladder. Ahead lay the last, vertical, kilometer, fortunately in a gravity field only a few per cent of Earth's. A thirty-minute rest, a careful check of oxygen, and they were ready for the final lap.

Norton made sure that all his men were safely ahead of him again, spaced out at twenty-meter intervals along the ladder. From now on it would be a slow, steady haul, extremely boring. The best technique was to empty the mind of all thoughts and to count the rungs as they drifted by—one hundred, two hundred, three hundred, four hundred . . .

He had just reached twelve hundred and fifty when he realized that something was wrong. The light shining on the vertical surface immediately in front of his eyes was the wrong color—and it was much too bright.

Norton did not even have time to check his ascent, or to call a warning to his men. Everything happened in less than a second.

In a soundless concussion of light, dawn burst upon Rama.

18

Dawn

THE LIGHT WAS so brilliant that for a full minute Norton had to keep his eyes clenched tightly shut. Then he risked opening them, and stared through barely parted lids at the wall a few centimeters in front of his face. He blinked several times, waited for the involuntary tears to drain away, and then turned slowly to behold the dawn.

He could endure the sight for only a few seconds; then he was forced to close his eyes again. It was not the glare that was intolerable—he could grow accustomed to that—but the awesome spectacle of Rama, now seen for the first time in its entirety.

Norton had known exactly what to expect; nevertheless, the sight had stunned him. He was seized by a spasm of uncontrollable trembling; his hands tightened around the rungs of the ladder with the violence of a drowning man clutching at a life belt. The muscles of his forearms began to knot, yet at the same time his legs—already fatigued by hours of steady climbing—seemed about to give way. If it had not been for the low gravity, he might have fallen.

Then his training took over, and he began to apply the first remedy for panic. Still keeping his eyes closed, and trying to forget the monstrous spectacle around him, he started to take deep, long breaths, filling his lungs with oxygen and washing the poisons of fatigue out of his system.

Presently he felt much better, but he did not open his eyes until he had performed one more action. It took a major effort of will to force his right hand to open—he had to talk to it as though it were a disobedient child—but presently he maneuvered it down to his waist, unclipped the safety belt from his harness, and hooked the buckle to the nearest rung. Now, whatever happened, he could not fall.

He took several more deep breaths; then, still keeping his eyes closed, he switched on his radio. He hoped his voice sounded calm and authoritative as he called: "Captain here. Is everyone OK?"

As he checked off the names one by one, and received answers—even if somewhat tremulous ones—from everybody, his own confidence and self-control came swiftly back to him. All his men were safe, and were looking to him for leadership. He was the commander once more.

"Keep your eyes closed until you're quite sure you can take it," he called. "The view is—overwhelming. If anyone finds that it's too much, keep on climbing without looking back. Remember, you'll soon be at zero gravity, so you can't possibly fall."

It was hardly necessary to point out such an elementary fact to trained spacemen, but Norton had to remind himself of it every few seconds. The thought of zero gravity was a kind of talisman, protecting him from harm. Whatever his eyes told him, Rama could not drag him down to destruction on the plain eight kilometers below.

It became an urgent matter of pride and self-esteem that he should open his eyes once more and look at the world around him. But first he had to get his body under control.

He let go of the ladder with *both* hands, and hooked his left arm under a rung. Clenching and unclenching his fists, he waited until the muscle cramps had faded away. When he felt quite comfortable, he opened his eyes and slowly turned to face Rama.

His first impression was one of blueness. The glare that filled the sky could not have been mistaken for sunlight; it might have been that of an electric arc. So Rama's sun, Norton told himself, must be hotter than ours. That should interest the astronomers.

And now he understood the purpose of those mysterious trenches, the Straight Valley and its five companions. They were nothing less than gigantic striplights. Rama had six linear suns, symmetrically ranged around its interior. From each a broad fan of light was aimed across the central axis, to shine upon the far side of the world. Norton wondered if they could be switched alternately to produce a cycle of light and darkness, or whether this was a planet of perpetual day.

Too much staring at those blinding bars of light had made his eyes hurt again; he was not sorry to have a good excuse to close them for a while. It was not until then, when he had almost recovered from this initial visual shock, that he was able to devote himself to a much more serious problem.

Who, or what, had switched on the lights of Rama?

By the most sensitive tests that man could apply to it, this world was sterile. But now something was happening that could not be explained by the action of natural forces. There might not be life here, but there could be consciousness, awareness; robots might be waking after a sleep of eons. Perhaps this outburst of light was an unprogrammed, random spasm—a last dying gasp of machines that were responding wildly to the warmth of a new sun and would soon lapse again into quiescence, this time forever.

Yet Norton could not believe such a simple explanation. Bits of the jigsaw puzzle were beginning to fall into place, though many were still missing: the absence of all signs of wear, for example, and the feeling of *newness*, as if Rama had just been created.

These thoughts might have inspired fear, even terror. Somehow, though, they did nothing of the sort. On the contrary, Norton felt a sense of exhilaration, almost of delight. There was far more here to discover than they had ever dared to hope. Wait, he said to himself, until the Rama Committee hears about *this!*

Then, with calm determination, he opened his eyes again and began a careful inventory of everything he saw.

First he had to establish some kind of reference system. He was looking at the largest enclosed space ever seen by man, and he needed a mental map to find his way around it.

The feeble gravity was little help, for with an effort of will he could switch "up" and "down" in any direction he pleased. But some directions were psychologically dangerous; whenever his mind skirted these, he had to vector it hastily away.

Safest of all was to imagine that he was at the bowl-shaped bottom of a gigantic well, sixteen kilometers wide and fifty deep. The advantage of this image was that there could be no danger of falling farther. Nevertheless, it had some serious defects.

He could pretend that the scattered towns and cities, and the differently colored and textured areas, were all securely fixed to the towering walls. The various complex structures that could be seen hanging from the dome overhead were perhaps no more disconcerting than the pendent candelabra in some great concert hall on Earth. What was quite unacceptable was the Cylindrical Sea.

There it was, halfway up the well shaft—a band of water, wrapped completely around it, with no visible means of support. There could be no doubt that it *was* water; it was a vivid blue, flecked with brilliant sparkles from the few remaining ice floes. But a vertical sea forming a complete circle twenty kilometers up in the sky was such an unsettling phenomenon that after a while he began to seek an alternative.

That was when his mind switched the scene through ninety degrees. Instantly, the deep well became a long tunnel, capped at each end. "Down" was obviously in the direction of the ladder and the stairway he had just ascended; and now, with this perspective, he was at last able to appreciate the true vision of the architects who had built this place.

He was clinging to the face of a curving, sixteen-kilometer-high cliff, the upper half of which overhung completely until it merged into the arched roof of what was now the sky. Beneath him, the ladder descended more than five hundred meters, until it ended at the first ledge or terrace. There the stairway began, continuing almost vertically at first in this low-gravity regime, then slowly becoming less and less steep until, after breaking at five more platforms, it reached the distant plain. For the first two or three kilometers he could see the individual steps, but thereafter they had merged into a continuous band.

The downward swoop of that immense stairway was so overwhelming that it was impossible to appreciate its true scale. Norton had once flown around Mount

Everest, and had been awed by its size. He reminded himself that this stairway was as high as the Himalayas, but the comparison was meaningless.

And no comparison at all was possible with the other two stairways, Beta and Gamma, which slanted up into the sky and then curved far out over his head. Norton had now acquired enough confidence to lean back and glance up at them—briefly. Then he tried to forget that they were there.

Too much thinking along these lines evoked yet a third image of Rama, which he was anxious to avoid at all costs. This was the viewpoint that regarded it once again as a vertical cylinder, or well—but now he was at the *top*, not the bottom, like a fly crawling upside down on a domed ceiling, with a fifty-kilometer drop immediately below. Every time he found this image creeping up on him, he needed all his will power not to cling to the ladder in mindless panic.

In time, he was sure, all these fears would ebb. The wonder and strangeness of Rama would banish its terrors, at least for men who were trained to face the realities of space. Perhaps no one who had never left Earth, and had never seen the stars all around him, could endure these vistas. But if any men could accept them, Norton told himself with grim determination, it would be the captain and crew of the *Endeavour*.

He looked at his chronometer. This pause had lasted only two minutes, but it had seemed a lifetime. Exerting barely enough effort to overcome his inertia and the fading gravitational field, he started to pull himself slowly up the last hundred meters of the ladder. Just before he entered the air lock and turned his back upon Rama, he made one final swift survey of the interior.

It had changed, even in the last few minutes; a mist was rising from the sea. For the first few hundred meters the ghostly white columns were tilted sharply forward in the direction of Rama's spin; then they started to dissolve in a swirl of turbulence, as the uprushing air tried to jettison its excess velocity. The trade winds of this cylindrical world were beginning to etch their patterns in its sky; the first tropical storm in unknown ages was about to break.

19

A Warning from Mercury

IT WAS THE first time in weeks that every member of the Rama Committee had made himself available. Professor Solomons had emerged from the depths of the Pacific, where he had been studying mining operations along the mid-ocean trenches. And to nobody's surprise, Dr. Taylor had reappeared, now that there was at least a possibility that Rama held something more newsworthy than lifeless artifacts.

The Chairman had fully expected Dr. Perera to be even more dogmatically assertive than usual, now that his prediction of a Raman hurricane had been confirmed. To His Excellency's great surprise, Perera was remarkably subdued, and accepted the congratulations of his colleagues in a manner as near to embarrassment as he was ever likely to achieve.

The exobiologist was, in fact, deeply mortified. The spectacular breakup of the Cylindrical Sea was a much more obvious phenomenon than the hurricane winds, yet he had completely overlooked it. To have remembered that hot air rises but to have forgotten that hot ice contracts was not an achievement of which he could be very proud. However, he would soon get over it and revert to his normal Olympian self-confidence.

When the Chairman offered him the floor, and asked what further climatic changes he expected, he was careful to hedge his bets.

"You must realize," he explained, "that the meteorology of a world as strange as Rama may have many other surprises. But if my calculations are correct, there will be no further storms, and conditions will soon be stable. There will be a slow temperature rise until perihelion—and beyond—but that won't concern us, because *Endeavour* will have had to leave long before then."

"So it should soon be safe to go back inside?"

"Er—probably. We should certainly know in forty-eight hours."

"A return is imperative," said the Ambassador from Mercury. "We have to learn everything we possibly can about Rama. The situation has now changed completely."

"I think we know what you mean, but would you care to elaborate?"

"Of course. Until now, we have assumed that Rama is lifeless—or at any rate uncontrolled. But we can no longer pretend that it is a derelict. Even if there are no life forms aboard, it may be directed by robot mechanisms, programmed to carry out some mission—perhaps one highly disadvantageous to us. Unpalatable though it may be, we must consider the question of self-defense."

There was a babble of protesting voices, and the Chairman had to hold up his hand to restore order.

"Let His Excellency finish!" he pleaded. "Whether we like the idea or not, it should be considered seriously."

"With all due respect to the Ambassador," said Taylor in his most disrespectful voice, "I think we can rule out as naïve the fear of malevolent intervention. Creatures as advanced as the Ramans must have correspondingly developed morals. Otherwise, they would have destroyed themselves—as we nearly did in the twentieth century. I've made that quite clear in my new book, *Ethos and Cosmos*. I hope you received your copy."

"Yes, thank you, though I'm afraid the pressure of other matters has not allowed me to read beyond the introduction. However, I'm familiar with the general thesis. We may have no malevolent intentions toward an ant heap, but if we want to build a house on the same site . . ."

"This is as bad as the Pandora party! It's nothing less than interstellar xenophobia!"

"Please, *gentlemen!* This is getting us nowhere. Mr. Ambassador, you still have the floor."

The Chairman glared across three hundred and eighty thousand kilometers of space at Conrad Taylor, who reluctantly subsided, like a volcano biding its time.

"Thank you," said the Ambassador from Mercury. "The danger may be unlikely, but where the future of the human race is involved we can take no chances. And, if I may say so, we Hermians may be particularly concerned. We may have more cause for alarm than anyone else."

Taylor snorted audibly, but was quelled by another glare from the Moon.

"Why Mercury, more than any other planet?" asked the Chairman.

"Look at the dynamics of the situation. Rama is already inside our orbit. It is only an assumption that it will go around the Sun and head on out again into space. Suppose it carries out a braking maneuver? If it does so, this will be at perihelion, about thirty days from now. My scientists tell me that if the entire velocity change is carried out there, Rama will end up in a circular orbit only twenty-five million kilometers from the Sun. From there, it could dominate the solar system."

For a long time nobody—not even Taylor—spoke a word. All the members of the committee were marshaling their thoughts about those difficult people the Hermians, so ably represented here by their ambassador.

To most people, Mercury was a fairly good approximation of Hell; at least, it would do until something worse came along. But the Hermians were proud of their bizarre planet, with its days longer than its years, its double sunrises and sunsets, its rivers of molten metal. By comparison, the Moon and Mars had been almost trivial challenges. Not until men landed on Venus (if they ever did) would they encounter an environment more hostile than that of Mercury.

And yet this world had turned out to be, in many ways, the key to the solar system. This seemed obvious in retrospect, but the Space Age had been almost a century old before the fact was realized. Now the Hermians never let anyone forget it.

Long before men reached the planet, Mercury's abnormal density hinted at the heavy elements it contained; even so, its wealth was a source of astonishment, and had postponed for a thousand years any fears that the key metals of human civilization would be exhausted. And these treasures were in the best possible place, where the power of the Sun was ten times greater than on frigid Earth.

Unlimited energy, unlimited metal: *that* was Mercury. Its great magnetic launchers could catapult manufactured products to any point in the solar system. It could also export energy, in synthetic transuranium isotopes or pure radiation. It had even been proposed that Hermian lasers would one day thaw out gigantic Jupiter, but this idea had not been well received on the other worlds. A technology that could cook Jupiter had too many tempting possibilities for interplanetary blackmail.

That such a concern had ever been expressed said a good deal about the general attitude toward the Hermians. They were respected for their toughness and engineering skills, and admired for the way in which they had conquered so fearsome a world. But they were not liked, and still less were they completely trusted.

At the same time it was possible to appreciate their point of view. The Hermians, it was often joked, sometimes behaved as if the Sun were their personal property. They were bound to it in an intimate love-hate relationship—as the Vikings had once been linked to the sea, the Nepalese to the Himalayas, the Eskimos to the tundra. They would be most unhappy if something came between them and the natural force that dominated and controlled their lives.

At last the Chairman broke the long silence. He remembered the Sun of India and shuddered to contemplate the Sun of Mercury. So he took the Hermians seriously indeed, even though he considered them uncouth technological barbarians.

"I think there is some merit in your argument, Mr. Ambassador," he said slowly. "Have you any proposals?"

"Yes, sir. Before we know what action to take, we must have the facts. We know the geography of Rama—if one can use that term—but we have no idea of its capabilities. And the key to the whole problem is this:

does Rama have a propulsion system? *Can it change orbit?* I would be very interested in Dr. Perera's views."

"I've given the subject a good deal of thought," answered the exobiologist. "Of course Rama must have been given its original impetus by some launching device, but that could have been an external booster. If it does have onboard propulsion, we've found no trace of it. Certainly there are no rocket exhausts, or anything similar, anywhere on the outer shell."

"They could be hidden."

"True, but there would seem little point in it. And where are the propellant tanks, the energy sources? The main hull is solid; we've checked that with seismic surveys. The cavities in the northern cap are all accounted for by the air-lock systems.

"That leaves the southern end of Rama, which Commander Norton has been unable to reach, owing to that ten-kilometer-wide band of water. There are all sorts of curious mechanisms and structures up on the South Pole—you've seen the photographs. What they are is anybody's guess.

"But I'm reasonably sure of this. If Rama does have a propulsion system, it's something completely outside our present knowledge. In fact, it would have to be the fabulous 'space drive' people have been talking about for two hundred years."

"You wouldn't rule that out?"

"Certainly not. If we can prove that Rama has a space drive—even if we learn nothing about its mode of operation—that would be a major discovery. At least we'd know that such a thing is possible."

"What *is* a space drive?" asked the Ambassador from Earth, rather plaintively.

"Any kind of propulsion system, Sir Robert, that doesn't work on the rocket principle. Antigravity—if it is possible—would do very nicely. At present we don't know where to look for such a drive, and most scientists doubt it exists."

"It doesn't," Professor Davidson interjected. "Newton settled *that*. You can't have action without reaction. Space drives are nonsense. Take it from me."

"You may be right," Perera replied with unusual blandness. "But if Rama doesn't have a space drive, it has no drive at all. There's simply no room for a conventional propulsion system, with its enormous fuel tanks."

"It's hard to imagine a whole world being pushed around," said Solomons. "What would happen to the objects inside it? Everything would have to be bolted down. Most inconvenient."

"Well, the acceleration would probably be very low. The biggest problem would be the water in the Cylindrical Sea. How would you stop that from . . ."

Perera's voice faded away, and his eyes glazed over. He seemed to be in the throes of incipient epileptic fit, or even a heart attack. His colleagues looked at him in alarm; then he made a sudden recovery, banged his fist on the table, and shouted: "Of course! That explains everything! The southern cliff—*now* it makes sense!"

"Not to me," grumbled the Lunar Ambassador, speaking for all the diplomats present.

"Look at this longitudinal cross section of Rama," Perera continued excitedly, unfolding his map. "Have you got your copies? The Cylindrical Sea is enclosed between two cliffs, which completely circle the interior of Rama. The one on the north is only fifty meters high. The southern one, on the other hand, is almost half a kilometer high. Why the big difference? No one's been able to think of a sensible reason.

"But suppose Rama *is* able to propel itself—accelerating so that the northern end is forward. The water in the sea would tend to move back; the level at the south would rise, perhaps hundreds of meters. Hence the cliff. Let's see . . ."

He started scribbling furiously. After an astonishingly short time—it could not have been more than twenty seconds—he looked up in triumph. "Knowing the height of those cliffs, we can calculate the maximum acceleration Rama can take. If it was more than two per cent of a gravity, the sea would slosh over into the southern continent."

"A fiftieth of a gee? That's not very much."

"For a mass of ten million megatons, it is. And it's all you need for astronomical maneuvering." '

"Thank you very much, Dr. Perera," said the Hermian Ambassador. "You've given us a lot to think about. Mr. Chairman, can we impress on Commander Norton the importance of looking at the south polar region?"

"He's doing his best. The sea is the obstacle, of course. They're trying to build some kind of raft—so that they can at least reach New York."

"The South Pole may be even more important. Meanwhile, I am going to bring these matters to the attention of the General Assembly. Do I have your approval?"

There were no objections, not even from Dr. Taylor. But just as the committee members were about to switch out of circuit, Sir Lewis raised his hand.

The old historian seldom spoke; when he did, everyone listened.

"Suppose we do find that Rama is—*active*—and has these capabilities. There is an old saying in military affairs that capability does not imply intention."

"How long should we wait to find what its intentions are?" asked the Hermian. "When we discover them, it may be far too late."

"It is already too late. There is nothing we can do to affect Rama. Indeed, I doubt if there ever was."

"I do not admit that, Sir Lewis. There are many things we can do—if it proves necessary. But the time is desperately short. Rama is a cosmic egg, being warmed by the fires of the Sun. It may hatch at any moment."

The Chairman of the committee looked at the Ambassador from Mercury in frank astonishment. He had seldom been so surprised in his diplomatic career. He would never have dreamed that a Hermian was capable of such a poetic flight of imagination.

20

Book of Revelation

WHEN ONE OF his crew called him "Commander," or, worse still, "*Mister* Norton," there was always something serious afoot. He could not recall that Boris Rodrigo had ever before addressed him in such a fashion, so this must be doubly serious. Even in normal times, Rodrigo was a grave and sober person.

"What's the problem, Boris?" he asked when the cabin door closed behind them.

"I'd like permission, Commander, to use ship priority for a direct message to Earth."

This *was* unusual, though not unprecedented. Routine signals went to the nearest planetary relay—at the moment, they were working through Mercury—and even though the transit time was only a matter of minutes, it was often five or six hours before a message arrived at the desk of the person for whom it was intended. Ninety-nine per cent of the time that was quite good enough; but, in an emergency, more direct and much more expensive channels could be employed at the captain's discretion.

"You know, of course, that you have to give me a good reason. All our available band width is already clogged with data transmission. Is this a personal emergency?"

"No, Commander. It is much more important than *that*. I want to send a message to the Mother Church."

Uh-uh, said Norton to himself. How do I handle this?

"I'd be glad if you'd explain."

It was not mere curiosity that prompted Norton's request, though that was certainly present. If he gave Rodrigo the priority he asked, he would have to justify his action.

The calm blue eyes stared into his. He had never known Rodrigo to lose control, to be other than completely self-assured. All the Cosmo Christers were like this; it was one of the benefits of their faith, and it helped to make them good spacemen. Sometimes, however, their unquestioning certainty was just a little annoying to those unfortunates who had not been vouchsafed the revelation.

"It concerns the purpose of Rama, Commander. I believe I have discovered it."

"Go on."

"Look at the situation. Here is a completely empty, lifeless world—yet it is suitable for human beings. It has water and an atmosphere we can breathe. It comes from the remote depths of space, aimed precisely at the solar system—something quite incredible, if it was a matter of pure chance. And it appears not only new; *it looks as if it has never been used.*"

We've all been through this dozens of times, Norton thought. What could Rodrigo add to it?

"Our faith has told us to expect such a visitation,

though we do not know exactly what form it will take.
The Bible gives hints. If this is not the Second Coming, it may be the Second Judgment; the story of
Noah describes the first. I believe that Rama is a
cosmic Ark, sent here to save—those who are worthy
of salvation."

There was silence for quite a while in the cabin. It
was not that Norton was at a loss for words; rather, he
could think of too many questions but was not sure
which ones it would be tactful to ask.

Finally he remarked, in as mild and noncommittal a
voice as he could manage: "That's a very interesting
concept, and though I don't go along with your faith,
it's a tantalizingly plausible one." He was not being
hypocritical or flattering; stripped of its religious over-
tones, Rodrigo's theory was at least as convincing as
half a dozen others he had heard. Suppose some catastrophe was about to befall the human race, and a benevolent higher intelligence knew all about it? That
would explain everything, very neatly. However, there
were still a few problems.

"A couple of questions, Boris. Rama will be at perihelion in three weeks; then it will round the Sun and
leave the solar system just as fast as it came in.
There's not much time for a Day of Judgment, or for
shipping across those who are—er—selected—however *that's* going to be done."

"Very true. So when it reaches perihelion, Rama
will have to decelerate and go into a parking orbit—
probably one with aphelion at Earth's orbit. There it
might make another velocity change, and rendezvous
with Earth."

This was disturbingly persuasive. If Rama wished to
remain in the solar system, it was going the right way
about it. The most efficient way to slow down was to
get as close to the Sun as possible, and carry out the
braking maneuver there. If there was any truth in

Rodrigo's theory, or some variant of it, it would soon be put to the test.

"One other point, Boris. What's controlling Rama now?"

"There is no doctrine to advise on that. It could be a pure robot. Or it could be—a spirit. That would explain why there are no signs of biological life forms."

"The Haunted Asteroid": why had that phrase popped up from the depths of memory? Then he recalled a silly story he had read years ago, but thought it best not to ask Rodrigo if he had ever seen it. He doubted if the other's tastes ran to that sort of reading.

"I'll tell you what we'll do, Boris," he said, abruptly making up his mind. He wanted to terminate this interview before it got too difficult, and thought he had found a good compromise. "Can you sum up your ideas in less than—oh, a thousand bits?"

"Yes, I think so."

"Well, if you can make it sound like a straightforward scientific theory, I'll send it, top priority, to the Rama Committee. Then a copy can go to your church at the same time, and everyone will be happy."

"Thank you, Commander. I really appreciate it."

"Oh, I'm not doing this to save my conscience. I'd just like to see what the committee makes of it. Even if I don't agree with you all along the line, you may have hit on something important."

"Well, we'll know at perihelion, won't we?"

"Yes. We'll know at perihelion."

When Rodrigo had left, Norton called the bridge and gave the necessary authorization. He thought he had solved the problem rather neatly; besides, just suppose that Rodrigo *was* right.

He might have increased his chances of being among the saved.

21

After the Storm

As THEY DRIFTED along the now familiar corridor of
the Alpha air-lock complex, Norton wondered if they
had let impatience overcome caution. They had waited
aboard *Endeavour* for forty-eight hours—two precious
days—ready for instant departure if events should justify it. But nothing had happened; the instruments left
in Rama had detected no unusual activity. Frustrating-
ly, the television camera on the hub had been blinded
by a fog that had reduced visibility to a few meters
and had only now started to retreat.

When they operated the final air-lock door and
floated out into the cat's cradle of guide ropes around
the hub, Norton was struck first by the change in the
light. It was no longer harshly blue, but was much
more mellow and gentle, reminding him of a bright,
hazy day on Earth.

He looked outward along the axis of the world, and

could see nothing except a glowing, featureless tunnel of white, reaching all the way to those strange mountains at the South Pole. The interior of Rama was completely blanketed by clouds, and nowhere was a break visible in the overcast. The top of the layer was quite sharply defined; it formed a smaller cylinder inside the larger one of this spinning world, leaving a central core, five or six kilometers wide, quite clear except for a few stray wisps of cirrus.

The immense tube of cloud was lit from within by the six artificial suns of Rama. The locations of the three on this northern continent were clearly defined by diffuse strips of light, but those on the far side of the Cylindrical Sea merged together into a continuous glowing band.

What is happening down beneath those clouds? Norton asked himself. But at least the storm, which had centrifuged them into such perfect symmetry about the axis of Rama, had now died away. Unless there were some other surprises, it would be safe to descend.

It seemed appropriate, on this return visit, to use the team that had made the first deep penetration into Rama. Sergeant Myron—like every other member of *Endeavour's* crew—now fully met Surgeon Commander Ernst's physical requirements; he even maintained, with convincing sincerity, that he was never going to wear his old uniforms again.

As Norton watched Mercer, Calvert, and Myron "swimming" quickly and confidently down the ladder, he reminded himself how much had changed. That first time, they had descended in cold and darkness; now, they were going toward light and warmth. And on all earlier visits they had been certain that Rama was dead. That might yet be true, in a biological sense. But something was stirring; and Boris Rodrigo's word would do as well as any other: the "spirit" of Rama was awake.

When they had reached the platform at the foot of the ladder and were preparing to start down the stairway, Mercer carried out his usual routine test of the atmosphere. There were some things that he never took for granted; even when the people around him were breathing perfectly comfortably, without aids, he had been known to stop for an air check before opening his helmet. When asked to justify such excessive caution, he had answered: "Because human senses aren't good enough, that's why. You may think you're fine, but you could fall flat on your face with the next deep breath."

He looked at his meter, and said, "Damn!"

"What's the trouble?" asked Calvert.

"It's broken—reading too high. Odd; I've never known that to happen before. I'll check it on my breathing circuit."

He plugged the compact little analyzer into the test point of his oxygen supply, then stood in thoughtful silence for a while. His companions looked at him with anxious concern; anything that upset Mercer was to be taken seriously indeed.

He unplugged the meter, used it to sample the Rama atmosphere again, then called Hub Control. "Skipper! Will you take an O_2 reading?"

There was a much longer pause than the request justified. Then Norton radioed back: "I think there's something wrong with my meter."

A slow smile spread across Mercer's face. "It's up fifty per cent, isn't it?"

"Yes. What does that mean?"

"It means that we can all take off our masks. Isn't that convenient?"

"I'm not sure," replied Norton, echoing the sarcasm

in Mercer's voice. "It seems too good to be true."
There was no need to say any more. Like all spacemen, Norton had a profound suspicion of things that
were too good to be true.

Mercer cracked his mask open a trifle and took a
cautious sniff. For the first time at this altitude, the air
was perfectly breathable. The musty, dead smell had
gone; so had the excessive dryness, which in the past
had caused several respiratory complaints. Humidity
was now an astonishing eighty per cent; doubtless the
thawing of the sea was responsible for this. There was
a muggy feeling in the air, though not an unpleasant
one. It was like a summer evening, Mercer thought, on
some tropical coast. The climate inside Rama had im-
proved dramatically during the last few days.

And why? The increased humidity was no problem;
the startling rise in oxygen was much more difficult to
explain. As he recommenced the descent, Mercer began a whole series of mental calculations. He had not
arrived at any satisfactory result by the time they entered the cloud layer.

It was a dramatic experience, for the transition was
abrupt. At one moment they were sliding downward in
clear air, gripping the smooth metal of the handrail so
that they would not gain speed too swiftly in this
quarter-of-a-gravity region. Then, suddenly, they shot
into a blinding white fog, and visibility dropped to a
few meters. Mercer put on the brakes so quickly that
Calvert almost bumped into him, and Myron did bump
into Calvert, nearly knocking him off the rail.

"Take it easy," said Mercer. "Spread out so we can
just see each other. And don't let yourself build up
speed, in case I have to stop suddenly."

In eerie silence they continued to glide downward
through the fog. Calvert could just see Mercer as a
vague shadow ten meters ahead, and when he looked

back, Myron was at the same distance behind him. In some ways, this was even spookier than descending in the complete darkness of the Raman night; then, at least, the searchlight beams had shown them what lay ahead. But *this* was like diving in poor visibility in the open sea.

It was impossible to tell how far they had traveled, but Calvert guessed they had almost reached the fourth level, when Mercer suddenly braked again. After they had bunched together, he whispered: "Listen! Don't you hear something?"

"Yes," said Myron, after a minute. "It sounds like the wind."

Calvert was not so sure. He turned his head back and forth, trying to locate the direction of the faint murmur that had come to them through the fog, but soon abandoned the attempt as hopeless.

They continued the slide, reached the fourth level, and started on toward the fifth. All the while the sound grew louder—and more hauntingly familiar. They were halfway down the fourth stairway when Myron called out: "Now do you recognize it?"

They should have identified it long ago, but it was not a sound they would ever have associated with any world except Earth. Coming out of the fog, from a source whose distance could not be guessed, was the steady thunder of falling water.

A few minutes later, the cloud ceiling ended as abruptly as it had begun. They shot out into the blinding glare of the Raman day, made more brilliant by the light reflected from the low-hanging clouds. There was the familiar curving plain—now made more acceptable to mind and senses because its full circle could no longer be seen. It was not too difficult to pretend that they were looking along a broad valley, and that the upward sweep of the sea was really an *outward* one.

They halted at the fifth and penultimate platform, to report that they were through the cloud cover and to make a careful survey. As far as they could tell, nothing had changed down there on the plain; but up here on the northern dome Rama had brought forth another wonder.

So there was the origin of the sound they had heard. Descending from some hidden source in the clouds three or four kilometers away was a waterfall, and for long minutes they stared at it silently, almost unable to believe their eyes. Logic told them that on this spinning world no falling object could move in a straight line, but there was something horribly unnatural about a curving waterfall that curved sideways, to end many kilometers away from the point directly below its source.

"If Galileo had been born in this world," said Mercer finally, "he'd have gone crazy working out the laws of dynamics."

"I thought I knew them," Calvert replied, "and I'm going crazy anyway. Doesn't it upset you, Prof?"

"Why should it?" said Myron. "It's a perfectly straight-forward demonstration of the Coriolis Effect. I wish I could show it to some of my students."

Mercer was staring thoughtfully at the globe-circling band of the Cylindrical Sea.

"Have you noticed what's happened to the water?" he said at last.

"Why—it's no longer so blue. I'd call it pea green. What does that signify?"

"Perhaps the same thing that it does on Earth. Laura called the sea an organic soup, waiting to be shaken into life. Maybe that's exactly what's happened."

"In a couple of days! It took millions of years on Earth."

"Three hundred and seventy-five million, according to the latest estimate. So *that's* where the oxygen's come from. Rama's shot through the anaerobic stage and has got to photosynthetic plants—in about forty-eight hours. I wonder what it will produce tomorrow?"

22

To Sail the Cylindrical Sea

WHEN THEY REACHED the foot of the stairway, they had another shock. At first it appeared that something had gone through the camp, overturning equipment, even collecting smaller objects and carrying them away. But after a brief examination their alarm was replaced by a rather shame-faced annoyance.

The culprit was only the wind. Though they had tied down all loose objects before they left, some ropes must have parted during exceptionally strong gusts. It was several days before they were able to retrieve all their scattered property.

Otherwise there seemed no major changes. Even the silence of Rama had returned, now that the ephemeral storms of spring were over. And out there at the edge of the plain was a calm sea, waiting for the first ship in a million years.

"Shouldn't one christen a new boat with a bottle of champagne?"

"Even if we had some on board I wouldn't allow such a criminal waste. Anyway, it's too late. We've already launched the thing."

"At least it does float. You've won your bet, Jimmy. I'll settle when we get back to Earth."

"It's got to have a name. Any ideas?"

The subject of these unflattering comments was now bobbing beside the steps leading down into the Cylindrical Sea. It was a small raft, constructed from six empty storage drums, held together by a light metal framework. Building it, assembling it at Camp Alpha, and hauling it on demountable wheels across more than ten kilometers of plain had absorbed the crew's entire energies for several days. It was a gamble that had better pay off.

The prize was worth the risk. The enigmatic towers of New York, gleaming there in the shadowless light five kilometers away, had taunted them ever since they had entered Rama. No one doubted that the city—or whatever it might be—was the real heart of this world. If they did nothing else, they must reach New York.

"We still don't have a name. Skipper, what about it?"

Norton laughed, then became suddenly serious. "I've got one for you. Call it *Resolution*."

"Why?"

"That was one of Cook's ships. It's a good name. May she live up to it."

There was a thoughtful silence; then Sergeant Barnes, who had been principally responsible for the design, asked for three volunteers. Everyone present held up a hand.

"Sorry—we have only four life jackets. Boris, Jimmy, Pieter—you've all done some sailing. Let's try her out."

No one thought it in the least peculiar that an executive sergeant was now taking charge of the proceedings. Ruby Barnes had the only master's certificate aboard; so that settled the matter. She had navigated racing trimarans across the Pacific, and it did not seem likely that a few kilometers of dead-calm water would present much of a challenge to her skills.

Ever since she had set eyes upon the sea, she had been determined to make this voyage. In all the thousands of years that man had had dealings with the waters of his own world, no sailor had ever faced anything remotely like this. In the last few days a silly little jingle had been running through her mind, and she could not get rid of it: "To sail the Cylindrical Sea. . . ." Well, that was precisely what she was going to do.

Her passengers took their places on the improvised bucket seats, and Ruby opened the throttle. The twenty-kilowatt motor started to whirr, the chain drives of the reduction gear blurred, and *Resolution* surged away, to the cheers of the spectators.

Ruby had hoped to get fifteen kph with this load, but would settle for anything over ten. A half-kilometer course had been measured along the cliff, and she made the round trip in five and a half minutes. Allowing for turning time, this worked out at twelve kph, and she was quite happy with that.

With no power, but with three energetic paddlers helping her own more skillful blade, Ruby was able to get a quarter of this speed. So even if the motor broke down, they could get back to shore in a couple of hours. The heavy-duty power cells could provide enough energy to circumnavigate the world, but she was carrying two spares, to be on the safe side. And now that the fog had completely burned away, even such a cautious mariner as Ruby was prepared to put to sea without a compass.

She saluted smartly as she stepped ashore. "Maiden voyage of *Resolution* successfully completed, sir. Now awaiting your instructions."

"Very good . . . Admiral. When will you be ready to sail?"

"As soon as stores can be loaded aboard, and the Harbor Master gives us clearance."

"Then we leave at dawn."

"Aye, aye, sir!"

Five kilometers of water does not seem much on a map; it is very different when one is in the middle of it. They had been cruising for only ten minutes, and the fifty-meter cliff facing the northern continent already seemed a surprising distance away. Yet, mysteriously, New York appeared hardly much closer than before.

Most of the time they paid little attention to the land; they were still too engrossed in the wonder of the sea. They no longer made the nervous jokes that had punctuated the start of the voyage. This new experience was too overwhelming.

Every time, Norton said to himself, I feel that I've grown accustomed to Rama, it produces some new wonder. As *Resolution* hummed steadily forward, it seemed again and again that they were caught in the trough of a gigantic wave, a wave that curved up on either side until it became vertical, then overhung until the two flanks met in a liquid arch sixteen kilometers above their heads. Despite everything that reason and logic told them, none of the voyagers could for long throw off the impression that at any minute those millions of tons of water would come crashing down from the sky.

Yet despite this, their main feeling was one of exhilaration; there was a sense of danger, without any *real* danger. Unless, of course, the sea itself produced more surprises.

That was a distinct possibility, for, as Mercer had guessed, the water was now alive. Every spoonful contained thousands of spherical, single-celled microorganisms, similar to the earliest forms of plankton that had existed in the oceans of Earth.

Yet they showed puzzling differences. They lacked a nucleus, as well as many of the other minimum requirements of even the most primitive terrestrial life forms. And although Laura Ernst—now doubling as research scientist and ship's doctor—had proved that they definitely generated oxygen, there were far too few of them to account for the augmentation of Rama's atmosphere. They should have existed in billions, not mere thousands.

Then she discovered that their numbers were dwindling rapidly, and must have been far higher during the first hours of the Raman dawn. It was as if there had been a brief explosion of life, recapitulating, on a trillionfold swifter time scale, the early history of Earth. Now, perhaps, it had exhausted itself; the drifting microorganisms were disintegrating, releasing their stores of chemicals back into the sea.

"If you have to swim for it," Dr. Ernst had warned the mariners, "keep your mouths closed. A few drops won't matter—if you spit them out right away. But all those weird organometallic salts add up to a fairly poisonous package, and I'd hate to have to work out an antidote."

This danger, fortunately, seemed unlikely. *Resolution* could stay afloat if any two of her buoyancy tanks were punctured. (When told of this, Calvert had muttered darkly: "Remember the *Titanic!*") And even if she sank, the crude but efficient life jackets would keep their heads above water. Although Dr. Ernst had been reluctant to give a firm ruling on this, she did not think that a few hours' immersion in the sea would be fatal; but she did not recommend it.

After twenty minutes of steady progress, New York was no longer a distant island. It was becoming a real place, and details they had seen only through telescopes and photo enlargements were now revealing themselves as massive, solid structures. It was now strikingly apparent that the "city," like so much of Rama, was triplicated. It consisted of three identical, circular complexes or superstructures, rising from a long, oval foundation. Photographs taken from the hub had also indicated that each complex was *itself* divided into three equal components, like a pie sliced into 120-degree portions. This would greatly simplify the task of exploration; presumably they had to examine only one-ninth of New York to see the whole of it. Even this would be a formidable undertaking. It would mean investigating at least a square kilometer of buildings and machinery, some of which towered hundreds of meters into the air.

The Ramans, it seemed, had brought the art of triple redundancy to a high degree of perfection. This was demonstrated in the air-lock system, the stairways at the hub, the artificial suns. And where it really mattered they had even taken the next step. New York appeared to be an example of triple-triple redundancy.

Ruby was steering *Resolution* toward the central complex, where a flight of steps led up from the water to the top of the wall or levee that surrounded the island. There was even a conveniently placed mooring post to which boats could be tied. When she saw this, Ruby became quite excited. Now she would never be content until she found one of the craft in which the Ramans sailed their extraordinary sea.

Norton was the first to step ashore. He looked back at his three companions and said, "Wait here on the boat until I get to the top of the wall. When I wave, Pieter and Boris will join me. You stay at the helm, Ruby, so that we can cast off at a moment's notice. If anything happens to me, report to Karl and follow his instructions. Use your best judgment—but no heroics. Understood!"

"Yes, Skipper. Good luck!"

Commander Norton did not really believe in luck; he never got into a situation until he had analyzed all the factors involved and had secured his line of retreat. But once again Rama was forcing him to break some of his cherished rules. Almost every factor here was unknown, as unknown as the Pacific and the Great Barrier Reef had been to his hero three and a half centuries ago. Yes, he could do with all the luck that happened to be lying around.

The stairway was a virtual duplicate of the one they had descended on the other side of the sea, where doubtless his friends were looking straight across at him through their telescopes. And "straight" was now the correct word; in this one direction, parallel to the axis of Rama, the sea was indeed completely flat. It might well be the only body of water in the universe of which this was true, for on all other worlds, every sea and lake must follow the surface of a sphere, with equal curvature in all directions.

"Nearly at the top," he reported, speaking for the record and for his intently listening second-in-command, five kilometers away. "Still completely quiet. Radiation normal. I'm holding the meter above my head, just in case this wall is acting as a shield for anything. And if there are any hostiles on the other side, they'll shoot that first."

He was joking, of course. And yet, why take any chances, when it was just as easy to avoid them?

When he took the last step, he found that the flat-topped embankment was about ten meters thick. On the inner side, an alternating series of ramps and stairways led down to the main level of the city, twenty meters below. In effect, he was standing on a high wall, which completely surrounded New York, and so was able to get a grandstand view of it.

It was a view almost stunning in its complexity, and his first act was to make a slow panoramic scan with his camera. Then he waved to his companions and radioed back across the sea: "No sign of any activity; everything quiet. Come on up—we'll start exploring."

23

N.Y., Rama

IT WAS NOT a city; it was a machine. Norton had come to that conclusion in ten minutes, and saw no reason to change it after they had made a complete traverse of the island. A city, whatever the nature of its occupants, surely had to provide some form of accommodation; there was nothing here of that nature, unless it was underground. And if that was the case, where were the entrances, the stairways, the elevators? He had not found anything that even qualified as a simple door.

The closest analogy to this place that he had ever seen on Earth was a giant chemical-processing plant. However, there were no stockpiles of raw materials, or any indications of a transport system to move them around. Nor could he imagine where the finished product would emerge—still less what that product could possibly be. It was all very baffling, and more than a little frustrating.

"Anybody care to make a guess?" he said at last, to all who might be listening. "If this is a factory, what does it make? And where does it get its raw materials?"

"I've a suggestion, Skipper," said Mercer, over on the far shore. "Suppose it uses the sea. According to Doc, that contains just about anything you can think of."

It was a plausible answer, and Norton had already considered it. There could well be buried pipes leading to the sea; in fact, there *must* be, for any conceivable chemical plant would require large quantities of water. But he had a suspicion of plausible answers; they were so often wrong.

"That's a good idea, Karl. But what does New York *do* with its sea water?"

For a long time nobody answered from ship, hub, or northern plain. Then an unexpected voice spoke.

"That's easy, Skipper. But you're all going to laugh at me."

"No, we're not, Ravi. Go ahead."

Ravi McAndrews, Chief Steward and Simp Master, was the last person on the *Endeavour* who would normally get involved in a technical discussion. His IQ was modest and his scientific knowledge was minimal, but he was no fool and he had a natural shrewdness that everyone respected.

"Well, it's a factory, all right, Skipper, and maybe the sea provides the raw material. After all, that's how it all happened on Earth, though in a different way. . . . I believe New York is a factory for making . . . Ramans."

Somebody, somewhere, snickered, but became quickly silent and did not identify himself.

"You know, Ravi," said his commander at last, "that theory is crazy enough to be true. And I'm not sure if I want to see it tested—at least, until I get back to the mainland."

This celestial New York was just about as wide as the island of Manhattan, but its geometry was totally different. There were few straight thoroughfares; it was a maze of short, concentric arcs, with radial spokes linking them. Luckily, it was impossible to lose one's bearings inside Rama; a single glance at the sky was enough to establish the north-south axis of the world.

They paused at almost every intersection to make a panoramic scan. When all these hundreds of pictures were sorted out, it would be a tedious but fairly straight-forward job to construct an accurate scale model of the city. Norton suspected that the resulting jigsaw puzzle would keep scientists busy for generations.

It was even harder to get used to the silence here than it had been out on the plain of Rama. A city-machine should make some sound; yet there was not even the faintest of electric hums, or the slightest whisper of mechanical motion. Several times Norton put his ear to the ground, or to the side of a building, and listened intently. He could hear nothing except the pounding of his own blood.

The machines were sleeping; they were not even ticking over. Would they ever wake again, and for what purpose? Everything was in perfect condition, as usual. It was easy to believe that the closing of a single circuit in some patient, hidden computer would bring all this maze back to life.

When at last they had reached the far side of the city, they climbed to the top of the surrounding levee and looked across the southern branch of the sea. For a long time Norton stared at the five-hundred-meter cliff that barred them from almost half of Rama— and, judging from their telescopic surveys, the most complex and varied half. From this angle it appeared an ominous, forbidding black, and it was easy to think of it as a prison wall surrounding a whole continent. Nowhere along its entire circle were there stairways or any other means of access.

He wondered how the Ramans reached their southern land from New York. Probably there was a transport system running beneath the sea, but they must also have aircraft, because there were many open areas here in the city that could be used for landing. To discover a Raman vehicle would be a major accomplishment, especially if they could learn to operate it. (Though could any conceivable power source still be functioning after several hundred thousand years?) There were numerous structures that had the functional look of hangars or garages, but they were all smooth and windowless, as if they had been sprayed with sealer. Sooner or later, Norton told himself grimly, we'll be forced to use explosives and laser beams. He was determined to put off this decision to the last possible moment.

His reluctance to use brute force was based partly on pride, partly on fear. He did not wish to behave like a technological barbarian, smashing what he could not understand. After all, he was an uninvited visitor in this world, and should act accordingly.

As for his fear, perhaps that was too strong a word; apprehension might be better. The Ramans seemed to have planned for everything. He was not anxious to discover the precautions they had taken to guard their property. When he sailed back to the mainland, it would be with empty hands.

24

Dragonfly

LIEUTENANT JAMES PAK was the most junior officer on board *Endeavour*, and this was only his fourth mission into deep space. He was ambitious, and due for promotion; he had also committed a serious breach of regulations. No wonder, therefore, that he took a long time to make up his mind.

It would be a gamble; if he lost, he could be in deep trouble. He would not only be risking his career; he might even be risking his neck. But if he succeeded, he would be a hero. What finally convinced him was neither of these arguments. It was the certainty that, if he did nothing at all, he would spend the rest of his life brooding over his lost opportunity.

Nevertheless, he was still hesitant when he asked Commander Norton for a private meeting.

What is it *this* time? Norton asked himself as he analyzed the uncertain expression on the young officer's

face. He remembered his delicate interview with Boris
Rodrigo; no, it wouldn't be anything like that. Pak
was certainly not the religious type. The only interests
he had ever shown outside his work were sport and
sex, preferably combined.

It could hardly be the former, and Norton hoped it
was not the latter. He had encountered most of the
problems that a commanding officer could encounter
in this department—except the classical one of an un-
scheduled birth during a mission. Though this situation was the subject of innumerable jokes, it had never
happened yet; but such gross incompetence was probably only a matter of time.

"Well, Jimmy, what is it?"

"I have an idea, Commander. I know how to reach
the southern continent—even the South Pole."

"I'm listening. How do you propose to do it?"

"Er—by flying there."

"Jimmy, I've had at least five proposals to do that
—more, if you count crazy suggestions from Earth.
We've looked into the possibility of adapting our spacesuit propulsors, but air drag would make them hopelessly inefficient. They'd run out of fuel before they
could go ten kilometers."

"I know that. But I have the answer."

Pak's attitude was a curious mixture of complete
confidence and barely suppressed nervousness. Norton
was quite baffled. What was the kid worried about?
Surely he knew his commanding officer well enough to
be certain that no reasonable proposal would be
laughed out of court.

"Well, go on. If it works, I'll see your promotion is
retroactive."

That little half-promise, half-joke didn't go down as
well as he had hoped. Jimmy gave a rather sickly
smile, made several false starts, then decided on an
oblique approach to the subject.

"You know, Commander, that I was in the Lunar Olympics last year."

"Of course. Sorry you didn't win."

"It was bad equipment; I know what went wrong. I have friends on Mars who've been working on it, in secret. We want to give everyone a surprise."

"Mars? But I didn't know—"

"Not many people do. The sport's still new there; it's only been tried in the Xante Sportsdome. But the best aerodynamicists in the solar system are on Mars. If you can fly in *that* atmosphere, you can fly anywhere.

"Now, my idea was that if the Martians could build a good machine, with all their know-how, it would *really* perform on the Moon—where gravity is only half as strong."

"That seems plausible, but how does it help us?" Norton was beginning to guess, but he wanted to give Jimmy plenty of rope.

"Well, I formed a syndicate with some friends in Port Lowell. They've built a fully aerobatic flyer, with some refinements that no one has ever seen before. In lunar gravity, under the Olympic dome, it should create a sensation."

"And win you the gold medal."

"I hope so."

"Let me see if I follow your train of thought correctly. A sky-bike that could enter the Lunar Olympics, at a sixth of a gravity, would be even more sensational inside Rama, with no gravity at all. You could fly it right along the axis, from the North Pole to the South—and back again."

"Yes—easily. The one-way trip would take three hours, nonstop. But of course you could rest whenever you wanted to, as long as you kept near the axis."

"It's a brilliant idea, and I congratulate you. What a

pity sky-bikes aren't part of regular Space Survey equipment."

Jimmy seemed to have some difficulty in finding words. He opened his mouth several times, but nothing happened.

"All right, Jimmy. As a matter of morbid interest, and purely off the record, how did you smuggle the thing aboard?"

"Er . . . 'recreational stores.' "

"Well, you weren't lying. And what about the weight?"

"It's only twenty kilograms."

"*Only!* Still, that's not as bad as I thought. In fact, I'm astonished you can build a bike at that weight."

"Some have been only fifteen, but they were too fragile and usually folded up when they made a turn. There's no danger of *Dragonfly* doing that. As I said, she's fully aerobatic."

"*Dragonfly*—nice name. So tell me just how you plan to use her; then I can decide whether a promotion or a court-martial is in order. Or both."

25

Maiden Flight

DRAGONFLY WAS CERTAINLY a good name. The long tapering wings were almost invisible, except when the light struck them from certain angles and was refracted into rainbow hues. It was as if a soap bubble had been wrapped around a delicate tracery of aerofoil sections; the envelope enclosing the little flyer was an organic film only a few molecules thick, yet strong enough to control and direct the movements of a fifty-kph air flow.

The pilot—who was also the power plant and the guidance system—sat on a tiny seat at the center of gravity, in a semireclining position to reduce air resistance. Control was by a single stick, which could be moved backward and forward, right and left; the only "instrument" was a piece of weighted ribbon attached to the leading edge, to show the direction of the relative wind.

Once the flyer had been assembled at the hub, Jimmy Pak would allow no one to touch it. Clumsy handling could snap one of the single-fiber structural members, and those glittering wings were an almost irresistible attraction to prying fingers. It was hard to believe that there was *really* something there.

As he watched Jimmy climb into the contraption, Norton began to have second thoughts. If one of those wire-sized struts snapped when *Dragonfly* was on the other side of the Cylindrical Sea, Jimmy would have no way of getting back—even if he was able to make a safe landing. They were also breaking one of the most sacrosanct rules of space exploration; a man was going *alone* into unknown territory, beyond all possibility of help. The only consolation was that he would be in full view and communication all the time; if he did meet with disaster, they would know exactly what had happened to him.

Yet this opportunity was far too good to miss. If one believed in fate or destiny, it would be challenging the gods themselves to neglect the only chance they might ever have of reaching the far side of Rama, and seeing at close quarters the mysteries of the South Pole. Jimmy knew what he was attempting, far better than anyone in the crew could tell him. This was precisely the sort of risk that had to be taken; if it failed, that was the luck of the game. You couldn't win them all.

"Now listen to me carefully, Jimmy," said Laura Ernst. "It's very important not to overexert yourself. Remember, the oxygen level here at the axis is still very low. If you feel breathless at any time, stop and hyperventilate for thirty seconds—but no longer."

Jimmy nodded absent-mindedly as he tested the controls. The whole rudder-elevator assembly, which formed a single unit on an outrigger five meters behind the rudimentary cockpit, began to twist around;

then the flap-shaped ailerons, halfway along the wing, moved alternately up and down.

"Do you want me to swing the prop?" asked Joe Calvert, unable to repress memories of two-hundred-year-old war movies. "Ignition! Contact!" Probably no one except Jimmy knew what he was talking about, but it helped to relieve the tension.

Very slowly, Jimmy started to move the foot pedals. The flimsy, broad fan of the airscrew—like the wing, a delicate skeleton covered with shimmering film—began to turn. By the time it had made a few revolutions, it had disappeared completely. And *Dragonfly* was on her way.

She lifted straight upward—or outward—from the hub, moving slowly along the axis of Rama. When she had traveled a hundred meters, Jimmy stopped pedaling. It was strange to see an obviously aerodynamic vehicle hanging motionless in mid-air. This must be the first time such a thing had ever happened, except possibly on a limited scale inside one of the larger space stations.

"How does she handle?" Norton called.

"Response good, stability poor. But I know what the trouble is—no gravity. We'll be better off a kilometer lower down."

"Now wait a minute—is that safe?"

By losing altitude, Jimmy would be sacrificing his main advantage. As long as he stayed precisely on the axis, he, and *Dragonfly*, would be completely weightless. He could hover effortlessly, or even go to sleep, if he wished. But as soon as he moved away from the central line around which Rama spun, the pseudo-weight of centrifugal force would reappear.

And so, unless he could maintain himself at this altitude, he would continue to lose height—and, at the same time, *to gain weight*. It would be an accelerating process, which could end in catastrophe. The gravity down on the plain of Rama was twice that in which *Dragonfly* had been designed to operate. Jimmy might be able to make a safe landing; he could certainly never take off again.

But he had already considered all this, and he answered confidently enough: "I can manage a tenth of a gee without any trouble. And she'll handle more easily in denser air."

In a slow, leisurely spiral, *Dragonfly* drifted across the sky, roughly following the line of Stairway Alpha down toward the plain. From some angles, the little sky-bike was almost invisible; Jimmy seemed to be sitting in mid-air pedaling furiously. Sometimes he moved in spurts of up to thirty kilometers an hour; then he would coast to a halt, getting the feel of the controls, before accelerating again. And he was always careful to keep a safe distance from the curving face of Rama.

It was soon obvious that *Dragonfly* handled much better at lower altitudes; she no longer rolled around at any angle, but stabilized so that her wings were parallel to the plain seven kilometers below. Jimmy completed several wide orbits, then started to climb upward again. He finally halted a few meters above his waiting colleagues and realized, a little belatedly, that he was not quite sure how to land his gossamer craft.

"Shall we throw you a rope?" Norton asked half seriously.

"No, Skipper, I've got to work this out myself. I won't have anyone to help me at the other end."

He sat thinking for a while, then started to ease *Dragonfly* toward the hub with short bursts of power. She quickly lost momentum between each, as air drag brought her to rest again. When he was only five meters away, and the sky-bike was still barely moving, Jimmy abandoned ship. He let himself float toward the nearest safety line in the hub webwork, grasped it, then swung around in time to catch the approaching bike with his hands. The maneuver was so neatly executed that it drew a round of applause.

"For my *next* act—" Joe Calvert began.

Jimmy was quick to disclaim any credit. "That was messy," he said. "But now I know how to do it. I'll take a sticky-bomb on a twenty-meter line. Then I'll be able to pull myself in wherever I want to."

"Give me your wrist, Jimmy," ordered the doctor, "and blow into this bag. I'll want a blood sample, too. Did you have any difficulty in breathing?"

"Only at this altitude. Hey, what do you want the blood for?"

"Sugar level; so I can tell how much energy you've used. We've got to make sure you can carry enough fuel for the mission. By the way, what's the endurance record for sky-biking?"

"Two hours twenty-five minutes three point six seconds. On the Moon, of course—a two-kilometer circuit in the Olympic Dome."

"And you think you can keep it up for six hours?"

"Easily, since I can stop for a rest at any time. Sky-biking on the Moon is at least twice as hard as it is here."

"OK, Jimmy—back to the lab. I'll give you a Go —No Go as soon as I've analyzed these samples. I don't want to raise false hopes, but I think you can make it."

A large smile of satisfaction spread across Jimmy's ivory-hued countenance. As he followed Surgeon Commander Ernst to the air lock, he called back to his companions: "Hands off, *please!* I don't want anyone putting his fist through the wings."

"I'll see to that, Jimmy," promised the Commander. "*Dragonfly* is off limits to *everybody*—including myself."

26

The Voice of Rama

THE REAL MAGNITUDE of his adventure did not hit Jimmy Pak until he reached the coast of the Cylindrical Sea. Until now, he had been over known territory; barring a catastrophic structural failure, he could always land and walk back to base in a few hours.

That option no longer existed. If he came down in the sea, he would probably drown, quite unpleasantly, in its poisonous waters. And even if he made a safe landing on the southern continent, it might be impossible to rescue him before *Endeavour* had to break away from Rama's sunward orbit.

He was also acutely aware that the foreseeable disasters were the ones most unlikely to happen. The totally unknown region over which he was flying might produce any number of surprises. Suppose there were flying creatures here who objected to his intrusion? He would hate to engage in a dogfight with anything larger than a pigeon. A few well-placed pecks could destroy *Dragonfly's* aerodynamics.

Yet if there were no hazards there would be no achievement, no sense of adventure. Millions of men would gladly have traded places with him now. He was going not only where no one had ever been before, but also where no one would ever go again. In all of history he would be the only human being to visit the southern regions of Rama. Whenever he felt fear brushing against his mind, he could remember that.

He had now grown accustomed to sitting in mid-air with the world wrapped around him. Because he had dropped two kilometers below the central axis, he had acquired a definite sense of "up" and "down." The ground was only six kilometers below, but the arch of the sky was ten kilometers overhead. The "city" of London was hanging up there near the zenith; New York, on the other hand, was the right way up, directly ahead.

"*Dragonfly,*" said Hub Control, "You're getting a little low. Twenty-two hundred meters from the axis."

"Thanks," he replied. "I'll gain altitude. Let me know when I'm back at twenty."

This was something he'd have to watch. There was a natural tendency to lose height, and he had no instruments to tell him exactly where he was. If he got too far away from the zero gravity of the axis, he might never be able to climb back to it. Fortunately, there was a wide margin for error, and there was always someone watching his progress through a telescope at the hub.

He was now well out over the sea, pedaling along at a steady twenty kilometers an hour. In five minutes, he would be over New York; already the island looked rather like a ship, sailing forever round and round the Cylindrical Sea.

When he reached New York he flew a circle over it,

stopping several times so that his little TV camera could send back steady, vibration-free images. The panorama of buildings, towers, industrial plants, power stations—or whatever they were—was fascinating but essentially meaningless. No matter how long he stared at its complexity, he was unlikely to learn anything. The camera would record far more details than he could possibly assimilate; and one day—perhaps years hence—some student might find in them the key to Rama's secrets.

After leaving New York, he crossed the other half of the sea in only fifteen minutes. Though he was not aware of it, he had been flying fast over water, but as soon as he reached the south coast he unconsciously relaxed, and his speed dropped by several kilometers an hour. He might be in wholly alien territory, but at least he was over land.

As soon as he had crossed the great cliff that formed the sea's southern limit, he panned the TV camera completely around the circle of the world.

"Beautiful!" said Hub Control. "This will keep the map makers happy. How are you feeling?"

"I'm fine—just a little fatigue, but no more than I expected. How far do you make me from the pole?"

"Fifteen point six kilometers."

"Tell me when I'm at ten; I'll take a rest then. And make sure I don't get low again. I'll start climbing when I've five to go."

Twenty minutes later the world was closing in upon him. He had come to the end of the cylindrical section and was entering the southern dome.

He had studied it for hours through the telescopes at the other end of Rama, and had learned its geography by heart. Even so, that had not fully prepared him for the spectacle all around him.

In almost every way the southern and northern ends of Rama differed completely. Here was no triad of stairways, no series of narrow, concentric plateaus, no sweeping curve from hub to plain. Instead, there was an immense central spike, more than five kilometers long, extending along the axis. Six smaller ones, half the size, were equally spaced around it; the whole assembly looked like a group of remarkably symmetrical stalactites, hanging from the roof of a cave; or, inverting the point of view, the spires of some Cambodian temple, set at the bottom of a crater.

Linking these slender, tapering towers, and curving down from them to merge eventually in the cylindrical plain, were flying buttresses that looked massive enough to bear the weight of a world. And this, perhaps, was their function, if they were indeed the elements of some exotic drive units, as had been suggested.

Jimmy approached the central spike cautiously, stopped pedaling while he was still a hundred meters away, and let *Dragonfly* drift to rest. He checked the radiation level and found only Rama's very low background. There might be forces at work here that no human instruments could detect, but that was another unavoidable risk.

"What can you see?" Hub Control asked anxiously.

"Just Big Horn. It's absolutely smooth—no markings—and the point's so sharp you could use it as a needle. I'm almost scared to go near it."

He was only half joking. It seemed incredible that so massive an object should taper to such a geometrically perfect point. Jimmy had seen collections of insects impaled upon pins, and he had no desire for his own *Dragonfly* to meet a similar fate.

He pedaled slowly forward until the spike had flared out to several meters in diameter, and stopped again. Opening a small container, he rather gingerly extracted a sphere about as big as a baseball and tossed it toward the spike. As it drifted away, it played out a barely visible thread.

The sticky-bomb hit the smoothly curving surface —and did not rebound. Jimmy gave the thread an experimental twitch, then a harder tug. Like a fisherman hauling in his catch, he slowly wound *Dragonfly* across to the tip of the appropriately christened Big Horn, until he was able to put out his hand and make contact with it.

"I suppose you could call this some kind of touchdown," he reported to Hub Control. "It feels like glass —almost frictionless, and slightly warm. The sticky-bomb worked fine. Now I'm trying the mike. . . . Let's see if the suction pad holds as well. . . . Plugging in the leads . . . Anything coming through?"

There was a long pause, then Hub Control said disgustedly: "Not a damn thing, except the usual thermal noises. Will you tap it with a piece of metal? Then at least we'll find if it's hollow."

"OK. Now what?"

"We'd like you to fly along the spike, making a complete scan every half-kilometer and looking out for anything unusual. Then, if you're sure it's safe, you might go across to one of the Little Horns. But only if you're certain you can get back to zero gee without any problems."

"Three kilometers from the axis—that's slightly above lunar gravity. *Dragonfly* was designed for that. I'll just have to work harder."

"Jimmy, this is the captain. I've got second thoughts on that. Judging by your pictures, the smaller spikes are just the same as the big one. Get the best coverage of them you can with the zoom lens. I don't want you leaving the low-gravity region—unless you see something that looks very important. Then we'll talk it over."

"OK, Skipper," said Jimmy, and perhaps there was just a trace of relief in his voice. "I'll stay close to Big Horn. Here we go again."

He felt he was dropping straight downward into a narrow valley between a group of incredibly tall and slender mountains. Big Horn now towered a kilometer above him, and the six spikes of the Little Horns were looming up all around. The complex of buttresses and flying arches that surrounded the lower slopes was approaching rapidly. He wondered if he could make a safe landing somewhere down there in that Cyclopean architecture. He could no longer land on Big Horn itself, for the gravity on its widening slopes was now too powerful to be counteracted by the feeble force of the sticky-bomb.

As he came ever closer to the South Pole, he began to feel more and more like a sparrow flying beneath the vaulted roof of some great cathedral—though no cathedral ever built had been even one-hundredth the size of this place. He wondered if it was indeed a religious shrine, or something remotely analogous, but quickly dismissed the idea. Nowhere in Rama had there been any trace of artistic expression; everything was purely functional. Perhaps the Ramans felt that they already knew the ultimate secrets of the universe, and were no longer haunted by the yearnings and aspirations that drove mankind.

That was a chilling thought, quite alien to Jimmy's usually not very profound philosophy. He felt an urgent need to resume human contact, and reported his situation back to his distant friends.

"Say again, *Dragonfly*," replied Hub Control. "We can't understand you; your transmission is garbled."

"I repeat—I'm near the base of Little Horn number six, and am using the sticky-bomb to haul myself in."

"Understand only partially. Can you hear me?"

"Yes, perfectly. Repeat, perfectly."

"Please start counting numbers."

"One, two, three, four . . ."

"Got part of that. Give us beacon for fifteen seconds, then go back to voice."

"Here it is."

Jimmy switched on the low-powered beacon that would locate him anywhere inside Rama, and counted off the seconds. When he went over to voice again, he asked plaintively: "What's happening? Can you hear me now?"

Presumably Hub Control didn't, because the controller then asked for fifteen seconds of TV. Not until Jimmy had repeated the question twice did the message get through.

"Glad you can hear us OK, Jimmy. But there's something very peculiar happening at your end. Listen."

Over the radio, he heard the familiar whistle of his own beacon, played back to him. For a moment it was perfectly normal; then a weird distortion crept into it. The thousand-cycle whistle became modulated by a deep, throbbing pulse so low that it was almost beneath the threshold of hearing. It was a kind of basso-profundo flutter in which each individual vibration could be heard. And the modulation was itself modulated; it rose and fell, rose and fell, with a period of about five seconds.

Never for a moment did it occur to Jimmy that there was something wrong with his radio transmitter. This was from outside; though what it was, and what it meant, was beyond his imagination.

Hub Control was not much wiser, but at least it had a theory.

"We think you must be in some kind of very intense field—probably magnetic—with a frequency of about ten cycles. It may be strong enough to be dangerous. Suggest you get out right away—it may be only local.

Switch on your beacon again, and we'll play it back to you. Then you can tell when you're getting clear of the interference."

Jimmy hastily jerked the sticky-bomb loose and abandoned his attempt to land. He swung *Dragonfly* around in a wide circle, listening as he did so to the sound that wavered in his earphones. After flying only a few meters, he could tell that its intensity was falling rapidly. As Hub Control had guessed, it was extremely localized.

He paused at the last spot where he could hear it, like a faint throbbing deep in his brain. So might a primitive savage have listened in awe-struck ignorance to the low humming of a giant power transformer. And even the savage might have guessed that the sound he heard was merely the stray leakage from colossal energies, fully controlled, but biding their time.

Whatever this sound meant, Jimmy was glad to be clear of it. This was no place, among the overwhelming architecture of the South Pole, for a lone man to listen to the voice of Rama.

27

Electric Wind

As JIMMY TURNED homeward, the northern end of
Rama seemed incredibly far away. Even the three
giant stairways were barely visible, as a faint Y etched
on the dome that closed the world. The band of the
Cylindrical Sea was a wide and menacing barrier,
waiting to swallow him, like Icarus, if his fragile wings
should fail.

But he had come all this way with no problems, and
though he was feeling slightly tired, he now felt that he
had nothing to worry about. He had not even touched
his food or water, and had been too excited to rest. On
the return journey, he would relax and take it easy. He
was also cheered by the thought that the homeward
trip could be twenty kilometers shorter than the outward one, for as long as he cleared the sea, he could
make an emergency landing anywhere in the Northern
Hemisphere. That would be a nuisance, because he

would have a long walk, and, much worse, would have to abandon *Dragonfly*, but it gave him a comforting safety margin.

He was now gaining altitude, climbing back toward the central spike. Big Horn's tapering needle still stretched for a kilometer ahead of him, and sometimes he felt it was the axis on which this whole world turned.

He had almost reached the tip of Big Horn when he became aware of a curious sensation. A feeling of foreboding, and, indeed, of physical as well as psychological discomfort, had come over him. He suddenly recalled—and this did nothing at all to help—a phrase he had once come across: *"Someone is walking over your grave."*

At first, he shrugged it off, and continued his steady pedaling. He certainly had no intention of reporting anything as tenuous as a vague malaise to Hub Control. But as it grew steadily worse he was tempted to do so. It could not possibly be psychological; if it was, his mind was much more powerful than he realized. And he could, quite literally, feel his skin beginning to crawl.

Now seriously alarmed, he stopped in mid-air to consider the situation. What made it all the more peculiar was the fact that this depressed, heavy feeling was not completely novel; he had known it before, but could not remember where.

He looked around him. Nothing had changed. The great spike of Big Horn was a few hundred meters above, with the other side of Rama spanning the sky beyond that. Eight kilometers below lay the complicated patchwork of the southern continent, full of wonders that no other man would ever see. In all the utterly alien, yet now familiar, landscape, he could find no cause for his discomfort.

Something was tickling the back of his hand. For a

moment, he thought an insect had landed there, and brushed it away without looking. He had only half completed the swift motion when he realized what he was doing and checked himself, feeling slightly foolish. Of course, no one had ever seen an insect in Rama. . . .

He lifted his hand, and stared at it, mildly puzzled because the tickling sensation was still there. It was then that he noticed that every individual hair was standing straight upright. All the way up his forearm it was the same—and so it was with his head, when he checked with an exploring hand.

So *that* was the trouble. He was in a tremendously powerful electric field. The oppressed, heavy sensation he had felt was that which sometimes precedes a thunderstorm on Earth.

The sudden realization of his predicament brought Jimmy near to panic. Never before in his life had he been in real physical danger. Like all spacemen, he had known moments of frustration with balky equipment, and times when, because of mistakes or inexperience, he had wrongly believed he was in a perilous situation. But none of these episodes had lasted more than a few minutes, and usually he was able to laugh at them almost at once.

This time there was no quick way out. He felt naked and alone in a suddenly hostile sky, surrounded by titanic forces that might discharge their furies at any moment. *Dragonfly*—already fragile enough—now seemed more insubstantial than the finest gossamer. The first detonation of the gathering storm would blast her to fragments.

"Hub Control," he said urgently, "there's a static charge building up around me. I think there's going to be a thunderstorm at any moment."

He had barely finished speaking when there was a flicker of light behind him; by the time he had counted ten, the first crackling rumble arrived. Three kilometers—that put it back around the Little Horns. He looked toward them and saw that every one of the six needles seemed to be on fire. Brush discharges, hundreds of meters long, were dancing from their points, as if they were giant lightning conductors.

What was happening back there could take place on an even larger scale near the tapering spike of Big Horn. His best move would be to get as far as possible from this dangerous structure, and to seek clear air. He started to pedal again, accelerating as swiftly as he could without putting too great a strain on *Dragonfly*. At the same time he began to lose altitude; even though this would mean entering the region of higher gravity, he was now prepared to take such a risk. Eight kilometers was much too far from the ground for his peace of mind.

The ominous black spike of Big Horn was still free of visible discharges, but he did not doubt that tremendous potentials were building up there. From time to time the thunder reverberated behind him, rolling round and round the circumference of the world. It suddenly occurred to Jimmy that it was strange to have such a storm in a perfectly clear sky. Then he realized that this was not a meteorological phenomenon at all. In fact, it might be only a trivial leakage of energy from some hidden source, deep in the southern cap of Rama. But why *now*? And, even more important, *what next*?

He was well past the tip of Big Horn, and hoped that he would soon be beyond the range of any lightning discharges. But now he had another problem: the air was becoming turbulent, and he had difficulty controlling *Dragonfly*. A wind seemed to have sprung up from nowhere, and if conditions became much worse, the sky-bike's fragile skeleton would be endangered.

He pedaled grimly on, trying to smooth out the buffeting by variations in power and movements of his body. Because *Dragonfly* was almost an extension of himself, he was partly successful; but he did not like the faint creaks of protest that came from the main spar, or the way in which the wings twisted with every gust.

And there was something else that worried him: a faint rushing sound, steadily growing in strength, that seemed to come from the direction of Big Horn. It sounded like gas escaping from a valve under great pressure, and he wondered if it had anything to do with the turbulence he was battling. Whatever its cause, it gave him yet further grounds for disquiet.

From time to time he reported these phenomena, rather briefly and breathlessly, to Hub Control. No one there could give him any advice or even suggest what might be happening; but it was reassuring to hear the voices of his friends, even though he was now beginning to fear that he would never see them again.

The turbulence was still increasing. It felt almost as if he was entering a jet stream—which he had once done, in search of a record, while flying a high-altitude glider on Earth. But what could possibly create a jet stream inside Rama?

He had asked himself the right question. As soon as he had formulated it, he knew the answer.

The sound he had heard was the electric wind carrying away the tremendous ionization that must be building up around Big Horn. Charged air was spraying out along the axis of Rama, and more air was flowing into the low-pressure region behind. He looked back at that gigantic and now doubly threatening needle, trying to visualize the boundaries of the gale that was blowing from it. Perhaps the best tactic would be to fly by ear, getting as far as possible away from the ominous hissing.

Rama spared him the necessity of choice. A sheet of flame burst out behind him, filling the sky. He had time to see it split into six ribbons of fire, stretching from the tip of Big Horn to each of the Little Horns. Then the concussion reached him.

28

Icarus

JIMMY HAD BARELY time to radio "The wing's buckling—I'm going to crash" when *Dragonfly* started to fold up gracefully around him. The left wing snapped cleanly in the middle, and the outer section drifted away like a gently falling leaf. The right wing put up a more complicated performance. It twisted around at the root, and angled back so sharply that its tip became entangled in the tail. Jimmy felt that he was sitting in a broken kite, slowly falling down the sky.

Yet he was not quite helpless; the airscrew still worked, and while he had power there was still some measure of control. He had perhaps five minutes in which to use it.

Was there any hope of reaching the sea? No—it was much too far away. Then he remembered that he was thinking in terrestrial terms; though he was a good swimmer, it would be hours before he could possibly be rescued, and in that time the poisonous waters would undoubtedly have killed him. His only hope was to come down on land. The problem of the sheer southern cliff, he would think about later—if there was any "later."

He was falling very slowly, here in this tenth-of-a-gravity zone, but would soon start to accelerate as he got farther away from the axis. However, air drag would complicate the situation, and would prevent him from building up too swift a rate of descent. *Dragonfly*, even without power, would act as a crude parachute. The few kilograms of thrust he could still provide might make all the difference between life and death; that was his only hope.

Hub had stopped talking; his friends could see exactly what was happening to him and knew that there was no way their words could help. Jimmy was now doing the most skillful flying of his life. It was too bad, he thought with grim humor, that his audience was so small, and could not appreciate the finer details of his performance.

He was going down in a wide spiral, and as long as its pitch remained fairly flat his chances of survival were good. His pedaling was helping to keep *Dragonfly* airborne, though he was afraid to exert maximum power in case the broken wings came comletely adrift. And every time he swung southward, he could appreciate the fantastic display that Rama had kindly arranged for his benefit.

The streamers of lightning still played from the tip of Big Horn down to the lesser peaks beneath, but now the whole pattern was rotating. The six-pronged crown of fire was turning against the spin of Rama, making one revolution every few seconds. Jimmy felt that he was watching a giant electric motor in operation, and perhaps that was not hopelessly far from the truth.

He was halfway down to the plain, orbiting in a flat spiral, when the fireworks display suddenly ceased. He could feel the tension drain from the sky and knew, without looking, that the hairs on his arms were no longer straining upright. There was nothing to distract or hinder him now, during the last few minutes of his fight for life.

Now that he could be certain of the general area in which he must land, he started to study it intently. Much of this region was a checkerboard of totally conflicting environments, as if a mad landscape gardener had been given a free hand and told to exercise his imagination to the utmost. The squares of the checkerboard were almost a kilometer on a side, and though most of them were flat, he could not be sure if they were solid because their colors and textures varied so greatly. He decided to wait until the last possible minute before making a decision—if, indeed, he had any choice.

When there were a few hundred meters to go, he made a last call to the Hub. "I've still got some control—will be down in half a minute—will call you then."

That was optimistic, and everyone knew it. But he refused to say good-by; he wanted his comrades to know that he had gone down fighting, and without fear.

Actually, he felt little fear, and this surprised him, for he had never thought of himself as a particularly brave man. It was almost as if he were watching the struggles of a complete stranger, and was not himself personally involved. Rather, he was studying an interesting problem in aerodynamics, and changing various parameters to see what would happen. Almost the only emotion he felt was a certain remote regret for lost opportunities—of which the most important was the forthcoming Lunar Olympics. One future at least was decided: *Dragonfly* would never show her paces on the Moon.

A hundred meters to go; his ground speed seemed acceptable, but how fast was he falling? And here was one piece of luck: the terrain was completely flat. He would put forth all his strength in a final burst of power, starting—NOW!

The right wing, having done its duty, finally tore off at the roots. *Dragonfly* started to roll over, and he tried to correct by throwing the weight of his body against the spin. He was looking directly at the curving arch of landscape sixteen kilometers away when he hit.

It seemed altogether unfair and unreasonable that the sky should be so hard.

29

First Contact

WHEN JIMMY RETURNED to consciousness, the first thing he became aware of was a splitting headache. He almost welcomed it; at least it proved that he was alive.

Then he tried to move, and at once a wide selection of aches and pains brought themselves to his attention. But as far as he could tell, nothing seemed to be broken.

After that he risked opening his eyes, but closed them at once when he found himself staring straight into the band of light along the ceiling of the world. As a cure for a headache, that view was not recommended.

He was still lying there, regaining his strength and wondering how soon it would be safe to open his eyes, when there was a sudden crunching noise from close at hand. Turning his head slowly toward the source of the sound, he risked a look—and almost lost consciousness again.

Not more than five meters away, a large crablike creature was apparently dining on the wreckage of poor *Dragonfly*. When Jimmy had recovered his wits, he rolled slowly and quietly away from the monster, expecting at every moment to be seized by its claws when it discovered that more appetizing fare was available. However, it took not the slightest notice of him; when he had increased their mutual separation to ten meters, he cautiously propped himself up in a sitting position.

From this greater distance, the thing did not appear quite so formidable. It had a low, flat body about two meters long and one wide, supported on six triple-jointed legs. Jimmy saw that he was mistaken in assuming that it had been eating *Dragonfly*; in fact, he could not see any sign of a mouth. The creature was actually doing a neat job of demolition, using scissorlike claws to chop the sky-bike into small pieces. A whole row of manipulators, which looked uncannily like tiny human hands, then transferred the fragments to a steadily growing pile on the animal's back.

But *was* it an animal? Though that had been Jimmy's first reaction, now he had second thoughts. There was a purposefulness about its behavior that suggested fairly high intelligence. He could see no reason why any creature of pure instinct should carefully collect the scattered pieces of his sky-bike—unless, perhaps, it was gathering material for a nest.

Keeping a wary eye on the crab, which still ignored him completely, Jimmy struggled to his feet. A few wavering steps demonstrated that he could walk, though he was not sure if he could outdistance those six legs. Then he switched on his radio, never doubting that it would still be operating. A crash that *he* could survive would not even have been noticed by its solid-state electronics.

"Hub Control," he said softly, "can you receive me?"

"Thank God! Are you OK?"

"Just a bit shaken. Take a look at this."

He turned his camera toward the crab, just in time to record the final demolition of *Dragonfly*'s wing.

"What the devil is it—and why is it chewing up your bike?"

"Wish I knew. It's finished with *Dragonfly*. I'm going to back away, in case it wants to start on me."

Jimmy slowly retreated, never taking his eyes off the crab. It was now moving round and round in a steadily widening spiral, apparently searching for fragments it might have overlooked, and so Jimmy was able to get an over-all view of it for the first time.

Now that the initial shock had worn off, he could appreciate that it was quite a handsome beast. The name "crab," which he had automatically given to it, was perhaps a little misleading. If it had not been so impossibly large, he might have called it a beetle. Its carapace had a beautiful metallic sheen; he would almost have been prepared to swear that it *was* metal.

That was an interesting idea. Could it be a robot, and not an animal? He stared at the crab intently with this thought in mind, analyzing all the details of its anatomy. Where it should have had a mouth was a collection of manipulators that reminded Jimmy strongly of the multi-purpose knives that are the delight of all red-blooded boys; there were pinchers, probes, rasps, and even something that looked like a drill. But this was not decisive. On Earth, the insect world had matched all these tools, and many more. The animal-or-robot question remained in perfect balance in his mind.

The eyes, which might have settled the matter, left it even more ambiguous. They were so deeply recessed in protective hoods that it was impossible to tell whether their lenses were made of crystal or of jelly. They were quite expressionless, and of a startling vivid blue. Though they had been directed toward Jimmy several times, they had never shown the slightest flicker of interest. In his perhaps biased opinion, that decided the level of the creature's intelligence. An entity —robot or animal—which could ignore a human being could not be very bright.

It had stopped its circling, and stood still for a few seconds, as if listening to some inaudible message. Then it set off, with a curious rolling gait, in the general direction of the sea. It moved in a perfectly straight line at a steady four or five kilometers an hour, and had already traveled a couple of hundred meters before Jimmy's still slightly shocked mind registered the fact that the last sad relics of his beloved *Dragonfly* were being carried away from him. He set off in hot and indignant pursuit.

His action was not wholly illogical. The crab was heading toward the sea—and if any rescue was possible, it could be only from this direction. Moreover, he wanted to discover what the creature would do with its trophy; that should reveal something about its motivation and intelligence.

Because he was bruised and stiff, it took Jimmy several minutes to catch up with the purposefully moving crab. When he had done so, he followed it at a respectful distance, until he felt sure that it did not resent his presence. It was then that he noticed his water flask and emergency-ration pack among the debris of *Dragonfly*, and felt instantly both hungry and thirsty.

There, scuttling away from him at a remorseless five kilometers an hour, was the only food and drink in all this half of the world. Whatever the risk, he had to get hold of it.

He cautiously closed in on the crab, approaching from the right rear. While he kept station with it, he studied the complicated rhythm of its legs, until he could anticipate where they would be at any moment. When he was ready, he muttered a quick, "Excuse *me*," and shot swiftly in to grab his property.

Jimmy had never dreamed that he would one day have to exercise the skills of a pickpocket, but he was delighted with his success. He was out again in less than a second, and the crab never slackened its steady pace.

He dropped back a dozen meters, moistened his lips from the flask, and started to chew a bar of meat concentrate. The little victory made him feel much happier; now he could even risk thinking about his somber future.

While there was life, there was hope; yet he could imagine no way in which he could possibly be rescued. Even if his colleagues crossed the sea, how could he reach them, half a kilometer below? "We'll find a way down *somehow*," Hub Control had promised. "That cliff can't go right around the world, without a break anywhere." He had been tempted to answer "Why not?" but had thought better of it.

One of the strangest things about walking inside Rama was that you could always see your destination. Here, the curve of the world did not hide; it *revealed*. For some time Jimmy had been aware of the crab's objective; up there in the land that seemed to rise before him was a half-kilometer-wide pit. It was one of three in the Southern Hemisphere; from the hub, it had been impossible to see how deep they were. All had been named after prominent lunar craters, and he was approaching Copernicus. The name was hardly appropriate, for there were no surrounding hills and no central peaks. This Copernicus was merely a deep shaft, or well, with perfectly vertical sides.

When he came close enough to look into it, Jimmy was able to see a pool of ominous leaden-green water at least half a kilometer below. This would put it just about level with the sea, and he wondered if they were connected.

Winding down the interior of the well was a spiral ramp, completely recessed into the sheer wall, so that the effect was rather like that of rifling in an immense gun barrel. There seemed to be a remarkable number of turns; not until Jimmy had traced them for several revolutions, getting more and more confused in the process, did he realize that there was not one ramp, but *three*, totally independent and 120 degrees apart. In any other background than Rama, the whole concept would have been an impressive architectural tour de force.

The three ramps led straight down into the pool and disappeared beneath its opaque surface. Near the water line Jimmy could see a group of black tunnels, or caves. They looked rather sinister, and he wondered if they were inhabited. Perhaps the Ramans were amphibious.

As the crab approached the edge of the well, Jimmy assumed that it was going to descend one of the ramps —perhaps taking the wreckage of *Dragonfly* to some entity who would be able to evaluate it. Instead, the creature walked straight to the brink, extended almost half its body over the gulf without any sign of hesitation—though an error of a few centimeters would have been disastrous—and gave a brisk shrug. The fragments of *Dragonfly* went fluttering down into the depths. There were tears in Jimmy's eyes as he watched them go. So much, he thought bitterly, for *this* creature's intelligence.

Having disposed of the garbage, the crab swung around and started to walk toward Jimmy, standing only about ten meters away. Am I going to get the same treatment? he wondered. He hoped the camera was not too unsteady as he showed Hub Control the rapidly approaching monster. "What do you advise?" he whispered anxiously, without much hope that he would get a useful answer. It was some small consolation to realize that he was making history, and his mind raced through the approved patterns for such a meeting. Until now, all of these had been purely theoretical. He would be the first man to check them in practice.

"Don't run until you're sure it's hostile," Hub Control whispered back at him. Run where? Jimmy asked himself. He thought he could outdistance the thing in a hundred-meter sprint, but he had a sick certainty that it could wear him down over the long haul.

Slowly, Jimmy held up his outstretched hands. Men had been arguing for two hundred years about this gesture; would every creature, everywhere in the universe, interpret this as "See—no weapons"? But no one could think of anything better.

The crab showed no reaction whatsoever, nor did it slacken its pace. Ignoring Jimmy completely, it walked straight past him and headed purposefully into the south. Feeling extremely foolish, the acting representative of *Homo sapiens* watched his First Contact stride away across the Raman plain, totally indifferent to his presence.

He had seldom been so humiliated in his life. Then his sense of humor came to the rescue. After all, it was no great matter to have been ignored by an animated garbage truck. It would have been worse if it had greeted him as a long-lost brother.

He walked back to the rim of Copernicus, and stared down into its opaque waters. For the first time, he noticed that vague shapes, some of them quite large, were moving slowly back and forth beneath the surface. Presently one of them headed toward the nearest spiral ramp, and something that looked like a multilegged tank started on the long ascent. At the rate it was going, Jimmy decided, it would take almost an hour to get here; if it was a threat, it was a very slow-moving one.

Then he noticed a flicker of much more rapid movement, near those cavelike openings down by the water line. Something was traveling swiftly along the ramp, but he could not focus clearly upon it, or discern any definite shape. It was as if he was looking at a small whirlwind or dust devil, about the size of a man.

He blinked and shook his head, keeping his eyes closed for several seconds. When he opened them again, the apparition was gone.

Perhaps the impact had shaken him up more than he had realized; this was the first time he had ever suffered from visual hallucinations. He would not mention it to Hub Control.

Nor would he bother to explore these ramps, as he had half thought of doing. It would obviously be a waste of energy.

The spinning phantom he had merely imagined seeing had nothing to do with his decision—nothing at all; for, of course, Jimmy did not believe in ghosts.

30

The Flower

JIMMY'S EXERTIONS HAD made him thirsty, and he was acutely conscious of the fact that in all this land there was no water that a man could drink. With the contents of his flask, he could probably survive a week—but for what purpose? The best brains of Earth would soon be focused on his problem, and doubtless Commander Norton would be bombarded with suggestions. But he could imagine no way in which he could lower himself down the face of that half-kilometer cliff. Even if he had a long-enough rope, there was no place to which he could attach it.

Nevertheless, it was foolish—and unmanly—to give up without a struggle. Any help would have to come from the sea, and while he was marching toward it he could carry on with his job as if nothing had happened. No one else would ever observe and photograph the varied terrains through which he must pass, and that would guarantee a posthumous immortality. Though he would have preferred many other honors, that was better than nothing.

He was only three kilometers from the sea as poor *Dragonfly* could have flown, but it seemed unlikely that he could reach it in a straight line; some of the terrain ahead of him might prove too great an obstacle. That was no problem, however, because there were plenty of alternative routes. He could see them all, spread out on the great curving map that swept up and away from him on either side.

He had plenty of time; he would start with the most interesting scenery, even if it took him off his direct route. About a kilometer away to the right was a square that glittered like cut glass, or a gigantic display of jewelry. It was probably this thought that triggered Jimmy's footsteps. Even a doomed man might reasonably be expected to take some slight interest in a few thousand square meters of gems.

He was not particularly disappointed when they turned out to be quartz crystals, millions of them, set in a bed of sand. The adjacent square of the checkerboard was rather more interesting. It was covered with an apparently random pattern of hollow metal columns, set close together and ranging in height from less than one to more than five meters. It was completely impassable; only a tank could have crashed through that forest of tubes.

Jimmy walked between the crystals and the columns until he came to the first crossroads. The square on the right was a huge rug or tapestry made of woven wire; he tried to prise a strand loose, but was unable to break it. On the left was a tesselation of hexagonal tiles, so smoothly inlaid that there were no visible joints between them. It would have appeared a continuous surface had the tiles not been colored all the hues of the rainbow. Jimmy spent many minutes trying to find two adjacent tiles of the same color, to see if he could then distinguish their boundaries, but he could not find a single example of such a coincidence.

As he did a slow pan right around the crossroads, he said plaintively to Hub Control: "What do you think this is? I feel I'm trapped in a giant jigsaw puzzle. Or is this the Raman Art Gallery?"

"We're as baffled as you, Jimmy. But there's never been any sign that the Ramans go in for art. Let's wait until we have some more examples before we jump to any conclusions."

The two examples he found at the next crossroads were not much help. One was completely blank—a smooth, neutral gray, hard but slippery to the touch. The other was a soft sponge, perforated with billions upon billions of tiny holes. He tested it with his foot, and the whole surface undulated sickeningly beneath him like a barely stabilized quicksand.

At the next crossroads he encountered something strikingly like a plowed field, except that the furrows were a uniform meter in depth, and the material of which they were made had the texture of a file or rasp. But he paid little attention to this, because the square adjacent to it was the most thought-provoking of all that he had seen. At last there was something that he could understand; and it was more than a little disturbing.

The entire square was surrounded by a fence, so conventional that he would not have looked at it twice had he seen it on Earth. There were posts, apparently of metal, five meters apart, with six strands of wire strung taut between them.

Beyond this fence was a second, identical one—and beyond that, a third. It was another example of Rama redundancy; whatever was penned inside this enclosure would have no chance of breaking out. There was no entrance—no gates that could be swung open to drive in the beast, or beasts, that were presumably kept here. Instead, there was a single hole, like a smaller version of Copernicus, in the center of the square.

Even in different circumstances, Jimmy would probably not have hesitated, but now he had nothing to lose. He quickly scaled all three fences, walked over to the hole, and peered into it.

Unlike Copernicus, this well was only fifty meters deep. There were three tunnel exits at the bottom, each of which looked large enough to accommodate an elephant. And that was all.

After staring for some time, Jimmy decided that the only thing that made sense about the arrangement was for the floor down there to be an elevator. But *what* it elevated he was never likely to know; he could only guess that it was quite large, and possibly quite dangerous.

During the next few hours, he walked more than ten kilometers along the edge of the sea, and the checkerboard squares had begun to blur together in his memory. He had seen some that were totally enclosed in tentlike structures of wire mesh, as if they were giant bird cages. There were others that seemed to be pools of congealed liquid, full of swirl patterns; however, when he tested them gingerly, they were quite solid. And there was one so utterly black that he could not even see it clearly; only the sense of touch told him that anything was there.

Yet now there was a subtle modulation into something he could understand. Ranging one after the other toward the south was a series of—no other word would do—*fields*. He might have been walking past an experimental farm on Earth. Each square was a smooth expanse of carefully leveled earth or dirt, the first he had ever seen in the metallic landscape of Rama.

The great fields were virgin, lifeless—waiting for crops that had never been planted. Jimmy wondered what their purpose could be, since it was incredible that creatures as advanced as the Ramans would engage in any form of agriculture; even on Earth, farming was no more than a popular hobby and a source of exotic luxury foods. But he could swear that these were potential farms, immaculately prepared. He had never seen dirt that looked so clean; each square was covered with a great sheet of tough, transparent plastic. He tried to cut through it to obtain a sample, but his knife would barely scratch the surface.

Farther inland were other fields, and on many of them were complicated constructions of rods and wires, presumably intended for the support of climbing plants. They looked bleak and desolate, like leafless trees in the depths of winter. The winter they had known must have been long and terrible indeed, and these few weeks of light and warmth might be only a brief interlude before it came again.

Jimmy never knew what made him stop and look more closely into the metal maze to the south. Unconsciously, his mind must have been checking every detail around him; it had noticed, in this fantastically alien landscape, something even more anomalous.

About a quarter of a kilometer away, in the middle of a trellis of wires and rods, glowed a single speck of color. It was so small and inconspicuous that it was almost at the limit of visibility; on Earth, no one would have looked at it twice. Yet undoubtedly one of the reasons he had noticed it now was because it reminded him of Earth.

He did not report to Hub Control until he was sure that there was no mistake, and that wishful thinking had not deluded him. Not until he was only a few meters away could he be completely sure that life as he knew it had intruded into the sterile, aseptic world of

Rama. Here, blooming in lonely splendor at the edge of the Southern Hemisphere, was a flower.

As he came closer, it was obvious to Jimmy that something had gone wrong. There was a hole in the sheathing that, presumably, protected this layer of dirt from contamination by unwanted life forms. Through this break extended a green stem, about as thick as a man's little finger, which twined its way up through the trelliswork. A meter from the ground it burst into an efflorescence of bluish leaves, shaped more like feathers than the foliage of any plant known to Jimmy. The stem ended, at eye level, in what he had first taken to be a single flower. Now he saw, with no surprise at all, that it was actually three flowers tightly packed together.

The petals were brightly colored tubes about five centimeters long; there were at least fifty in each bloom, and they glittered with such metallic blues, violets, and greens that they seemed more like the wings of a butterfly than anything in the vegetable kingdom. Jimmy knew practically nothing about botany, but he was puzzled to see no trace of any structures resembling pistils or stamens. He wondered if the likeness to terrestrial flowers might be a pure coincidence; perhaps this was someting more akin to a coral polyp. In either case, it would seem to imply the existence of small, air-borne creatures to serve either as fertilizing agents or as food.

It did not really matter. Whatever the scientific definition, to Jimmy this was a flower. The strange miracle, the un-Ramanlike accident, of its existence here reminded him of all that he would never see again; and he was determined to possess it.

That would not be easy. It was more than ten meters away, separated from him by a latticework made of thin rods. They formed a cubic pattern, repeated over and over, less than forty centimeters on a side.

Jimmy would not have been flying sky-bikes unless he had been slim and wiry, so he knew he could crawl through the interstices of the grid. But getting out again might be quite a different matter. It would certainly be impossible for him to turn around; so he would have to retreat backward.

Hub Control was delighted with his discovery when he had described the flower and scanned it from every available angle. There was no objection when he said: "I'm going after it." Nor did he expect there to be; his life was now his own, to do with as he pleased.

He stripped off all his clothes, grasped the smooth metal rods, and started to wriggle into the framework. It was a tight fit; he felt like a prisoner escaping through the bars of his cell. When he had inserted himself completely into the lattice he tried backing out again, just to see if there were any problems. It was considerably more difficult, since he now had to use his outstretched arms for pushing instead of pulling, but he saw no reason why he should get helplessly trapped.

Jimmy was a man of action and impulse, not of introspection. As he squirmed uncomfortably along the narrow corridor of rods, he wasted no time asking himself just why he was performing so quixotic a feat. He had never been interested in flowers in his whole life, yet now he was gambling his last energies to collect one.

It was true that this specimen was unique, and of enormous scientific value. But he really wanted it because it was his last link with the world of life, and the planet of his birth.

Yet when the flower was within his grasp, he had sudden qualms. Perhaps it was the only flower that grew in the whole of Rama. Was he justified in collecting it?

If he needed any excuse, he could console himself

with the thought that the Ramans themselves had not included it in their plans. It was obviously a freak, growing ages too late—or too soon. But he did not really require an excuse and his hesitation was only momentary. He reached out, grasped the stem, and gave a sharp jerk.

The flower came away easily enough. He also collected two of the leaves before starting to back slowly through the lattice. Now that he had only one free hand, progress was extremely difficult, even painful, and he soon had to pause to regain his breath. It was then that he noticed that the feathery leaves were closing, and the headless stem was slowly unwinding itself from its supports. As he watched with a mixture of fascination and dismay, he saw that the whole plant was steadily retreating into the ground, like a mortally injured snake crawling back into its hole.

I've murdered something beautiful, Jimmy said to himself. But then, Rama had killed him. He was only collecting what was his rightful due.

31

Terminal Velocity

COMMANDER NORTON HAD never yet lost a man, and he had no intention of losing one now. Even, before Jimmy had set off for the South Pole he had been considering ways of rescuing him in the event of accident. The problem had turned out to be so difficult, however, that he had found no answer. All that he had managed to do was to eliminate every obvious solution.

How does one climb a half-kilometer vertical cliff, even in reduced gravity? With the right equipment, and training, it would be easy enough. But there were no piton-guns aboard *Endeavour,* and no one could think of any other practical way of driving the necessary hundreds of spikes into that hard mirror surface.

He had glanced briefly at more exotic solutions, some frankly crazy. Perhaps a simp, fitted with suction pads, could make the ascent. But even if this scheme was practical, how long would it take to manufacture and test such equipment—and to train a simp to use it? He doubted if a man would have the necessary strength to perform the feat.

Then there was more advanced technology. The EVA propulsion units were tempting, but their thrust was too small, since they were designed for zero-gee operation. They could not possibly lift the weight of a man, even against Rama's modest gravity.

Could an EVA thruster be sent up on automatic control, carrying only a rescue line? He had tried out this idea on Sergeant Myron, who had promptly shot it down. There were, the engineer pointed out, severe stability problems; they might be solved, but it would take a long time, much longer than they could afford.

What about balloons? There seemed a faint possibility here, if they could devise an envelope and a sufficiently compact source of heat. This was the only approach that Norton had not dismissed when the problem suddenly ceased to be one of theory and became a matter of life and death, dominating the news in all the inhabited worlds.

While Jimmy was making his trek along the edge of the sea, half the crackpots in the solar system were trying to save him. At Fleet Headquarters all the suggestions were considered, and about one in a thousand was forwarded to *Endeavour*. Dr. Carlisle Perera's arrived twice—once via the Survey's own network, and once by PLANETCOM, RAMA PRIORITY. It had taken the scientist approximately five minutes of thought and one millisecond of computer time.

At first Norton thought it was a joke in very poor taste. Then he saw the sender's name and the attached calculations, and did a quick double take.

He handed the message to Karl Mercer. "What do you think of this?" he asked, in as noncommittal a tone of voice as he could manage.

Karl read it swiftly, then said, "Well, I'm damned! He's right, of course."

"Are you *sure?*"

"He was right about the storm, wasn't he? We should have thought of this; it makes me feel a fool."

"You have company. The next problem is—how do we break it to Jimmy?"

"I don't think we should . . . until the last possible minute. That's how I'd prefer it if I was in his place. Just tell him we're on the way."

Though he could look across the full width of the Cylindrical Sea, and knew the general direction from which *Resolution* was coming, Jimmy did not spot the tiny craft until it had already passed New York. It seemed incredible that it could carry six men, and whatever equipment they had brought to rescue him.

When it was only a kilometer away, he recognized Commander Norton, and started waving. A little later the Skipper spotted him and waved back.

"Glad to see you're in good shape, Jimmy," he radioed. "I promised we wouldn't leave you behind. Now do you believe me?"

Not quite, Jimmy thought; until this moment he had still wondered if this was all a kindly plot to keep up his morale. But the Commander would not have crossed the sea just to say good-by. He must have worked out *something*.

"I'll believe you, Skipper," he said, "when I'm down there on the deck. *Now* will you tell me how I'm going to make it?"

Resolution was slowing down a hundred meters from the base of the cliff. As far as Jimmy could tell, she carried no unusual equipment—though he was not sure what he had expected to see.

"Sorry about that, Jimmy, but we didn't want you to have too many things to worry about."

Now *that* sounded ominous; what the devil did he mean?

Resolution came to a halt fifty meters out and five hundred below. Jimmy had almost a bird's-eye view of the Commander as he spoke into his microphone.

"This is it, Jimmy. You'll be perfectly safe, but it will require nerve. We know you've got plenty of that. *You're going to jump.*"

"Five hundred meters!"

"Yes, but at only half a gee."

"So! Have you ever fallen two hundred and fifty on Earth?"

"Shut up, or I'll cancel your next leave. You should have worked this out for yourself. It's just a question of terminal velocity. In this atmosphere you can't reach more than ninety kilometers an hour—whether you fall two hundred or two thousand meters. Ninety's a little high for comfort, but we can trim it some more. This is what you'll have to do, so listen carefully."

"I will," said Jimmy. "It had better be good."

He did not interrupt the Commander again, and made no comment when Norton had finished. Yes, it made sense, and was so absurdly simple that it would take a genius to think of it. And, perhaps, someone who did not expect to do it himself.

Jimmy had never tried high-diving or made a delayed parachute drop, which would have given him some psychological preparation for this feat. One could tell a man that it was perfectly safe to walk a plank across an abyss, yet even if the structural calculations were impeccable he might still be unable to do it. Now Jimmy understood why the Commander had been so evasive about the details of the rescue. He had been given no time to brood, or to think of objections.

"I don't want to hurry you," said Norton's persuasive voice from half a kilometer below, "but the sooner the better."

Jimmy looked at his precious souvenir, the only flower in Rama. He wrapped it carefully in his grimy handkerchief, knotted the fabric, and tossed it over the edge of the cliff.

It fluttered down with reassuring slowness, but it also took a very long time, getting smaller, and smaller, and smaller, until he could no longer see it. But then *Resolution* surged forward, and he knew that it had been spotted.

"Beautiful!" exclaimed the Commander enthusiastically. "I'm sure they'll name it after you. OK—we're waiting."

Jimmy stripped off his shirt—the only upper garment anyone ever wore in this now tropical climate— and stretched it thoughtfully. Several times on his trek he had almost discarded it; now it might help to save his life.

For the last time, he looked back at the hollow world he alone had explored, and the distant, ominous pinnacles of the Big and Little Horns. Then, grasping the shirt firmly with his right hand, he took a running jump as far out over the cliff as he could.

Now there was no particular hurry; he had a full twenty seconds in which to enjoy the experience. But he did not waste any time, as the wind strengthened around him and *Resolution* slowly expanded in his field of view. Holding his shirt with both hands, he stretched his arms above his head, so that the rushing air filled the garment and blew it into a hollow tube.

As a parachute, it was hardly a success. The few kilometers an hour it subtracted from his speed were useful, but not vital. It was doing a much more important job: keeping his body vertical, so that he would arrow straight into the sea.

He still had the impression that he was not moving at all, but that the water below was rushing up toward him. Once he had committed himself, he had no sense of fear; indeed, he felt a certain indignation against the Skipper for keeping him in the dark. Did he *really* think that he would have been scared to jump if he'd had to brood over it too long?

At the last moment he let go of his shirt, took a deep breath, and grabbed his mouth and nose with his hands. As he had been instructed, he stiffened his body into a rigid bar, and locked his feet together. He would enter the water as cleanly as a falling spear.

"It will be just the same," the Commander had promised, "as stepping off a diving board on Earth. Nothing to it—*if* you make a good entry."

"And if I don't?" he had asked.

"Then you'll have to go back and try again."

Something slapped him across the feet—hard, but not viciously. A million slimy hands were tearing at his body; there was a roaring in his ears, a mounting pressure, and even though his eyes were tightly closed, he could tell that darkness was falling as he arrowed down into the depths of the Cylindrical Sea.

With all his strength, he started to swim upward toward the fading light. He could not open his eyes for more than a single blink; the poisonous water felt like acid when he did so. He seemed to have been struggling for ages, and more than once he had a nightmare fear that he had lost his orientation and was really swimming downward. Then he would risk another quick glimpse, and every time the light was stronger.

His eyes were still clenched tightly shut when he broke water. He gulped a precious mouthful of air, rolled over on his back, and looked around.

Resolution was heading toward him at top speed. Within seconds, eager hands had grabbed him and dragged him aboard.

"Did you swallow any water?" was the Commander's anxious question.

"I don't think so."

"Rinse your mouth out with this, anyway. That's fine. How do you feel?"

"I'm not really sure. I'll let you know in a minute. Oh . . . thanks, everybody." The minute was barely up when Jimmy was only too sure how he felt.

"I'm going to be sick," he confessed miserably.

His rescuers were incredulous. "In a dead calm—on a flat sea?" protested Sergeant Barnes, who seemed to regard Jimmy's plight as a direct reflection on her skill.

"I'd hardly call it *flat*," said the Commander, waving his arm around at the band of water that circled the sky. "But don't be ashamed. You may have swallowed some of that stuff. Get rid of it as quickly as you can."

Jimmy was still straining, unheroically and unsuccessfully, when there was a flicker of light in the sky behind them. All eyes turned toward the South Pole, and Jimmy instantly forgot his sickness. The Horns had started their fireworks display again.

There were the kilometer-long streamers of fire, dancing from the central spike to its smaller companions. Once again they began their stately rotation, as if invisible dancers were winding their ribbons around an electric Maypole. But now they began to accelerate, moving faster and faster, until they blurred into a flickering cone of light.

It was a spectacle more awe-inspiring than any they had yet seen here, and it brought with it a distant crackling roar, which added to the impression of overwhelming power. The display lasted for about five minutes; then it stopped as abruptly as if someone had turned a switch.

"I'd like to know what the Rama Committee make of *that*," Norton muttered to no one in particular.

"Has anyone here got any theories?"

There was no time for an answer, because at that moment Hub Control called in great excitement.

"*Resolution!* Are you OK? Did you feel that?"

"Feel *what?*"

"We think it was an earthquake. It must have happened the minute those fireworks stopped."

"Any damage?"

"I don't think so. It wasn't really violent—but it shook us up a bit."

"We felt nothing at all. But we wouldn't, out here in the sea."

"Of course—silly of me. Anyway, everything seems quiet now . . . until next time."

"Yes, until next time," Norton echoed. The mystery of Rama was steadily growing; the more they discovered about it, the less they understood.

There was a sudden shout from the helm. "Skipper —look—up there in the sky!"

Norton lifted his eyes and swiftly scanned the circuit of the sea. He saw nothing until his gaze had almost reached the zenith and he was staring at the other side of the world.

"My God," he whispered slowly, as he realized that the "next time" was already almost here.

A tidal wave was racing toward them down the eternal curve of the Cylindrical Sea.

32

The Wave

EVEN IN THAT moment of shock, Norton's first concern was for his ship.

"*Endeavour!*" he called. "Situation report!"

"All OK, Skipper" was the reassuring answer from Exec. "We felt a slight tremor, but nothing that could cause any damage. There's been a small change of attitude; the bridge says about point two degrees. They also think the spin rate has altered slightly. We'll have an accurate reading on that in a couple of minutes."

So it's beginning to happen, Norton said to himself, and a lot earlier than we expected; we're still a long way from perihelion and the logical time for an orbit change. But some kind of trim was undoubtedly taking place—and there might be more shocks to come.

Meanwhile, the effects of this first one were all too obvious, up there on the curving sheet of water that seemed perpetually falling from the sky. The wave was about ten kilometers away, and stretched the full width of the sea from northern to southern shore. Near the land it was a foaming wall of white, but in deeper water it was a barely visible blue line, moving much faster than the breakers on either flank. The drag of the shoreward shallows was already bending it into a bow, with the central portion getting farther and farther ahead.

"Sergeant," said Norton urgently, "this is *your* job. What can we do?"

Sergeant Barnes had brought the raft completely to rest and was studying the situation intently. Her expression, Norton was relieved to see, showed no trace of alarm—rather, a certain zestful excitement, like that of a skilled athlete about to accept a challenge.

"I wish we had some soundings," she said. "If we're in deep water there's nothing to worry about."

"Then we're all right. We're about four kilometers from shore."

"I hope so, but I want to study the situation."

She applied power again and swung *Resolution* around until it was just under way, heading directly toward the approaching wave. Norton judged that the swiftly moving central portion would reach them in less than five minutes, but he could also see that it presented no serious danger. It was only a racing ripple a fraction of a meter high, and would scarcely rock the boat. The walls of foam lagging far behind it were the real menace.

Suddenly, in the very center of the sea, a line of breakers appeared. The wave had clearly hit a submerged wall, several kilometers in length, not far below the surface. At the same time, the breakers on the two flanks collapsed as they ran into deeper water.

Antislosh plates, Norton told himself—exactly the same as in *Endeavour's* own propellant tanks, but on a thousandfold greater scale. There must be a complex pattern of them all around the sea, to damp out any waves as quickly as possible. The only thing that matters now is: are we right on top of one?

Sergeant Barnes was one jump ahead of him. She brought *Resolution* to a full stop and threw out the anchor. It hit bottom at only five meters.

"Haul it up!" she called to her crewmates. "We've got to get away from here!"

Norton agreed heartily. But in which direction? The Sergeant was headed full speed *toward* the wave, which was now only five kilometers away. For the first time, he could hear the sound of its approach—a distant, unmistakable roar, which he had never expected to hear inside Rama. Then it changed in intensity. The central portion was collapsing again, and the flanks again were building up.

He tried to estimate the distance between the submerged baffles, assuming that they were spaced at equal intervals. If he was right, there should be one more to come; if they could station the raft in the deep water between them, they would be perfectly safe.

Sergeant Barnes cut the motor and threw out the anchor again. It went down thirty meters without hitting bottom.

"We're OK," she said, with a sigh of relief. "But I'll keep the motor running."

Now there were only the lagging walls of foam along the coast. Out here in the central sea it was calm again, apart from the inconspicuous blue ripple still speeding toward them. The Sergeant was just holding *Resolution* on course toward the disturbance, ready to pour on full power at a moment's notice.

Then, only two kilometers ahead of them, the sea started to foam once more. It humped up in white-maned fury, and now its roaring seemed to fill the world. Upon the sixteen-kilometer-high wave of the

Cylindrical Sea, a smaller ripple was superimposed, like an avalanche thundering down a mountain slope. And that ripple was quite large enough to kill them.

Sergeant Barnes must have seen the expressions on the faces of her crewmates. She shouted above the roar: "What are you scared about! I've ridden bigger ones than this." That was not quite true; nor did she add that her earlier experience had been in a well-built surfboat, not an improvised raft. "But if we *have* to jump, wait until I tell you. Check your life jackets."

She's magnificent, like a Viking warrior going into battle, and obviously enjoying every minute, thought the Commander. And she's probably right—unless we've miscalculated badly.

The wave continued to rise, curving upward and over. The slope above them probably exaggerated its height, but it looked enormous, an irresistible force of nature that would overwhelm everything in its path.

Then, within seconds, it collapsed, as if its foundations had been pulled out from underneath it. It was over the submerged barrier, in deep water again. When it reached them a minute later, *Resolution* merely bounced up and down a few times before Sergeant Barnes swung her around and set off at top speed toward the north.

"Thanks, Ruby—that was splendid. But will we get home before it comes around for the second time?"

"Probably not; it will be back in about twenty minutes. But it will have lost all its strength then. We'll scarcely notice it."

Now that the wave had passed, they could relax and enjoy the voyage—though no one would be completely at ease until they were back on land. The disturbance had left the water swirling in random eddies, and had also stirred up a most peculiar acidic smell—"like crushed ants," as Jimmy put it well. Though unpleasant, the odor caused none of the attacks of seasickness that might have been expected. It was something so alien that human physiology could not respond to it.

A minute later, the wave front hit the next underwater barrier as it climbed away from them and up the sky. This time, seen from the rear, the spectacle was unimpressive, and the voyagers were ashamed of their previous fears. They began to feel themselves masters of the Cylindrical Sea.

The shock was therefore all the greater when, not more than a hundred meters away, something like a slowly rotating wheel began to rear up out of the water. Glittering metallic spokes, five meters long, emerged dripping, spun for a moment in the fierce Raman glare, and splashed back. It was as if a giant starfish, with tubular arms, had broken the surface.

At first sight it was impossible to tell whether it was an animal or a machine. Then it flopped over and lay half-awash, bobbing up and down in the gentle aftermath of the wave.

Now they could see that there were nine arms, apparently jointed, radiating from a central disc. Two of the arms were broken, snapped off at the outer joint. The others ended at a complicated collection of manipulators that reminded Jimmy strongly of the crab he had encountered. The two creatures came from the same line of evolution, or the same drawing board.

At the middle of the disc was a small turret, bearing three large eyes. Two were closed, one open—and even that appeared to be blank and unseeing. No one doubted that they were watching the death throes of some strange monster, tossed up to the surface by the submarine disturbance that had just passed.

Then they saw that it was not alone. Swimming around it, and snapping at its still feebly moving limbs, were two small beasts like overgrown lobsters.

They were efficiently chopping up the monster, and it did nothing to resist, though its own claws seemed quite capable of dealing with the attackers.

Again Jimmy was reminded of the crab that had demolished *Dragonfly*. He watched intently as the one-sided conflict continued and quickly confirmed his impression.

"Look, Skipper," he whispered. "Do you see—they're not eating it. They don't even have any mouths. *They're simply chopping it to pieces.* That's exactly what happened to *Dragonfly*."

"You're right. They're dismantling it . . . like . . . like a broken machine." Norton wrinkled his nose. "But no dead machine ever smelled like that."

Then another thought struck him. "My God—suppose they start on us! Ruby, get us back to shore as quickly as you can!"

Resolution surged forward with reckless disregard for the life of her power cells. Behind them, the nine spokes of the great starfish—they could think of no better name for it—were clipped steadily shorter, and presently the weird tableau sank back into the depths of the sea.

There was no pursuit, but they did not breathe comfortably again until *Resolution* had drawn up to the landing stage and they had stepped thankfully ashore.

As he looked back across that mysterious and now sinister band of water, Norton grimly determined that no one would ever sail it again. There were too many unknowns, too many dangers.

He looked back upon the towers and ramparts of New York and the dark cliff of the continent beyond. They were safe now from inquisitive man.

He would not tempt the gods of Rama again.

33

Spider

FROM NOW ON, Norton had decreed, there would always be at least three people at Camp Alpha, and one of them would always be awake. In addition, all exploring parties would follow the same routine. Potentially dangerous creatures were on the move inside Rama, and though none had shown active hostility, a prudent commander would take no chances.

As an extra safeguard, there was always an observer up on the hub, keeping watch through a powerful telescope. From this vantage point, the whole interior of Rama could be surveyed, and even the South Pole appeared to be only a few hundred meters away. The territory around any group of explorers was to be kept under regular observation; in this way, it was hoped to eliminate any possibility of surprise. It was a good plan—and it failed completely.

After the last meal of the day, and just before the 2200 sleep period, Norton, Rodrigo, Calvert, and Laura Ernst were watching the regular evening news telecast beamed specially to them from the transmitter at Inferno, Mercury. They had been particularly interested in seeing Jimmy's film of the Southern Hemisphere, and the return across the Cylindrical Sea—an episode that had excited all viewers. Scientists, news commentators, and members of the Rama Committee had given their opinions, most of them contradictory. No one could agree whether the crablike creature Jimmy had encountered was an animal, a machine, a genuine Raman, or something that fitted none of these categories.

They had just been watching, with a distinctly queasy feeling, the giant starfish being demolished by its predators, when they discovered that they were no longer alone. There was an intruder in the camp.

Laura Ernst noticed it first. She froze, then said: "Don't move, Bill. Now look slowly to the right."

Norton turned his head. Ten meters away was a slender-legged tripod surmounted by a spherical body no larger than a soccer ball. Set around the body were three large, expressionless eyes, apparently giving 360 degrees of vision, and trailing beneath it were three whiplike tendrils. The creature was not quite as tall as a man and looked far too fragile to be dangerous, but that did not excuse their carelessness in letting it sneak up on them unawares. It reminded Norton of nothing so much as a three-legged spider or daddy longlegs, and he wondered how it had solved the problem—never attempted by any creature on Earth—of tripedal locomotion.

"What do you make of it, Doc?" he whispered, turning off the voice of the TV newscaster.

"Usual Raman threefold symmetry. I don't see how it could hurt us, though those whips might be unpleasant—and they could be poisonous, like a coelenterate's. Sit tight and see what it does."

After regarding them impassively for several minutes, the creature suddenly moved, and now they could understand why they had failed to observe its arrival. It was *fast*, and it covered the ground with such an extraordinary spinning motion that the human eye and mind had real difficulty in following it.

As far as Norton could judge—and only a high-speed camera could settle the matter—each leg in turn acted as a pivot around which the creature whirled its body. And he was not sure, but it also seemed to him that every few "steps" it reversed its direction of spin, while the three whips flickered over the ground like lightning as it moved. Its top speed—though this also was hard to estimate—seemed to be at least thirty kilometers an hour.

It swept swiftly around the camp, examining every item of equipment, delicately touching the improvised beds and chairs and tables, communication gear, food containers, electrosans, cameras, water tanks, tools—there seemed to be nothing that it ignored except the four watchers. Clearly, it was intelligent enough to draw a distinction between humans and their inanimate property; its actions gave the unmistakable impression of an extremely methodical curiosity or inquisitiveness.

"I wish I could examine it!" Laura exclaimed in frustration as the creature continued its swift pirouette. "Shall we try to catch it?"

"How?" Calvert asked, reasonably enough.

"You know the way primitive hunters bring down fast-moving animals with a couple of weights whirling around at the end of a rope? It doesn't even hurt them."

"That I doubt," said Norton. "But even if it worked, we can't risk it. We don't know how intelligent this creature is—and a trick like that could easily break its legs. Then we would be in real trouble, from Rama, Earth, and everyone else."

"But I've got to have a specimen!"

"You may have to be content with Jimmy's flower —unless one of these creatures co-operates with you. Force is out. How would you like it if something landed on Earth and decided that *you* would make a nice specimen for dissection?"

"I don't want to dissect it," said Laura, not at all convincingly. "I only want to examine it."

"Well, alien visitors might have the same attitude toward you, but you could have a very uncomfortable time before you believed them. We must make no move that could possibly be regarded as threatening."

He was quoting from ship's orders, of course, and Laura knew it. The claims of science had a lower priority than those of space diplomacy.

In fact there was no need to bring in such elevated considerations; it was merely a matter of good manners. They were all visitors here, and had never even asked permission to come inside.

The creature seemed to have finished its inspection. It made one more high-speed circuit of the camp, then shot off at a tangent, toward the stairway.

"I wonder how it's going to manage the steps?" Laura mused. Her question was quickly answered: the spider ignored them completely and headed up the gently sloping curve of the ramp without slackening its speed.

"Hub Control," said Norton, "you may have a visitor shortly. Take a look at Stairway Alpha, section six. And incidentally, thanks a lot for keeping such a good watch on us."

It took a minute for the sarcasm to sink in. Then the hub observer started to make apologetic noises.

"Er . . . I can just see *something*, Skipper, now you tell me it's there. But what is it?"

"Your guess is as good as mine," Norton answered as he pressed the General Alert button. "Camp Alpha calling all stations. We've just been visited by a creature like a three-legged spider, with very thin legs, about two meters high, small spherical body, travels very fast, with a spinning motion. Appears harmless but inquisitive. It may sneak up on you before you notice it. Please acknowledge."

The first reply came from London, fifteen kilometers to the east.

"Nothing unusual here, Skipper."

From the same distance to the west, Rome answered, sounding suspiciously sleepy.

"Same here, Skipper. Uh . . . just a moment . . ."

"What is it?"

"I put my pen down a minute ago—and it's gone! What . . . oh!"

"Talk sense!"

"You won't believe this, Skipper. I was making some notes—you know I like writing, and it doesn't disturb anybody—and I was using my favorite ballpoint; it's nearly two hundred years old. Well, now it's lying on the ground, about five meters away! I've got it. Thank goodness it isn't damaged."

"And how do you suppose it got there?"

"Er . . . I may have dozed off for a minute. It's been a hard day."

Norton sighed, but refrained from comment; there were so few of them, and they had so little time in which to explore a world. Enthusiasm could not always overcome exhaustion, and he wondered if they were taking unnecessary risks. Perhaps he should not split his men up into such small groups and try to cover so much territory. But he was always conscious of the swiftly passing days and the unsolved mysteries around them. He was becoming more and more certain that something was about to happen, and that they would have to abandon Rama even before it reached perihelion—the moment of truth when any orbit change must surely take place.

"Now listen, Hub, Rome, London—everyone," he said. "I want a report every half-hour through the night. We must assume that from now on we may have visitors at any time. Some of them may be dangerous, but at all costs we have to avoid . . . incidents. You all know the directives on this subject."

That was true enough; it was part of their training. Yet perhaps none of them had ever really believed that the long-theorized "physical contact with intelligent aliens" would occur in their lifetimes—still less that they would experience it themseves.

Training was one thing, reality another, and no one could be sure that the ancient human instincts of self-preservation would not take over in an emergency. Yet it was essential to give every entity they encountered in Rama the benefit of the doubt, up to the last possible minute—and even beyond.

Commander Norton did not want to be remembered by history as the man who started the first interplanetary war.

Within a few hours there were hundreds of the spiders, and they were all over the plain. Through the telescope it could be seen that the Southern Hemisphere was also infested with them, but not, it seemed, the island of New York.

They took no further notice of the explorers, and after a while the explorers took little notice of them—though from time to time Norton detected a predatory gleam in his Surgeon Commander's eye. Nothing would please her better, he was sure, than for one of the spiders to have an unfortunate accident, and he would not put it past her to arrange such a thing in the interests of science.

It seemed virtually certain that the spiders could not be intelligent; their bodies were far too small to contain much in the way of brains, and indeed it was hard to see where they stored all the energy to move. Yet their behavior was curiously purposeful and co-ordinated. They appeared to be everywhere, but they never visited the same place twice. Norton frequently had the impression that they were *searching* for something. Whatever it was, they did not seem to have discovered it.

They went all the way up to the central hub, scorning the three great stairways. How they managed to ascend the vertical sections, even under almost zero gravity, was not clear. Laura theorized that they were equipped with suction pads.

And then, to her obvious delight, she got her eagerly desired specimen. Hub Control reported that a spider had fallen down the vertical face and was lying, dead or incapacitated, on the first platform. Laura's time up from the plain was a record that would never be beaten.

When she arrived at the platform she found that, despite the low velocity of impact, the creature had broken all its legs. Its eyes were open, but it showed no reactions to any external tests. Even a fresh human corpse would have been livelier, Laura thought. As soon as she got her prize back to the *Endeavour,* she started to work with her dissecting kit.

The spider was so fragile that it almost came to pieces without her assistance. She disarticulated the legs, then started on the delicate carapace, which split along three great circles and opened up like a peeled orange.

After some moments of blank incredulity—for

there was nothing that she could recognize or identify —she took a series of careful photographs. Then she picked up her scalpel.

Where to start cutting? She felt like closing her eyes and stabbing at random, but that would not have been very scientific.

The blade went in with practically no resistance. A second later, Surgeon Commander Ernst's most unlady-like yell echoed the length and breadth of *Endeavour*.

It took an annoyed Sergeant McAndrews a good twenty minutes to calm down the startled simps.

34

His Excellency Regrets...

"As you are all aware, gentlemen," said the Martian Ambassador, "a great deal has happened since our last meeting. We have much to discuss—and to decide. I'm therefore particularly sorry that our distinguished colleague from Mercury is not here."

That last statement was not altogether accurate. Dr. Bose was not particularly sorry that His Excellency the Hermian Ambassador was absent. It would have been much more truthful to say that he was worried. All his diplomatic instincts told him that something was happening, and though his sources of information were excellent he could gather no hints as to what it might be.

The Ambassador's letter of apology had been courteous and entirely uncommunicative. His Excellency had regretted that urgent and unavoidable business had kept him from attending the meeting, either in person or by video. Dr. Bose found it hard to think of anything more urgent, or more important, than Rama.

"Two of our members have statements to make. I would first like to call on Professor Davidson."

There was a rustle of excitement among the other scientists on the committee. Most of them had felt that the astronomer, with his well-known cosmic viewpoint, was not the right man to be chairman of the Space Advisory Council. He sometimes gave the impression that the activities of intelligent life were an unfortunate irrelevance in the majestic universe of stars and galaxies, and that it was bad manners to pay too much attention to them. This had not endeared him to exobiologists such as Dr. Perera, who took exactly the opposite view. For them, the only purpose of the universe was the production of intelligence, and they were apt to talk sneeringly about purely astronomical phenomena. "Mere dead matter" was one of their favorite phrases.

"Mr. Ambassador," the scientist began, "I have been analyzing the curious behavior of Rama during the last few days, and would like to present my conclusions. Some of them are rather startling."

Dr. Perera looked surprised, then a little smug. He strongly approved of anything that startled Davidson.

"First of all, there was the remarkable series of events when that young lieutenant"—he pronounced it "leftenant"—"flew over to the Southern Hemisphere. The electrical discharges themselves, though spectacular, are not important; it is easy to show that they contained relatively little energy. But they coincided with a change in Rama's rate of spin, and its attitude—that is, its orientation in space. *This* must have involved an enormous amount of energy; the discharges which nearly cost Mr. . . . er . . . Pak his life were merely a minor by-product—perhaps a nuisance that had to be minimized by those giant lightning conductors at the South Pole.

"I draw two conclusions from this. When a spacecraft—and we must call Rama a spacecraft, despite its fantastic size—makes a change of attitude, that usually means it is about to make a change of orbit. We must therefore take seriously the views of those who believe that Rama may be preparing to become another planet of our sun, instead of going back to the stars.

"If this is the case, *Endeavour* must obviously be prepared to cast off—is that what spaceships do?—at a moment's notice. She may be in very serious danger while she is still physically attached to Rama. I imagine that Commander Norton is already well aware of this possibility, but I think we should send him an additional warning."

"Thank you very much, Professor Davidson. Yes —Professor Solomons?"

"I'd like to comment on that," said the science historian. "Rama seems to have made a change of spin *without* using any jets or reaction devices. This leaves only two possibilities, it seems to me.

"The first one is that it has internal gyroscopes, or their equivalent. They must be enormous. Where are they?

"The second possibility—which would turn all our physics upside down—is that it has a reactionless propulsion system. The so-called space drive, which Professor Davidson doesn't believe in. If this is the case, Rama may be able to do almost anything. We will be quite unable to anticipate its behavior, even on the gross physical level."

The diplomats were obviously somewhat baffled by this exchange, and the astronomer refused to be drawn. He had gone out on enough limbs for one day.

"I'll stick to the laws of physics, if you don't mind, until I'm forced to give them up. If we've not found any gyroscopes in Rama, we may not have looked hard enough, or in the right place."

Bose could see that Perera was getting impatient. Normally the exobiologist was as happy as anyone else to engage in speculation; but now, for the first time, he had some solid facts. His long-impoverished science had become wealthy overnight.

"Very well. If there are no other comments, I know that Dr. Perera has some important information."

"Thank you, Mr. Ambassador. As you've all seen, we have at last obtained a specimen of a Rama life form, and have observed several others at close quarters. Surgeon Commander Ernst, *Endeavour's* medical officer, has sent a full report on the spiderlike creature she dissected. I must say at once that some of her results are baffling, and in any other circumstances I would have refused to believe them.

"The spider is definitely organic, though its chemistry differs from ours in many respects. It contains considerable quantities of light metals. Yet I hesitate to call it an animal, for several fundamental reasons.

"In the first place, it seems to have no mouth, no stomach, no gut—no method of ingesting food. Also no air intakes, no lungs, no blood, no reproductive system . . .

"You may wonder what it *has* got. Well, there's a simple musculature, controlling its three legs and the three whiplike tendrils or feelers. There's a brain—fairly complex, mostly concerned with the creature's remarkably developed triocular vision. But eighty per cent of the body consists of a honeycomb of large cells, and this is what gave Dr. Ernst such an unpleasant surprise when she started her dissection. If she'd been luckier, she might have recognized it in time, because it's the one Raman structure that *does* exist on Earth—though only in a handful of marine animals.

"Most of the spider is simply a battery, much like

that found in electric eels and rays. But in this case it's apparently not used for defense. *It's the creature's source of energy.* And that is why it has no provisions for eating and breathing; it doesn't need such primitive arrangements. And incidentally, this means that it would be perfectly at home in a vacuum.

"So we have a creature which, to all intents and purposes, is nothing more than a mobile eye. It has no organs of manipulation; those tendrils are much too feeble. If I had been given its specifications, I would have said it's merely a reconnaissance device.

"Its behavior certainly fits that description. All the spiders ever do is run around and look at things. That's all they *can* do.

"But the other animals are different. The crab, the starfish, the sharks—for want of better words—these can obviously manipulate their environment, and appear to be specialized for various functions. I assume that they are also electrically powered, since, like the spider, they appear to have no mouths.

"I'm sure you'll appreciate the biological problems raised by all this. Could such creatures evolve naturally? I really don't think so. They appear to be *designed*, like machines, for specific jobs. If I had to describe them, I would say that they are robots—biological robots—something that has no analogy on Earth.

"If Rama is a spaceship, perhaps they are part of its crew. As to how they are born—or created—that's something I can't tell you. But I can guess that the answer's over there in New York. If Commander Norton and his men can wait long enough, they may encounter increasingly more complex creatures, with unpredictable behavior. Somewhere along the line they may meet the Ramans themselves—the real makers of this world.

"And when *that* happens, gentlemen, there will be no doubt about it at all."

35

Special Delivery

COMMANDER NORTON WAS sleeping soundly when his personal communicator dragged him away from happy dreams. He had been holidaying with his family on Mars, flying past the awesome, snow-capped peak of Nix Olympica, mightiest volcano in the solar system. Little Billie had started to say something to him; now he would never know what it was.

The dream faded; the reality was his executive officer, up on the ship.

"Sorry to wake you, Skipper," said Kirchoff. "Triple-A priority from headquarters."

"Let me have it," Norton answered sleepily.

"I can't. It's in code—Commander's Eyes Only."

Norton was instantly awake. He had received such a message only three times in his whole career, and on each occasion it had meant trouble.

"Damn!" he said. "What do we do now?"

The Exec did not bother to answer. Each understood the problem perfectly; it was one that ship's orders had never anticipated. Normally, a commander was never more than a few minutes away from his office and the code book in his personal safe. If he started now, Norton might get back to the ship—exhausted —in four or five hours. That was not the way to handle a Triple-A priority.

"Jerry," he said at length, "who's on the switchboard?"

"No one. I'm making the call myself."

"Recorder off?"

"By an odd breach of regulations, yes."

Norton smiled. Jerry was the best exec he had ever worked with; he thought of everything.

"OK. You know where my key is. Call me back."

He waited as patiently as he could for the next ten minutes, trying, without much success, to think of other problems. He hated wasting mental effort; it was unlikely that he could guess the message that was coming, and he would know its contents soon enough. *Then* he could start worrying effectively.

When Kirchoff called back, he was obviously speaking under considerable strain.

"It's not really *urgent*, Skipper. An hour won't make any difference. But I prefer to avoid radio. I'll send it down by messenger."

"But *why* . . . oh, very well. I trust your judgment. Who will carry it through the air locks?"

"I'm going myself. I'll call you when I reach the hub."

"Which leaves Laura in charge."

"For one hour, at the most. I'll get right back to the ship."

A medical officer did not have the specialized training to be acting captain, any more than a captain could be expected to perform an operation. In emergencies, the two jobs had sometimes been successfully switched; but it was not recommended. Well, one order had already been broken tonight.

"For the record, you never leave the ship. Have you waked Laura?"

"Yes. She's delighted to have the opportunity."

"Lucky that doctors are used to keeping secrets. Oh, have you sent the acknowledgment?"

"Of course, in your name."

"Then I'll be waiting."

Now it was quite impossible to avoid anxious anticipation. "Not *really* urgent—but I prefer to avoid radio . . ."

One thing was certain: the Commander was not going to get much more sleep this night.

36

Biot Watcher

SERGEANT PIETER ROUSSEAU knew why he had volunteered for this job; in many ways, it was a realization of a childhood dream. He had become fascinated by telescopes when he was only six or seven years old, and much of his youth had been spent collecting lenses of all shapes and sizes. These he had mounted in cardboard tubes, making instruments of ever-increasing power, until he was familiar with the Moon and planets, the nearer space stations, and the entire landscape within thirty kilometers of his home.

He had been lucky in his place of birth, among the mountains of Colorado. In almost every direction, the view was spectacular and inexhaustible. He had spent hours exploring, in perfect safety, the peaks that every year took their toll of careless climbers. Though he had seen much, he had imagined even more; he had liked to pretend that over each crest of rock, beyond the reach of his telescope, were magic kingdoms full of wonderful creatures. And so for years he had avoided visiting the places his lenses brought to him, because he knew that the reality could not live up to the dream.

Now, on the central axis of Rama, he could survey marvels beyond the wildest fantasies of his youth. A whole world lay spread out before him—a small one, it was true, yet a man could spend a lifetime exploring four thousand square kilometers, even when it was dead and changeless.

But now life, with all its infinite possibilities, had come to Rama. If the biological robots were not living creatures, they were certainly very good imitations.

No one knew who invented the word "biot"; it seemed to come into instant use, by a kind of spontaneous generation. From his vantage point on the hub, Rousseau was Biot Watcher in Chief, and he was beginning, so he believed, to understand some of their behavior patterns.

The spiders were mobile sensors, using vision, and probably touch, to examine the whole interior of Rama. At one time there had been hundreds of them rushing around at high speed, but after less than two days most had disappeared. Now it was quite unusual to see even one.

They had been replaced by a whole menagerie of much more impressive creatures, and it had been no minor task to think of suitable names for them. There were the "window cleaners," with large padded feet, who were apparently polishing their way the whole length of Rama's six artificial suns. Their enormous shadows, cast right across the diameter of the world, sometimes caused temporary eclipses on the far side.

The crab that had demolished *Dragonfly* seemed to be a "scavenger." A relay chain of identical creatures had approached Camp Alpha and carried off all the debris that had been neatly stacked on the outskirts; they would have carried off everything else if Norton and Mercer had not stood firm and defied them. The confrontation had been anxious but brief. Thereafter, the scavengers seemed to understand what they were allowed to touch, and arrived at regular intervals to see if their services were required. It was a most convenient arrangement, and indicated a high degree of intelligence—on the part of either the scavengers themselves or some controlling entity elsewhere.

Garbage disposal on Rama was simple: everything was thrown into the sea, where it was presumably broken down into forms that could be used again. The process was rapid. *Resolution* had disappeared overnight, to the great annoyance of Ruby Barnes. Norton had consoled her by pointing out that it had done its job magnificently and he would never have allowed anyone to use it again. The sharks might not be as discriminating as the scavengers.

No astronomer discovering an unknown planet could have been happier than Rousseau was when he spotted a new type of biot and secured a good photo of it through his telescope. Unfortunately, it seemed that all the interesting species were over at the South Pole, where they were performing mysterious tasks around the horns. Something that looked like a centipede with suction pads could be seen from time to time exploring Big Horn itself, while Rousseau had caught a glimpse of a burly creature around the lower peaks that could have been a cross between a hippopotamus and a bulldozer. And there was even a double-necked giraffe, which apparently acted as a mobile crane.

Presumably Rama, like any ship, required testing, checking, and repairing after its immense voyage. The crew was already hard at work. When would the passengers appear?

Biot-classifying was not Rousseau's main job. His orders were to keep watch on the two or three exploring parties that were always out, to see that they did not get into trouble, and to warn them if anything approached. He alternated every six hours with anyone else who could be spared, though more than once he had been on duty for twelve hours at a stretch. As a result, he now knew the geography of Rama better than any other man who would ever live. It was as familiar to him as the Colorado mountains of his youth.

When Lieutenant Commander Kirchoff emerged from Air-Lock Alpha, Rousseau knew at once that something unusual was happening. Personnel transfers never occurred during the sleeping period, and it was now past midnight by mission time. Then Rousseau remembered how short-handed they were, and was shocked by a much more startling irregularity.

"Jerry—who's in charge of the ship?"

"I am," said the Exec coldly as he flipped open his helmet. "You don't think I'd leave the bridge while I'm on watch, do you?"

He reached into his suit carryall and pulled out a small can bearing the label CONCENTRATED ORANGE JUICE. TO MAKE FIVE LITERS.

"You're good at this, Pieter. The Skipper is waiting for it."

Rousseau hefted the can, then said, "I hope you've put enough mass inside it. Sometimes they get stuck on the first terrace."

"Well, you're the expert."

That was true enough. The hub observers had had plenty of practice sending down small items that had been forgotten or were needed in a hurry. The trick was to get them safely past the low-gravity region, and then to see that the Coriolis Effect did not carry them too far away from the camp during the eight-kilometer roll downhill.

Rousseau anchored himself firmly, grasped the can, and hurled it down the face of the cliff. He did not aim directly toward Camp Alpha, but almost thirty degrees away from it.

Almost immediately, air resistance robbed the can of its initial speed, but then the pseudo-gravity of Rama took over and it started to move downward at a constant velocity It hit once near the base of the ladder, and did a slow-motion bounce which took it clear of the first terrace.

"It's OK now," said Rousseau. "Like to make a bet?"

"No" was the prompt reply. "You know the odds."

"You're no sportsman. But I'll tell you now—it will stop within three hundred meters of the camp."

"That doesn't sound very close."

"You might try it sometime. I once saw Joe miss by a couple of kilometers."

The can was no longer bouncing; gravity had become strong enough to glue it to the curving face of the north dome. By the time it had reached the second terrace it was rolling along at twenty or thirty kilometers an hour, and had reached nearly the maximum speed that friction would allow.

"Now we'll have to wait," said Rousseau, seating himself at the telescope so that he could keep track of the messenger. "It will be there in ten minutes. Ah, here comes the Skipper. I've got used to recognizing people from this angle. Now he's looking up at us."

"I believe that telescope gives you a sense of power."

"Oh, it does. I'm the only person who knows everything that's happening in Rama. At least, I *thought* I did," he added plaintively, giving Kirchoff a reproachful look.

"If it will keep you happy, the Skipper found he'd run out of toothpaste."

After that, conversation languished; but at last Rousseau said: "Wish you'd taken that bet. He's only got to walk fifty meters. Now he sees it. Mission complete."

"Thanks, Pieter—a very good job. Now you can go back to sleep."

"Sleep! I'm on watch until 0400."

"Sorry—you *must* have been sleeping. Or how else could you have dreamed all this?"

SPACE SURVEY H.Q. TO COMMANDER SSS ENDEAVOUR. PRIORITY AAA. CLASSIFICATION YOUR EYES ONLY. NO PERMANENT RECORD.

SPACEGUARD REPORTS ULTRA-HIGH-SPEED VEHICLE APPARENTLY LAUNCHED MERCURY TEN TO TWELVE DAYS AGO ON RAMA INTERCEPT. IF NO ORBIT CHANGE ARRIVAL PREDICTED DATE 322 DAYS 15 HOURS. MAY BE NECESSARY YOU EVACUATE BEFORE THEN. WILL ADVISE FURTHER. C IN C.

Norton read the message half a dozen times to memorize the date. It was hard to keep track of time inside Rama; he had to look at his calendar watch to see that it was now Day 315. That might leave them only one week.

The message was chilling, not only for what it said, but also for what it implied. The Hermians had made a clandestine launch, which in itself was a breach of space law. The conclusion was obvious: their "vehicle" could only be a missile.

But *why?* It was inconceivable—well, almost inconceivable—that they would risk endangering *Endeavour*. So presumably he would receive ample warning from the Hermians themselves. In an emergency he could leave at a few hours' notice, though he would do so only under extreme protest, at the direct orders of the Commander in Chief.

Slowly, and thoughtfully, he walked across to the improvised life-support complex and dropped the message into an elcctrosan. The brilliant flare of laser light bursting out through the crack beneath the seat cover told him that the demands of security were satisfied. It was too bad, he told himself, that all problems could not be disposed of so swiftly and hygienically.

37

Missile

THE MISSILE WAS still five million kilometers away when the glare of its plasma braking jets became clearly visible in *Endeavour*'s main telescope. By that time the secret was out, and Norton had reluctantly ordered the second and perhaps final evacuation of Rama. But he had no intention of leaving until events gave him no alternative.

When it had completed its braking maneuver, the unwelcome guest from Mercury was only fifty kilometers from Rama and apparently carrying out a survey through its TV cameras. These were clearly visible—one fore and one aft—as were several small omniantennas and one large directional dish, aimed steadily at the distant star of Mercury. Norton wondered what instructions were coming down that beam and what information was going back.

Yet the Hermians could learn nothing that they did

not already know; all that *Endeavour* had discovered had been broadcast throughout the solar system. This spacecraft, which had broken all speed records to get here, could be only an extension of its makers' will, an instrument of their purpose. That purpose would soon be known, for in three hours the Hermian Ambassador to the United Planets would be addressing the General Assembly.

Officially, the missile did not exist. It bore no identification marks and was not radiating on any standard beacon frequency. This was a serious breach of law, but even SPACEGUARD had not yet issued a formal protest. Everyone was waiting, with nervous impatience, to see what Mercury would do next.

It had been three days since the missile's existence —and origin—had been announced. All that time, the Hermians had remained stubbornly silent. They could be good at that when it suited them.

Some psychologists had claimed that it was almost impossible to understand fully the mentality of anyone born and bred on Mercury. Forever exiled from Earth by its three-times-more-powerful gravity, Hermians could stand on the Moon and look across the narrow gap to the planet of their ancestors, even of their own parents, but they could never visit it. And so, inevitably, they claimed that they did not want to.

They pretended to despise the soft rains, the rolling fields, the lakes and seas, the blue skies—all the things that they could know only through recordings. Because their planet was drenched with such solar energy that the daytime temperature often reached six hundred degrees, they affected a rather swaggering toughness that did not bear a moment's serious examination. In fact, they tended to be physically weak, since they could survive only if they were totally insulated from their environment. Even if he could have tolerated the gravity, a Hermian would have been quickly incapacitated by a hot day in any equatorial country on Earth.

Yet in matters that really counted, they *were* tough. The psychological pressures of that ravening star so close at hand, the engineering problems of tearing into a stubborn planet and wrenching from it all the necessities of life—these had produced a Spartan and in many ways highly admirable culture. You could rely on the Hermians; if they promised something, they would do it, though the bill might be considerable. It was their own joke that if the Sun ever showed signs of going nova they would contract to get it under control —once the fee had been settled. It was a non-Hermian joke that any child who showed signs of interest in art, philosophy, or abstract mathematics was plowed straight back into the hydroponic farms. As far as criminals and psychopaths were concerned, this was not a joke at all. Crime was one of the luxuries that Mercury could not afford.

Commander Norton had been to Mercury once, had been enormously impressed, like most visitors, and had acquired many Hermian friends. He had fallen in love with a girl in Port Lucifer, and had even contemplated signing a three-year contract, but parental disapproval of anyone from outside the orbit of Venus had been too strong. It was just as well.

"Triple-A message from Earth, Skipper," said the bridge. "Voice and back-up text from Commander in Chief. Ready to accept?"

"Check and file text; let me have the voice."

"Here it comes."

Admiral Hendrix sounded calm and matter-of-fact, as if he were issuing a routine fleet order, instead of handling a situation unique in the history of space. But then, he was not ten kilometers from the bomb.

"C in C to Commander, *Endeavour*. This is a quick summary of the situation as we see it now. You know that the General Assembly meets at 1400 and you'll be listening to the proceedings. It is possible that you may then have to take action immediately, without consultation; hence this briefing.

"We've analyzed the photos you have sent us. The vehicle is a standard space probe, modified for high-impulse and probably laser-riding for initial boost. Size and mass are consistent with fusion bomb in the five-hundred- to one-thousand-megaton range. The Hermians use up to one hundred megatons routinely in their mining operations, so they would have had no difficulty in assembling such a warhead.

"Our experts also estimate that this would be the minimum size necessary to assure destruction of Rama. If it was detonated against the thinnest part of the shell, underneath the Cylindrical Sea, the hull would be ruptured, and the spin of the body would complete its disintegration.

"We assume that the Hermians, if they are planning such an act, will give you ample time to get clear. For your information, the gamma-ray flash from such a bomb could be dangerous to you up to a range of a thousand kilometers.

"But that is not the most serious danger. The fragments of Rama, weighing tons and spinning off at almost a thousand kilometers an hour, could destroy you at an *unlimited* distance. We therefore recommend that you proceed along the spin axis, since no fragments will be thrown off in that direction. Ten thousand kilometers should give an adequate safety margin.

"This message cannot be intercepted; it is going by multiple-pseudo-random routing, so I can talk in clear English. Your reply may not be secure, so speak with discretion and use code when necessary. I will call you immediately after the General Assembly discussion. Message concluded. C in C, out."

38

General Assembly

ACCORDING TO THE history books—though no one could really believe it—there had been a time when the old United Nations had 172 members. The United Planets had only seven; and that was sometimes bad enough. In order of distance from the Sun, they were Mercury, Earth, Luna, Mars, Ganymede, Titan, and Triton.

The list contained numerous omissions and ambiguities which presumably the future would rectify. Critics never tired of pointing out that most of the United Planets were not planets at all, but satellites. And how ridiculous that the four giants Jupiter, Saturn, Uranus, and Neptune were not included.

But no one lived on the Gas Giants, and quite possibly no one ever would. The same might be true of the other major absentee, Venus. Even the most enthusiastic of planetary engineers agreed that it would take centuries to tame Venus; meanwhile, the Hermians kept their eyes on it, and doubtless brooded over long-range plans.

Separate representation for Earth and Luna had also been a bone of contention. The other members argued that it put too much power in one corner of the solar system. But there were more people on the Moon than on all the other worlds except Earth itself, and it *was* the meeting place of the U.P. Moreover, Earth and Moon hardly ever agreed on anything, so they were not likely to constitute a dangerous bloc.

Mars held the asteroids in trust, except for the Icarian group (supervised by Mercury), and a handful with perihelions beyond Saturn and thus claimed by Titan. One day the larger asteroids, such as Pallas, Vesta, Juno, and Ceres, would be important enough to have their own ambassadors, and the membership of the U.P. would then reach two figures.

Ganymede represented not only Jupiter—and therefore more mass than all the rest of the solar system put together—but also the remaining fifty or so Jovian satellites, if one included temporary captures from the asteroid belt—though lawyers were still arguing over this. In the same way, Titan took care of Saturn, its rings, and the other thirty-plus satellites.

The situation for Triton was even more complicated. The large moon of Neptune was the outermost body in the solar system under permanent habitation; as a result, its Ambassador wore a considerable number of hats. He represented Uranus and its eight moons (none yet occupied); Neptune and its other three satellites; Pluto and its solitary moon; and lonely, moonless Persephone. If there were planets beyond Persephone they, too, would be Triton's responsibility. And as if that was not enough, the Ambassador from Outer Darkness, as he was sometimes called, had been heard to ask plaintively: "What about comets?" It was generally felt that this problem could be left for the future to solve.

And yet, in a real sense that future was already here. By some definitions, Rama *was* a comet. They were the only other visitors from the interstellar deeps, and many had traveled on hyperbolic orbits even closer to the Sun than Rama's. Any space lawyer could make a good case out of that—and the Hermian Ambassador was one of the best.

"We recognize His Excellency the Ambassador from Mercury."

Because the delegates were arranged counterclockwise in order of distance from the Sun, the Hermian was on the President's extreme right. Up to the very last minute he had been interfacing with his computer; now he removed the synchronizing spectacles that allowed no one else to read the message on the display screen. He picked up his sheaf of notes and rose briskly to his feet.

"Mr. President, distinguished fellow delegates, I would like to begin with a brief summary of the situation which now confronts us."

From some delegates, that phrase "a brief summary" would have evoked silent groans from all listeners; but everyone knew that Hermians meant exactly what they said.

"The giant spaceship or artificial asteroid which has been christened Rama was detected over a year ago, in the region beyond Jupiter. At first it was believed to be a natural body, moving on a hyperbolic orbit that would take it around the Sun and on to the stars.

"When its true nature was discovered, the Solar Survey vessel *Endeavour* was ordered to rendezvous with it. I am sure we will all want to congratulate Commander Norton and his crew for the efficient way in which they have carried out their unique assignment.

"At first, it was believed that Rama was dead—frozen for so many hundreds of thousands of years that there was no possibility of revival. This may still be true, in a strictly biological sense. There seems general agreement, among those who have studied the matter, that no living organism of any complexity can survive more than a few centuries of suspended animation. Even at absolute zero, residual quantum effects eventually erase too much cellular information to make revival possible. It therefore appeared that, although Rama was of enormous archeological importance, it did not present any major astropolitical problems.

"It is now obvious that this was a very naïve attitude, though even from the first there were some who pointed out that Rama was too precisely aimed at the Sun for pure chance to be involved.

"Even so, it might have been argued—indeed, it was argued—that here was an experiment that had failed. Rama had reached the intended target, but the controlling intelligence had not survived. This view also seems very simple-minded; it surely underestimates the entities we are dealing with.

"What we failed to take into account was the possibility of nonbiological survival. If we accept Dr. Perera's very plausible theory, which certainly fits all the facts, the creatures who have been observed inside Rama did not exist until a short time ago. Their patterns, or templates, were stored in some central information bank, and when the time was ripe they were manufactured from available raw materials—presumably the organometallic soup of the Cylindrical Sea. Such a feat is still somewhat beyond our own ability, but does not present any theoretical problems. We know that solid-state circuits, unlike living matter, can store information without loss for indefinite periods of time.

"So Rama is now in full operating condition, serving the purpose of its builders—whoever they may be. From our point of view it does not matter if the Ramans themselves have all been dead for a million years, or whether they, too, will be re-created, to join their servants, at any moment. With or without them, their will is being done, and will continue to be done.

"Rama has now given proof that its propulsion system is still operating. In a few days, it will be at perihelion, where it would logically make any major orbit change. We may therefore soon have a new planet—moving through the solar space over which my government has jurisdiction. Or it may, of course, make additional changes and occupy a final orbit at any distance from the Sun. It could even become a satellite of a major planet, such as Earth.

"We are therefore, fellow delegates, faced with a whole spectrum of possibilities, some of them very serious indeed. It is foolish to pretend that these creatures *must* be benevolent and will not interfere with us in any way. If they come to our solar system, they need something from it. Even if it is only scientific knowledge—consider how that knowledge may be used.

"What confronts us now is a technology hundreds, perhaps thousands, of years in advance of ours, and a *culture* that may have no points of contact with ours whatsoever. We have been studying the behavior of the biological robots—the biots—inside Rama, as shown in the films that Commander Norton has relayed, and we have arrived at certain conclusions, which we wish to pass on to you.

"On Mercury we are perhaps unlucky in having no indigenous life forms to observe. But, of course, we have a complete record of terrestrial zoology, and we find in it one striking parallel with Rama.

"This is the termite colony. Like Rama, it is an artificial world with a controlled environment. Like Rama, its functioning depends upon a whole series of specialized biological machines: workers, builders, farmers —*warriors*. And although we do not know if Rama has a queen, I suggest that the island known as New York serves a similar function.

"Now it would obviously be absurd to press this analogy too far; it breaks down at many points. But I put it to you for this reason: What degree of co-operation or understanding would ever be possible between human beings and termites? When there is no conflict of interest, we tolerate each other. But when either needs the other's territory or resources, no quarter is given.

"Thanks to our technology and our intelligence, we can always win if we are sufficiently determined. But sometimes it is not easy, and there are those who believe that final victory may go to the termites.

"With this in mind, consider now the appalling threat that Rama may—I do not say *must*—present to human civilization. What steps have we taken to counter it, if the worst eventuality should occur? None whatsoever. We have merely talked and speculated and written learned papers.

"Well, my fellow delegates, Mercury has done more than this. Acting under the provisions of Clause 34 of the Space Treaty of 2057, which entitles us to take any steps necessary to protect the integrity of our solar space, we have dispatched a high-energy nuclear device to Rama. We will indeed be happy if we never have to utilize it. But now, at least, we are not helpless —as we were before.

"It may be argued that we have acted unilaterally, without prior consultation. We admit that. But does anyone here imagine—with all respect, Mr. President —that we could have secured any such agreement in the time available? We consider that we are acting not only for ourselves, but also for the whole human race. All future generations may one day thank us for our foresight.

"We recognize that it would be a tragedy—even a crime—to destroy an artifact as wonderful as Rama. If there is any way in which this can be avoided, *without risk to humanity*, we will be very happy to hear of it. We have not found one, and time is running out.

"Within the next few days, before Rama reaches perihelion, the choice will have to be made. We will, of course, give ample warning to *Endeavour*, but we would advise Commander Norton always to be ready to leave at an hour's notice. It is conceivable that Rama may undergo further dramatic transformations at any moment.

"That is all, Mr. President, fellow delegates. I thank you for your attention. I look forward to your co-operation."

39

Command Decision

"WELL, BORIS, HOW do the Hermians fit into your theology?"

"Only too well, Commander," replied Lieutenant Rodrigo with a humorless smile. "It's the age-old conflict between the forces of good and the forces of evil. And there are times when men have to take sides in such a conflict."

I knew it would be something like that, Norton thought. This situation must have been a shock to Boris, but he would not have resigned himself to passive acquiescence. The Cosmo Christers were energetic, competent people. Indeed, in some ways they were remarkably like the Hermians.

"I take it you have a plan, Boris."

"Yes, Commander. It's really quite simple. We merely have to disable the bomb."

"Oh. And how do you propose to do that?"

"With a small pair of wire cutters."

If this had been anyone else, Norton would have assumed that he was joking. But not Boris Rodrigo.

"Now just a minute! It's bristling with cameras. Do you suppose the Hermians will just sit and watch you?"

"Of course; that's all they *can* do. When the signal reaches them, it will be far too late. I can easily finish the job in ten minutes."

"I see. They certainly *will* be mad. But suppose the bomb is booby-trapped so that interference sets it off?"

"That seems very unlikely. What would be the purpose? This bomb was built for a specific deep-space mission, and it will be fitted with all sorts of safety devices to prevent detonation *except* on a positive command. But that's a risk I'm prepared to take—and it can be done without endangering the ship. I've worked everything out."

"I'm sure you have," said Norton. The idea was fascinating, almost seductive in its appeal; he particularly liked the idea of the frustrated Hermians, and would give a good deal to see their reactions when they realized, too late, what was happening to their deadly toy.

But there were other complications, and they seemed to multiply as Norton surveyed the problem. He was facing by far the most difficult, and the most crucial, decision of his entire career.

And that was a ridiculous understatement. He was faced with the most difficult decision *any* commander had ever had to make. The future of the entire human race might well depend upon it. For just suppose the Hermians were right?

When Rodrigo had left, Norton switched on the DO NOT DISTURB sign. He could not remember when he had last used it and was mildly surprised that it was working. Now, in the heart of his crowded, busy ship, he was completely alone—except for the portrait of Captain James Cook, gazing at him down the corridors of time.

It was impossible to consult with Earth; he had already been warned that any messages might be tapped, perhaps by relay devices on the bomb itself. That left the whole responsibility in his hands.

There was a story he had heard somewhere about a President of the United States—was it Truman or Pérez?—who had a sign on his desk saying "The buck stops here." Norton was not quite certain what a buck was, but he knew when one had stopped at his desk.

He could choose to do nothing, and wait until the Hermians advised him to leave. How would that look in the histories of the future? Though Norton was not greatly concerned with posthumous fame or infamy, he would not care to be remembered forever as the accessory to a cosmic crime that it had been in his power to prevent.

And the plan was flawless. As he would have expected, Rodrigo had worked out every detail, anticipated every possibility, even the remote danger that the bomb might be triggered when tampered with. If that happened, *Endeavour* could still be safe, behind the shield of Rama. As for Rodrigo himself, he seemed to regard the possibility of instant apotheosis with complete equanimity.

Yet even if the bomb was successfully disabled, that would be far from the end of the matter. The Hermians might try again, unless some way could be found of stopping them. But at least weeks of time would have been bought; Rama would be far past perihelion before another missile could possibly reach it. By then the worst fears of the alarmists might have been disproved. Or the reverse . . .

To act or not act—that was the question. Never before had Norton felt such a close kinship with the

Prince of Denmark. Whatever he did, the possibilities for good or evil seemed in perfect balance. He was faced with the most morally difficult of all decisions. If his choice was wrong he would know very quickly. But if he was right he might never be able to prove it.

It was no use relying any further on logical arguments and the endless mapping of alternative futures. That way, one could go around in circles forever. The time had come to listen to his inner voices.

He returned the calm, steady gaze of Cook from across the centuries.

"I agree with you, Captain," he whispered. "The human race has to live with its conscience. Whatever the Hermians argue, survival is not everything."

He pressed the call button for the bridge circuit and said slowly, "Lieutenant Rodrigo, I'd like to see you."

Then he closed his eyes, hooked his thumbs in the restraining straps of his chair, and prepared to enjoy a few moments of total relaxation. It might be some time before he would experience it again.

40

Saboteur

THE SCOOTER HAD been stripped all of all unnecessary equipment; it was now merely an open framework holding together propulsion, guidance, and life-support systems. Even the seat for the second pilot had been removed, for every kilogram of extra mass had to be paid for in mission time.

That was one of the reasons, though not the most important, why Rodrigo had insisted on going alone. It was such a simple job that there was no need for extra hands, and the mass of a passenger would cost several minutes of flight time. Now the stripped-down scooter could accelerate at over a third of a gravity; it could make the trip from *Endeavour* to the bomb in four minutes. That left six to spare. It should be sufficient.

Rodrigo looked back only once when he had left the ship. He saw that, as planned, it had lifted from the central axis and was thrusting gently away across the spinning disc of the North Face. By the time he reached the bomb, it would have placed the thickness of Rama between them.

He took his time flying over the polar plain. There was no hurry here, because the bomb's cameras could not yet see him, and he could therefore conserve fuel. Then he drifted over the curving rim of the world—and there was the missile, glittering in sunlight fiercer even than that shining on the planet of its birth.

Rodrigo had already punched in the guidance instructions. Now he initiated the sequence, and the scooter spun on its gyros and came up to full thrust in a matter of seconds. At first the sensation of weight seemed crushing; then Rodrigo adjusted to it. He had, after all, comfortably endured twice as much inside Rama, and had been born under three times as much on Earth.

The huge, curving exterior wall of the fifty-kilometer cylinder was slowly falling away beneath him as the scooter aimed itself directly at the bomb. Yet it was impossible to judge Rama's size, since it was completely smooth, and so lacking in features that it was difficult to tell that it was spinning.

One hundred seconds into the mission he was approaching the halfway point. The bomb was too far away to show any details, but it was much brighter against the jet-black sky. It was strange to see no stars —not even brilliant Earth or dazzling Venus. The dark filters which protected his eyes against the deadly glare made that impossible. Rodrigo guessed that he was breaking a record; probably no other man had ever engaged in extra-vehicular work so close to the Sun. It was lucky for him that solar activity was low.

At two minutes ten seconds, the flip-over light started flashing, thrust dropped to zero, and the scooter spun through 180 degrees. Full thrust was back in an

instant, but now he was decelerating at the same mad
rate of three meters per second squared—rather better
than that, in fact, since he had lost almost half his propellant mass. The bomb was twenty-five kilometers
away. He would be there in another two minutes. He
had hit a top speed of fifteen hundred kph—which, for
a space scooter, was utter insanity, and probably another record. But this was hardly a routine EVA, and
he knew precisely what he was doing.

The bomb was growing; and now he could see the
main antenna, holding steady on the invisible star of
Mercury. Along that beam the image of his approaching scooter had been flashing at the speed of light for
the last three minutes. There were still two to go before it reached Mercury.

What would the Hermians do when they saw him?
There would be consternation, of course. They would
realize instantly that he had made a rendezvous with
the bomb several minutes before they even knew he
was on the way. Probably some stand-by observer
would call higher authority; that would take more
time. But even in the worst possible case—even if the
officer on duty had authority to detonate the bomb
and pressed the button immediately—it would take
another five minutes for the signal to arrive.

Though Rodrigo was not gambling on it—Cosmo
Christers never gambled—he was quite sure that there
would be no such instantaneous reaction. The Hermians would hesitate to destroy a reconnaissance vehicle
from Endeavour, even if they suspected its motives.
They would certainly attempt some form of communication first—and that would mean more delay.

And there was an even better reason: they would
not waste a gigaton bomb on a mere scooter. Wasted it
would be if it was detonated twenty kilometers from
its target. They would have to move it first. Oh, he
had plenty of time. . . . But he would continue to as-

sume the worst. He would act as if the triggering impulse were going to arrive in the shortest possible time —just five minutes.

As the scooter closed in across the last few hundred meters, Rodrigo quickly matched the details he could now see with those he had studied in the photographs taken at long range. What had been only a collection of pictures became hard metal and smooth plastic—no longer abstract, but a deadly reality.

The bomb was a cylinder about ten meters long and three in diameter—by a strange coincidence, almost the same proportions as those of Rama. It was attached to the framework of the carrier vehicle by an open latticework of short I beams. For some reason, probably to do with the location of the center of mass, it was supported at *right angles* to the axis of the carrier, so that it conveyed an appropriately sinister hammer-head impression. It was indeed a hammer, one powerful enough to smash a world.

From each end of the bomb a bundle of braided cables ran along the cylindrical side and disappeared through the latticework into the interior of the vehicle. All communication and control was here, there was no antenna of any kind on the bomb itself. Rodrigo had only to cut those two sets of cables and there would be nothing left but harmless inert metal.

Although this was exactly what he had expected, it seemed a little too easy. He glanced at his watch; it would be another thirty seconds before the Hermians, even if they had been watching when he rounded the edge of Rama, could know of his existence. He had an absolutely certain five minutes for uninterrupted work, and a ninety-nine-per-cent probability of much longer than that.

As soon as the scooter had drifted to a complete halt, Rodrigo grappled it to the missile framework so that the two formed a rigid structure. That took only seconds. He had already chosen his tools and was out of the pilot's seat at once, only slightly hampered by the stiffness of his heavy-insulation suit.

The first thing he found himself inspecting was a small metal plate bearing this inscription:

DEPARTMENT OF POWER ENGINEERING
Section D
47 Sunset Boulevard
Vulcanopolis, 17464
For information apply to Henry K. Jones

Rodrigo suspected that in a very few minutes Mr. Jones might be rather busy.

The heavy wire cutters made short work of the cable. As the first strands parted, Rodrigo gave scarcely a thought to the fires of Hell that were pent up only centimeters away. If his actions triggered them, he would never know.

He glanced again at his watch; this had taken less than a minute, which meant that he was on schedule. Now for the back-up cable, and then he could head for home, in full view of the furious and frustrated Hermians.

He was just beginning to work on the second cable assembly when he felt a faint vibration in the metal he was touching. Startled, he looked back along the body of the missile.

The characteristic blue-violet glow of a plasma thruster in action was hovering around one of the attitude-control jets. The bomb was preparing to move.

The message from Mercury was brief, and devastating. It arrived two minutes after Rodrigo had disappeared around the edge of Rama.

COMMANDER ENDEAVOUR FROM MERCURY SPACE CON-
TROL, INFERNO WEST. YOU HAVE ONE HOUR FROM RE-
CEIPT OF THIS MESSAGE TO LEAVE VICINITY OF RAMA.
SUGGEST YOU PROCEED MAXIMUM ACCELERATION ALONG
SPIN AXIS, REQUEST ACKNOWLEDGMENT. MESSAGE ENDS.

Norton read it with sheer disbelief, followed by anger. He felt a childish impulse to radio back that all
his crew were inside Rama and it would take hours to
get everyone out. But that would achieve nothing—except perhaps to test the will and nerve of the Hermians.

And why, several days before perihelion, had they
decided to act? He wondered if the mounting pressure
of public opinion was becoming too great and they
had decided to present the rest of the human race with
a *fait accompli*. It seemed an unlikely explanation, because such sensitivity would have been uncharacteris-
tic.

There was no way in which he could recall Rodrigo,
for the scooter was now in the radio shadow of Rama
and would be out of contact until they were in line of
sight again. That would not be until the mission was
completed—or had failed.

He would have to wait it out. There was still plenty
of time, a full fifty minutes. Meanwhile, he had decided on the most effective answer to Mercury.

He would ignore the message completely, and see
what the Hermians did next.

Rodrigo's first sensation when the bomb started to
move was not one of physical fear; it was something
much more devastating. He believed that the universe
operated according to strict laws, which not even God
could disobey—much less the Hermians. No message
could travel faster than light; he was five minutes
ahead of anything that Mercury could do.

This could only be a coincidence—fantastic, and perhaps deadly, but no more than that. By chance, a control signal must have been sent to the bomb at about the time he was leaving *Endeavour*. While he was traveling fifty kilometers, it had covered eighty million.

Or perhaps this was only an automatic change of attitude, to counter overheating somewhere in the vehicle. There were places where the skin temperature approached fifteen hundred degrees, and he had been very careful to keep in the shadows as far as possible.

A second thruster started to fire, checking the spin given by the first. No, this was *not* a mere thermal adjustment. The bomb was reorientating itself to point toward Rama.

Useless to wonder *why* this was happening, at this precise moment in time. There was one thing in his favor. The missile was a low-acceleration device; a tenth of a gee was the most that it could manage. He could hang on.

He checked the grapples attaching the scooter to the bomb framework, and rechecked the safety line on his own suit. A cold anger was growing in him, adding to his determination. Did this maneuver mean that the Hermians were going to explode the bomb without warning, giving *Endeavour* no chance to escape? That seemed incredible, an act not only of brutality but also of folly, calculated to turn the rest of the solar system against them. And what would have made them ignore the solem promise of their own Ambassador?

Whatever their plan, they would not get away with it.

The second message from Mercury was identical with the first, and arrived ten minutes later. So they had extended the deadline. Norton still had one hour. And they had obviously waited until a reply from *En-*

deavour could have reached them before calling him again.

Now there was another factor. By this time they must have seen Rodrigo and would have had several minutes in which to take action. Their instructions could already be on the way. They could arrive at any second.

He should be preparing to leave. At any moment the sky-filling bulk of Rama might become incandescent along the edges, blazing with a transient glory that would far outshine the Sun.

When the main thrust came on, Rodrigo was securely anchored. Only twenty seconds later it cut off again. He did a quick mental calculation; the delta vee could not have been more than fifteen kilometers an hour. The bomb would take over an hour to reach Rama; perhaps it was only moving in close to get a quicker reaction. If so, that was a wise precaution. But the Hermians had left it too late.

He glanced at his watch, though by now he was almost aware of the time without having to check. On Mercury, they would now be seeing him heading purposefully toward the bomb, and less than two kilometers away from it. They could have no doubt of his intentions, and would be wondering if he had already carried them out.

The second set of cables went as easily as the first. Like any good workman, Rodrigo had chosen his tools well. The bomb was disarmed; or, to be more accurate, it could no longer be detonated by remote command.

Yet there was one other possibility, and he could not afford to ignore it. There were no external contact fuses, but there might be internal ones that would be armed by the shock of impact. The Hermians still had control over their vehicle's movement, and so could crash it into Rama whenever they wished. Rodrigo's work was not yet finished.

Five minutes from now, in that control room somewhere on Mercury, they would see him crawling back along the exterior of the missile, carrying the modest-sized wire cutters that had neutralized the mightiest weapon ever built by man. He was almost tempted to wave at the camera, but decided that it would seem undignified. After all, he was making history, and millions would watch this scene in the years to come—unless, of course, the Hermians destroyed the recording in a fit of pique. He would hardly blame them.

He reached the mounting of the long-range antenna and drifted hand-over-hand along it to the big dish. His faithful cutters made short work of the multiplex feed system, chewing up cables and laser wave guides alike. When he made the last snip, the antenna started to swing slowly around. The unexpected movement took him by surprise, until he realized that he had destroyed its automatic lock on Mercury. Just five minutes from now the Hermians would lose all contact with their servant. Not only was it impotent; now it was blind and deaf.

Rodrigo climbed slowly back to the scooter, released the shackles, and swung it around until the forward bumpers were pressing against the missile, as close as possible to its center of mass. He brought thrust up to full power, and held it there for twenty seconds.

Pushing against many times its own mass, the scooter responded very sluggishly. When Rodrigo cut the thrust back to zero he took a careful reading of the bomb's new velocity vector.

It would miss Rama by a wide margin—and it

could be located again with precision at any future time. It was, after all, a valuable piece of equipment.

Rodrigo was a man of almost pathological honesty. He would not like the Hermians to accuse him of losing their property.

41

Hero

"DARLING," BEGAN NORTON, "this nonsense has cost us more than a day, but at least it's given me a chance to talk to you.

"I'm still in the ship, and she's heading back to station at the polar axis. We picked up Boris an hour ago, looking as if he'd just come off duty after a quiet watch. I suppose neither of us will ever be able to visit Mercury again, and I'm wondering if we're going to be treated as heroes or villains when we get back to Earth. But *my* conscience is clear; I'm sure we did the right thing. I wonder if the Ramans will ever say 'thank you.'

"We can stay here only two more days. Unlike Rama, we don't have a kilometer-thick skin to protect us from the Sun. The hull's already developing dangerous hot spots and we've had to put out some local screening. I'm sorry—I didn't want to bore you with my problems.

"So there's time for just one more trip into Rama, and I intend to make the most of it. But don't worry, I'm not taking any chances."

He stopped the recording. That, to say the least, was stretching the truth. There was danger and uncertainty about every moment inside Rama; no man could ever feel really at home there, in the presence of forces beyond his understanding. And on this final trip, now that he knew they would never return and that no future operations would be jeopardized, he intended to press his luck just a little further.

"In forty-eight hours, then, we'll have completed this mission. What happens after that is uncertain; as you know, we've used virtually all our fuel getting into this orbit. I'm still waiting to hear if a tanker can rendezvous with us in time to get back to Earth, or whether we'll have to make planet-fall on Mars. Anyway, I should be home by Christmas. Tell Junior I'm sorry I can't bring a baby biot; there's no such animal.

"We're all fine, but we're very tired. I've earned a long leave after all this, and we'll make up for lost time. Whatever they say about me, you can claim you're married to a hero. How many wives have a husband who saved a world?"

As always, he listened carefully to the tape before duping it, to make sure that it was applicable to both his families. It was strange to think that he did not know which of them he would see first. Usually his schedule was determined at least a year in advance, by the inexorable movements of the planets themselves.

But that was in the days before Rama. Now nothing would ever be the same again.

42

Temple of Glass

"IF WE TRY it," said Karl Mercer, "do you think the biots will stop us?"

"They may; that's one of the things I want to find out. Why are you looking at me like that?"

Mercer gave his slow, secret grin, which was liable to be set off at any moment by a private joke he might or might not share with his shipmates.

"I was wondering, Skipper, if you think you own Rama. Until now, you've vetoed any attempt to cut into buildings. Why the switch? Have the Hermians given you ideas?"

Norton laughed, then suddenly checked himself. It was a shrewd question, and he was not sure if the obvious answers were the right ones.

"Perhaps I have been ultracautious—I've tried to avoid trouble. But this is our last chance. If we're forced to retreat, we won't have lost much."

"Assuming that we retreat in good order."

"Of course. But the biots have never shown hostility. And except for the spiders, I don't believe there's anything here that can catch us if we do have to run for it."

"*You* may run, Skipper, but I intend to leave with dignity. And incidentally, I've decided why the biots are so polite to us."

"It's a little late for a new theory."

"Here it is, anyway. They think we're Ramans. They can't tell the difference between one oxy-eater and another."

"I don't believe they're *that* stupid."

"It's not a matter of stupidity. They've been programmed for their particular jobs, and we simply don't come into their frame of reference."

"Perhaps you're right. We may find out—as soon as we start work on London."

Joe Calvert had always enjoyed those old bank-robbery movies, but he had never expected to be involved in one. Yet this was, essentially, what he was doing now.

The deserted streets of London seemed full of menace, though he knew that was only his guilty conscience. He did not *really* believe that the sealed and windowless structures ranged all around them were full of watchful inhabitants, waiting to emerge in angry hordes as soon as the invaders laid a hand on their property. In fact, he was quite certain that this whole complex, like all the other towns, was merely some kind of storage area.

But a second fear, also based on innumerable ancient crime dramas, could be better grounded. Though there might be no clanging alarm bells and screaming sirens, it was reasonable to assume that Rama would have some kind of warning system. How otherwise did the biots know when and where their services were needed?

"Those without goggles, turn your backs," ordered Willard Myron. There was a smell of nitric oxides as the air itself started to burn in the beam of the laser torch, and a steady sizzling as the fiery knife sliced toward secrets that had been hidden since the birth of man.

Nothing material could resist this concentration of power, and the cut proceeded smoothly at a rate of several meters a minute. In a remarkably short time, a section large enough to admit a man had been sliced out.

Since the cutaway section showed no sign of moving, Myron tapped it gently—then harder—then banged on it with all his strength. It fell inward with a hollow, reverberating crash.

Once again, as he had done during that first entrance into Rama, Norton remembered the archeologist who had opened the old Egyptian tomb. He did not expect to see the glitter of gold; in fact, he had no preconceived ideas at all as he crawled through the opening, his flashlight held in front of him.

A Greek temple made of glass—that was his first impression. The building was filled with row upon row of vertical crystalline columns, about a meter wide and stretching from floor to ceiling. There were hundreds of them, marching away into the darkness beyond the reach of his light.

He walked toward the nearest column and directed his beam into its interior. Refracted as through a cylindrical lens, the light fanned out on the far side to be focused and refocused, getting fainter with each repetition, in the array of pillars beyond. He felt that he was in the middle of some complicated demonstration in optics.

"Very pretty," said the practical Mercer, "but what

does it mean? Who needs a forest of glass pillars?"

Norton rapped gently on the column. It sounded solid, though more metallic than crystalline. He was completely baffled, and so he followed a piece of useful advice he had heard long ago: "When in doubt, say nothing and move on."

As he reached the next column, which looked exactly like the first, he heard an exclamation of surprise from Mercer.

"I could have sworn this pillar was empty. Now there's something inside it."

Norton glanced quickly back. "Where?" he said. "I don't see anything."

He followed the direction of Mercer's pointing finger. It was aimed at nothing; the column was completely transparent.

"You can't see it?" said Mercer incredulously. "Come around to this side. Damn—now I've lost it!"

"What's going on here?" demanded Calvert. It was several minutes before he got even an approximation of an answer.

The columns were not transparent from every angle or under all illuminations. As one walked around them, objects would suddenly flash into view, apparently embedded in their depths like flies in amber, and would then disappear again. There were dozens of them, all different. They looked absolutely real and solid, yet many seemed to occupy the identical volume of space.

"Holograms," said Calvert. "Just like a museum on Earth."

That was the obvious explanation, and therefore Norton viewed it with suspicion. His doubts grew as he examined the other columns, and conjured up the images stored in their interiors.

Hand tools (though for huge and peculiar hands),

containers, small machines with keyboards that appeared to have been made for more than five fingers, scientific instruments, startingly conventional domestic utensils, including knives and plates that apart from their size would not have attracted a second glance on any terrestrial table: they were all there, with hundreds of less identifiable objects, often jumbled up together in the same pillar. A museum, surely, would have some logical arrangement, some segregation of related items. This seemed to be a completely random collection of hardware.

They had photographed the elusive images inside a score of the crystal pillars when the sheer variety of items gave Norton a clue. Perhaps this was not a collection but a *catalog*, indexed according to some arbitrary but perfectly logical system. He thought of the wild juxtapositions that any dictionary or alphabetized list will give, and tried the idea on his companions.

"I see what you mean," said Mercer. "The Ramans might be equally surprised to find us putting . . . ah . . . camshafts next to cameras."

"Or books beside boots," added Calvert after several seconds of hard thinking. One could play this game for hours, he decided, with increasing degrees of impropriety.

"That's the idea," replied Norton. "This may be an indexed catalog for 3-D images—templates—solid blueprints, if you like to call them that."

"For what purpose?"

"Well, you know the theory about the biots—the idea that they don't exist until they're needed and then they're created—synthesized—from patterns stored somewhere?"

"I see," said Mercer, and he went on slowly and thoughtfully: "So when a Raman needs a left-handed blivet, he punches out the correct code number and a copy is manufactured from the pattern in here."

"Something like that. But please don't ask me about the practical details."

The pillars through which they had been moving had been steadily growing in size, and were now more than two meters in diameter. The images were correspondingly larger. It was obvious that, for doubtless excellent reasons, the Ramans believed in sticking to a one-to-one scale. Norton wondered how they stored anything *really* big, if this was the case.

To increase their rate of coverage, the four explorers had now spread out through the crystal columns and were taking photographs as quickly as they could get their cameras focused on the fleeting images. This was an astonishing piece of luck, Norton told himself, though he felt that he had earned it; they could not possibly have made a better choice than this Illustrated Catalog of Raman Artifacts. And yet, in another way, it could hardly have been more frustrating. There was nothing actually *here* except impalpable patterns of light and darkness. These apparently solid objects did not really exist.

Even knowing this, more than once Norton felt an almost irresistible urge to laser his way into one of the pillars so that he could have something material to take back to Earth. It was the same impulse, he thought wryly, that would prompt a monkey to grab the reflection of a banana in a mirror.

He was photographing what seemed to be some kind of optical device when Calvert's shout started him running through the pillars.

"Skipper—Karl—Will—look at *this!*"

Calvert was prone to sudden enthusiasms, but what he had found now was enough to justify any amount of excitement.

Inside one of the two-meter columns was an elaborate harness, or uniform, obviously made for a vertically standing creature much taller than a man. A very narrow central metal band apparently surrounded the waist, thorax, or some division unknown to terrestrial zoology. From this rose three slim columns, tapering outward and ending in a perfectly circular belt, an impressive meter in diameter. Loops equally spaced along it could be intended only to go around upper limbs or arms—*three* of them.

There were numerous pouches, buckles, bandoliers from which tools (or weapons?) protruded, pipes and electrical conductors, even small black boxes that would have looked perfectly at home in an electronics lab on Earth. The whole arrangement was almost as complex as a spacesuit, though it obviously provided only partial covering for the creature wearing it.

And was that creature a Raman? Norton asked himself. We'll probably never know; but it must have been intelligent, because no mere animal could cope with all that sophisticated equipment.

"About two and a half meters high," said Mercer thoughtfully, "not counting the head—whatever *that* was like."

"With three arms—and presumably three legs. The same plan as the spiders, on a much more massive scale. Do you suppose that's a coincidence?"

"Probably not. We design robots in our own image; we might expect the Ramans to do the same."

Myron, unusually subdued, was looking at the display with something like awe. "Do you suppose they know we're here?" he half whispered.

"I doubt it," said Mercer. "We've not even reached their threshold of consciousness—though the Hermians certainly had a good try."

They were standing there, unable to drag themselves away, when Rousseau called from the hub, his voice full of urgent concern.

"Skipper, you'd better get outside."

"What is it—biots heading this way?"

"No. Something much more serious. *The lights are going out.*"

43

Retreat

WHEN HE HASTILY emerged from the hole they had lasered, it seemed to Norton that the six suns of Rama were as brilliant as ever. Surely, he thought, Rousseau must have made a mistake—though that was not like him at all.

But Rousseau had anticipated just this reaction. "It happened so slowly," he explained apologetically, "that it was a long time before I noticed any difference. But there's no doubt about it—I've taken a meter reading. The light level's down forty per cent."

Now, as his eyes readjusted themselves after the gloom of the glass temple, Norton could believe him. The long day of Rama was drawing to its close.

It was as warm as ever, yet Norton felt himself shivering. He had known this sensation once before, during a beautiful summer day on Earth. There had been an inexplicable weakening of light, as if darkness was falling or the sun had lost its strength, though there was not a cloud in the sky. Then he had remembered that a partial eclipse had begun.

"This is it," he said grimly. "We're going home. Leave all the equipment behind—we won't need it again."

Now, he hoped, one piece of planning was about to prove its worth. He had selected London for this raid because no other town was so close to a stairway. The foot of Beta was only four kilometers away.

They set off at the steady loping trot that was the most comfortable mode of traveling at half a gravity. Norton set a pace that, he estimated, would get them to the edge of the plain without exhaustion and in the minimum of time. He was acutely aware of the eight kilometers they would still have to climb when they had reached Stairway Beta, but he would feel much safer when they had actually started the ascent.

The first tremor came when they had almost reached the stairway. It was very slight, and instinctively Norton turned toward the south, expecting to see another display of fireworks around the horns. But Rama never seemed to repeat itself exactly. If there were any electrical discharges above those needle-sharp mountains, they were too faint to be seen.

"Bridge," he called, "did you notice that?"

"Yes, Skipper—very small shock. Could be another attitude change. We're watching the rate gyro. Nothing yet . . . Just a minute! Positive reading! Can just detect it—less than a microradian per second, but holding."

So Rama was beginning to turn, though with almost imperceptible slowness. Those earlier shocks might have been a false alarm, but this, surely, was the real thing.

"Rate increasing. Five microrad. Hello, did you feel *that* shock?"

"We certainly did. Get all ship's systems operational. We may have to leave in a hurry."

"Do you expect an orbit change already? We're still a long way from perihelion."

"I don't think Rama works by our textbooks. Nearly at Beta. We'll rest there for five minutes."

Five minutes was utterly inadequate, yet it seemed an age, for there was now no doubt that the light was failing, and failing fast.

Though they were all equipped with flashlights, the thought of darkness here was now intolerable. They had grown so accustomed psychologically to the endless day that it was hard to remember the conditions under which they had first explored this world. They felt an overwhelming urge to escape—to get out into the light of the Sun, a kilometer away on the other side of these cylindrical walls.

"Hub Control," called Norton, "is the searchlight operating? We may need it in a hurry."

"Yes, Skipper. Here it comes."

A reassuring spark of light started to shine eight kilometers above their heads. Even against the now fading day of Rama, it looked surprisingly feeble; but it had served them before, and would guide them once again if they needed it.

This, Norton was grimly aware, would be the longest and most nerve-racking climb they had ever made. Whatever happened, it would be impossible to hurry; if they overexerted themselves they would simply collapse somewhere on that vertiginous slope, and would have to wait until their protesting muscles permitted them to continue. By this time they must be one of the fittest crews that had ever carried out a space mission, but there were limits to what flesh and blood could do.

After an hour's steady plodding they had reached the fourth section of the stairway, about three kilometers from the plain. From now on it would be much easier; gravity was already down to a third of Earth value. Although there had been minor shocks from time to time, no other unusual phenomena had occurred and there was still plenty of light. They began to feel more optimistic, and even to wonder if they had left too soon. One thing was certain, however: there was no going back. They had all walked for the last time on the Central Plain of Rama.

It was while they were taking a ten-minute rest on the fourth platform that Calvert exclaimed: "What's that noise, Skipper?"

"Noise? I don't hear anything."

"High-pitched whistle, dropping in frequency. You *must* hear it."

"Your ears are younger than mine. Oh, now I do."

The whistle seemed to come from everywhere. Soon it was loud, even piercing, and falling swiftly in pitch. Then it suddenly stopped.

A few seconds later it came again, repeating the same sequence. It had all the mournful, compelling quality of a lighthouse siren sending out its warnings into the fog-shrouded night. There was a message here, and an urgent one. It was not designed for their ears, but they understood it. Then, as if to make doubly sure, it was reinforced by the lights themselves.

They dimmed almost to extinction, then started to flash. Brilliant beads, like ball lightning, raced along the six narrow valleys that had once illuminated this world. They moved from both poles toward the sea in a synchronized, hypnotic rhythm that could have only one meaning. "To the sea!" the lights were calling. "To the sea!" And the summons was hard to resist; there was not a man who did not feel a compulsion to turn back, and to seek oblivion in the waters of Rama.

"Hub Control!" Norton called urgently. "Can you see what's happening?"

The voice of Rousseau came back to him. He sounded awed, and more than a little frightened.

"Yes, Skipper. I'm looking across at the Southern Hemisphere. There are scores of biots over there—including some big ones. Cranes, bulldozers . . . lots of scavengers. And they're all rushing back to the sea faster than I've ever seen them move before. There goes a crane—right over the edge! Just like Jimmy, but going down a lot quicker . . . It smashed to pieces when it hit. . . . And here come the sharks; they're tearing into it. . . . Ugh, it's not a pleasant sight. . . .

"Now I'm looking at the plain. There's a bulldozer that seems to have broken down. . . . It's going round and round in circles. Now a couple of crabs are tearing into it, pulling it to pieces. . . . Skipper, I think you'd better get back right away."

"Believe me," Norton said with deep feeling, "we're coming just as quickly as we can."

Rama was battening down the hatches, like a ship preparing for a storm. That was Norton's overwhelming impression, though he could not have put it on a logical basis. He no longer felt completely rational. Two compulsions were warring in his mind: the need to escape and the desire to obey those bolts of lightning that flashed across the sky, ordering him to join the biots in their march to the sea.

One more section of stairway. Another ten-minute pause, to let the fatigue poisons drain from his muscles. Then on again. Another two kilometers to go, but better not to think about that. . . .

The maddening sequence of descending whistles abruptly ceased. At the same moment the fireballs racing along the slots of the Straight Valleys stopped their seaward strobing; Rama's six linear suns were once more continuous bands of light.

But they were fading fast, and sometimes they flickered, as if tremendous jolts of energy were being drained from waning power sources. From time to time there were slight tremors underfoot. The bridge reported that Rama was still swinging with imperceptible slowness, like a compass needle responding to a weak magnetic field. This was perhaps reassuring; it was when Rama *stopped* its swing that Norton would really begin to worry.

All the biots had gone, so Rousseau reported. In the whole interior of Rama, the only movement was that of human beings, crawling with painful slowness up the curving face of the north dome.

Norton had long since overcome the vertigo he had felt on that first ascent, but now a new fear was beginning to creep into his mind. They were so vulnerable here, on this endless climb from plain to hub. Suppose that Rama, when it had completed its attitude change, started to accelerate?

Presumably its thrust would be along the axis. If it was in the southward direction, that would be no problem; they would be held a little more firmly against the slope they were ascending. But if it was toward the north, they might be swept off into space, to fall back eventually on the plain far below.

He tried to reassure himself with the thought that any possible acceleration would be very feeble. Dr. Perera's calculations had been most convincing. Rama could not possibly accelerate at more than a fiftieth of a gravity, or the Cylindrical Sea would climb the southern cliff and flood an entire continent. But Perera had been in a comfortable study back on Earth, not with kilometers of overhanging metal apparently about to crash down upon his head. And perhaps Rama was designed for periodic flooding.

No, that was ridiculous. It was absurd to imagine that all these trillions of tons could suddenly start moving with sufficient acceleration to shake him loose. Nevertheless, for the remainder of the ascent Norton never let himself get far from the security of the hand-rail.

Lifetimes later, the stairway ended. Only a few hundred meters of vertical, recessed ladder were left. It was no longer necessary to climb this section, since one man at the hub, hauling on a cable, could easily hoist another against the rapidly diminishing gravity. Even at the bottom of the ladder a man weighed less than five kilos; at the top, virtually zero.

So Norton relaxed in the sling, grasping a rung from time to time to counter the feeble Coriolis force trying to push him off the ladder. He almost forgot his knotted muscles as he had his last view of Rama.

It was about as bright now as the light of a full moon on Earth. The over-all scene was perfectly clear, but he could no longer make out the finer details. The South Pole was now partially obscured by a glowing mist; only the peak of Big Horn protruded through it —a small, black dot, seen exactly head on.

The carefully mapped but still unknown continent beyond the sea was the same apparently random patchwork that it had always been. It was too fore-shortened, and too full of complex detail, to reward visual examination, and Norton scanned it only briefly.

He swept his gaze around the encircling band of the sea, and noticed for the first time a regular pattern of disturbed water, as if waves were breaking over reefs set at geometrically precise intervals. Rama's maneuvering was having some effect, but a slight one. He was sure that Sergeant Barnes would have sailed forth happily under these conditions had he asked her to cross the sea in her lost *Resolution*.

New York, London, Paris, Moscow, Rome . . . He said farewell to all the cities of the Northern Hemisphere, and hoped the Ramans would forgive him for the damage he had done. Perhaps they would understand that it was all in the cause of science.

Then, finally, he was at the hub, and eager hands reached out to grab him and to hurry him through the air locks. His overstrained legs and arms were trembling so uncontrollably that he was almost unable to help himself, and he was content to be handled like a half-paralyzed invalid.

The sky of Rama contracted above him as he descended into the central crater of the hub. When the door of the inner air lock shut off the view forever, he found himself thinking: How strange that night should be falling, now that Rama is closest to the Sun!

44

Space Drive

A HUNDRED KILOMETERS was an adequate safety margin, Norton had decided. Rama was now a huge black rectangle, exactly broadside on, eclipsing the Sun. He had used this opportunity to fly *Endeavour* completely into shadow, so that the load could be taken off the ship's cooling systems and some overdue maintenance could be carried out. Rama's protective cone of darkness might disappear at any moment, and he intended to make as much use of it as he could.

Rama was still turning. It had now swung through almost fifteen degrees, and it was impossible to believe that some major orbit change was not imminent. On the United Planets, excitement had reached a pitch of hysteria, but only a faint echo of this came to *Endeavour*. Physically and emotionally, her crew was exhausted; apart from a skeleton watch, everyone had slept for twelve hours after take-off from the North

Pole base. On doctor's orders, Norton himself had used electrosedation. Even so, he had dreamed that he was climbing an infinite stairway.

The second day back on the ship, everything had almost returned to normal, and the exploration of Rama already seemed part of another life. Norton started to deal with the accumulated office work and to make plans for the future; but he refused the requests for interviews that had somehow managed to insinuate themselves into the Survey and even SPACEGUARD radio circuits. There were no messages from Mercury, and the U.P. General Assembly had adjourned its session, though it was ready to meet again at an hour's notice.

Norton was having his first good night's sleep, thirty hours after leaving Rama, when he was rudely shaken back to consciousness. He cursed groggily, opened a bleary eye at Karl Mercer, and then, like any good commander, was instantly wide awake.

"It's stopped turning?"

"Yes. Steady as a rock."

"Let's go to the bridge."

The whole ship was awake. Even the simps knew that something was afoot, and made anxious, meeping noises until McAndrews reassured them with swift hand signals. As Norton slipped into his chair and fastened the restraints around his waist, he wondered if this might be yet another false alarm.

Rama was now foreshortened into a stubby cylinder, and the searing rim of the Sun had peeked over one edge. Norton jockeyed *Endeavour* gently back into the umbra of the artificial eclipse, and saw the pearly splendor of the corona reappear across a background of the brighter stars. There was one huge prominence, at least half a million kilometers high, that had climbed so far from the Sun that its upper branches looked like a tree of crimson fire.

So now we have to wait, Norton told himself. The important thing is not to get bored, to be ready to re-act at a moment's notice, to keep all the instruments aligned and recording, no matter how long it takes.

This was strange! The star field was shifting, almost as if he had actuated the roll thrusters. But he had touched no controls, and if there had been any real movement he would have sensed it at once.

"Skipper!" said Calvert urgently from the nav posi-tion. "We're rolling—look at the stars! *But I'm get-ting no instrument readings!*"

"Rate gyros operating?"

"Perfectly normal. I can see the zero jitter. But we're rolling several degrees a second!"

"That's impossible!"

"Of course it is—but look for yourself."

When all else failed, a man had to rely on eyeball instrumentation. Norton could not doubt that the star field was indeed slowly rotating. There went Sirius, across the rim of the port. Either the universe, in a re-version to pre-Copernican cosmology, had suddenly decided to revolve around *Endeavour;* or the stars were standing still, and the ship was turning.

The second explanation seemed rather more likely, yet it involved apparently insoluble paradoxes. If the ship was really turning at this rate he would have *felt* it—literally by the seat of his pants, as the old saying went. And the gyros could not all have failed, simulta-neously and independently.

Only one answer remained. Every atom of *Endea-vour* must be in the grip of some force—and only a powerful gravitational field could produce this effect. At least, no other *known* field could.

Suddenly, the stars vanished. The blazing disc of the Sun had emerged from behind the shield of Rama, and its glare had driven them from the sky.

"Can you get a radar reading? What's the Doppler?"

Norton was fully prepared to find that this, too, was inoperative, but he was wrong.

Rama was under way at last, accelerating at the modest rate of 0.015 gravities. Dr. Perera, Norton thought, would be pleased; he had predicted a maximum of 0.02. And *Endeavour* was somehow caught in its wake like a piece of flotsam whirling round and round behind a speeding ship.

Hour after hour that acceleration held constant. Rama was falling away from *Endeavour* at steadily increasing speed. As the distance grew, the anomalous behavior of the ship slowly ceased; the normal laws of inertia started to operate again. They could only guess at the energies in whose backlash they had been briefly caught, and Norton was thankful that he had stationed *Endeavour* at a safe distance before Rama had switched on its drive.

As to the nature of that drive, one thing was now certain, even though all else was mystery. There were no jets of gas, no beams of ions or plasma thrusting Rama into its new orbit. No one put it better than Sergeant Professor Myron, when he said, in shocked disbelief: "There goes Newton's Third Law."

It was Newton's Third Law, however, upon which *Endeavour* had to depend the next day, when she used her very last reserves of propellant to bend her own orbit outward from the Sun. The change was slight, but it would increase her perihelion distance by ten million kilometers. That was the difference between running the ship's cooling system at ninety-five-percent capacity and a certain fiery death.

When they had completed their own maneuver, Rama was two hundred thousand kilometers away, and difficult to see against the glare of the Sun. But they could obtain accurate radar measurements of its orbit. And the more they observed, the more puzzled they became.

They checked the figures over and over again, until there was no escaping the unbelievable conclusion. It looked as if all the fears of the Hermians, the heroism of Rodrigo, and the rhetoric of the General Assembly had been utterly in vain.

What a cosmic irony, thought Norton as he looked at his final figures, if after a million years of safe guidance, Rama's computers had made one trifling error —perhaps changing the sign of an equation from plus to minus.

Everyone had been so certain that Rama would lose speed, so that it could be captured by the Sun's gravity and thus become a new planet of the solar system. It was doing just the opposite.

It was gaining speed—and in the worst possible direction. Rama was falling ever more swiftly into the Sun.

45

Phoenix

As THE DETAILS of its new orbit became more and more clearly defined, it was hard to see how Rama could possibly escape disaster. Only a handful of comets had ever passed as close to the Sun; at perihelion it would be less than half a million kilometers above that inferno of fusing hydrogen. No solid material could withstand the temperature of such an approach. The tough alloy that composed Rama's hull would start to melt at ten times that distance.

Endeavour had now passed its own perihelion, to everyone's relief, and was slowly increasing its distance from the Sun. Rama was far ahead on its closer, swifter orbit, and already appeared well inside the outermost fringes of the corona. The ship would have a grandstand view of the drama's final stage.

Then, five million kilometers from the Sun, and still

accelerating, Rama started to spin its cocoon. Until now, it had been visible under the maximum power of *Endeavour's* telescopes as a tiny bright bar; suddenly it began to scintillate, like a star seen through horizon mists. It almost seemed as if it was disintegrating. When he saw the image breaking up, Norton felt a poignant sense of grief at the loss of so much wonder. Then he realized that Rama was still there, but that it was surrounded by a shimmering haze.

And then it was gone. In its place was a brilliant, starlike object, showing no visible disc—as if Rama had contracted into a tiny ball.

It was some time before they figured out what had happened. Rama had indeed disappeared. It was now surrounded by a perfectly reflecting sphere, about a hundred kilometers in diameter. All that they could now see was the reflection of the Sun itself on the curved portion that was closest to them. Behind this protective bubble, Rama was presumably safe from the solar inferno.

As the hours passed, the bubble changed its shape. The image of the Sun became elongated, distorted. The sphere was turning into an ellipsoid, its long axis pointed in the direction of Rama's flight. It was then that the first anomalous reports started coming in from the robot observatories, which, for almost two hundred years, had been keeping a permanent watch on the Sun.

Something was happening to the solar magnetic field in the region around Rama. The million-kilometer-long lines of force that threaded the corona and drove its wisps of fiercely ionized gas at speeds that sometimes defied even the crushing gravity of the Sun were shaping themselves around that glittering ellipsoid. Nothing was yet visible to the eye, but the orbiting instruments reported every change in magnetic flux and ultraviolet radiation.

And presently even the eye could see the changes in the corona. A faintly glowing tube or tunnel, a hundred thousand kilometers long, had appeared high in the outer atmosphere of the Sun. It was slightly curved, bending along the orbit Rama was tracing, and Rama itself—or the protective cocoon around it —was visible as a glittering bead racing faster and faster down that ghostly tube through the corona.

For it was still gaining speed. Now it was moving at more than two thousand kilometers a second, and there was no question of its ever remaining a captive of the Sun. Now, at last, the Ramans' strategy was obvious. They had come so close to the Sun merely to tap its energy at the source and to speed themselves even faster on the way to their ultimate, unknown goal.

Soon it seemed that they were tapping more than energy. No one could ever be certain of this, because the nearest observing instruments were thirty million kilometers away, but there were definite indications that matter was flowing from the Sun *into Rama itself*, as if it was replacing the leakage and losses of ten thousand centuries in space.

Faster and faster Rama swept around the Sun, moving more swiftly than any object that had ever traveled through the solar system. In less than two hours its direction of motion had swung through more than ninety degrees, and it had given a final, almost contemptuous proof of its total lack of interest in all the worlds whose peace of mind it had so rudely disturbed.

It was dropping out of the ecliptic, down into the southern sky, far below the plane in which all the planets move. Though that, surely, could not be its ultimate goal, it was aimed squarely at the Greater Magellanic Cloud, and the lonely gulfs beyond the Milky Way.

46

Interlude

"COME IN," SAID Commander Norton absent-mindedly, at the quiet knock on his door.

"Some news for you, Bill. I wanted to give it first, before the crew gets into the act. And anyway, it's my department."

Norton still seemed far away. He was lying with his hands clasped under his head, eyes half shut, cabin light low—not really drowsing, but lost in some reverie or private dream.

He blinked once or twice, and was suddenly back in his body.

"Sorry, Laura, I don't understand. What's it all about?"

"Don't say you've forgotten!"

"Stop teasing, you wretched woman. I've had a few things on my mind recently."

Surgeon Commander Ernst slid a captive chair across in its slots and sat down beside him.

"Though interplanetary crises come and go, the wheels of Martian bureaucracy grind steadily away. But I suppose Rama helped. Good thing you didn't have to get permission from the Hermians as well."

Light was dawning. "Oh—Port Lowell has issued the permit!"

"Better than that. It's already being acted on." Laura glanced at the slip of paper in her hand. "Immediate," she read. "Probably right now your new son is being conceived. Congratulations."

"Thank you. I hope he hasn't minded the wait."

Like every astronaut, Norton had been sterilized when he entered the service. For a man who would spend years in space, radiation-induced mutation was not a risk; it was a certainty. The spermatozoon that had just delivered its cargo of genes on Mars, two hundred million kilometers away, had been frozen for thirty years, awaiting its moment of destiny.

Norton wondered if he would be home in time for the birth. He had earned rest, relaxation, and such normal family life as an astronaut could ever know. Now that the mission was essentially over, he was beginning to unwind, and to think once more about his own future, and that of both his families. Yes, it would be good to be home for a while, and to make up for lost time—in many ways.

"This visit," protested Laura rather feebly, "was purely in a professional capacity."

"After all these years," replied Norton, "we know each other better than that. Anyway, you're off duty now." This situation, he knew, was doubtless being repeated throughout the ship. Even though they were weeks from home, the end-of-mission "orbital orgy" would be in full swing.

"*Now* what are you thinking?" demanded Laura, much later. "You're not becoming sentimental, I hope."

"Not about us. About Rama. I'm beginning to miss it."

"Thanks very much for the compliment."

Norton tightened his arms around her. One of the nicest things about weightlessness, he often thought, was that you could really hold someone all night without cutting off the circulation. There were those who claimed that love at one gee was so ponderous that they could no longer enjoy it.

"It's a well-known fact, Laura, that men, unlike women, have *two*-track minds. But seriously—well, *more* seriously—I do feel a sense of loss."

"I can understand that."

"Don't be so clinical; that's not the only reason. Oh, never mind." He gave up. It was not easy to explain, even to himself.

He had succeeded on this mission beyond all reasonable expectation. What his men had discovered in Rama would keep scientists busy for decades. And, above all, he had done it without a single casualty.

But he had also failed. One might speculate endlessly, but the nature and the purpose of the Ramans was still utterly unknown. They had used the solar system as a refueling stop, a booster station—call it what you will; and had then spurned it completely, on their way to more important business. They would probably never even know that the human race existed. Such monumental indifference was worse than any deliberate insult.

When Norton had glimpsed Rama for the last time, a tiny star hurtling outward beyond Venus, he knew that part of his life was over. He was just fifty-five, but he felt he had left his youth down there on the curving Central Plain, among mysteries and wonders now receding inexorably beyond the reach of man. Whatever honors and achievements the future brought him, for the rest of his life he would be haunted by a sense of anticlimax and the knowledge of opportunities missed.

So he told himself; but even then, he should have known better.

And on far-off Earth, Dr. Carlisle Perera had as yet told no one of how he had wakened from a restless sleep with the message from his subconscious echoing in his brain:

The Ramans do everything in threes.

ABOUT THE AUTHOR

Arthur C. Clarke was born at Minehead, Somerset, England in 1917 and is a graduate of King's College, London, where he obtained First Class Honors in physics and mathematics. He is past chairman of the British Interplanetary Society, a member of the Academy of Astronautics, the Royal Astronomical Society, and many other scientific organizations. During the Second World War, as an RAF officer, he was in charge of the first radar talk-down ("G.C.A.") equipment during its experimental trials.

Author of more than forty books, in 1962 he went to New Delhi to receive the £ 1,000 Kalinga Prize for science writing from the Director-General of UNESCO. In 1962 he was awarded a gold medal by the Franklin Institute for having originated communications satellites in a technical paper published in 1945. This described in detail the geostationary satellite system now used by all commercial comsats.

Ten million copies of his books have been printed in over thirty languages. An article on comsats in *Life* was awarded the Aviation-Space Writers' 1965 prize as the best aerospace reporting of the year in any medium, and in 1969 he won the American Association for the Advancement of Science-Westinghouse science writing prize. He shared an Oscar nomination with Stanley Kubrick in 1969 for *2001: A Space Odyssey*, and has won the two top science fiction awards, the Hugo and Nebula.

He has contributed to *Playboy, Look, Time, Reader's Digest, Holiday Horizon,* and *The New York Times.*

For the past twenty years, Mr. Clarke's hobby has been underwater exploration along the Great Barrier Reef of Australia and off the coast of Ceylon, where he has resided since 1956. Eleven of his books have been concerned with this work, which has also been the subject of TV features. In 1961 his colleagues discovered a man-of-war which had sunk in 1702 off the coast of Ceylon with at least a ton of silver aboard: the account of its salvage is described in *The Treasure of the Great Reef* and *Indian Ocean Treasure*.

Mr. Clarke joined Walter Cronkite and Captain Wally Schirra on CBS-TV during the Apollo 11, 12, and 15 missions. He has appeared with David Frost, Hugh Downs, Dick Cavett, Patrick Moore, and many other radio and TV personalities.